Skyrook Gorge - Prey

Ken Ra

For KatKat.

CONTENTS

CONTENTS

Ken Ra

CONTENTS

Skyrook Gorge

ACKNOWLEDGMENTS

A big thank-you to the talented Elaine Aneira for creating the covers of this book. Accurately capturing my vision was quite a feat, and I could not have been more pleased with the result. Shout-out to Marleen Burckgard for the fire photograph Elaine incorporated into the image.

Additional thanks to everyone who encouraged me and everyone who supported me by purchasing a copy of the first book.

A final thanks to my awesome cats and everyone who purchases this book.

CHAPTER 1

The year was 2038. Twenty-year-old Pradhan was in a Kalari dueling his instructor – Gurukkal Dhimant. The two men were dueling with maduvus (weapons consisting of two steel horns and a metal plate for shielding). Pradhan was clean shaven with short black hair. He possessed no unusual features, however anyone else in the room could feel the anger radiating from within his soul. Dhimant, the Gurukkal of the Kalari, was an older man of at least sixty. His once dark skin was now a pale brown and his thick beard had only one layer of black hairs holding their color above the mountain of silver. Dhimant's head was shaven, revealing the discolored erosion across his skin.

The two men clashed their weapons with an unnatural speed for some time before Pradhan witnessed an opportunity to disarm his master. He successfully executed the attack and caused Dhimant's maduvu to fly across the dojo.

Pradhan lunged his weapon in toward Dhimant's neck. Dhimant sensed Pradhan's overconfidence and swung his arm beneath his pupil's. With minimal effort he grabbed Pradhan's maduvu and tore it from his hand. Pradhan didn't know how to react as his master then kicked him onto his back. Dhimant jabbed the maduvu toward Pradhan's face – stilling the weapon as the point rested within the first layer his skin. Pradhan frowned, but admitted defeat.

Pradhan caught his breath before speaking in Tamil. "That was our longest spar, master!"

"So?" Dhimant asked, also speaking Tamil.

"So! I held up against you for-" Pradhan's sass was interrupted as his master spoke.

"Why is that relevant?" Dhimant growled. "You still lost. Had this been a real fight you would be dead, and I would still be standing unscathed. You accomplished nothing other than wasting time. The point of a fight is to win, and win as quickly as you can. So, you can draw out a fight, swell. You risk depleting your own stamina. More performances means more opportunities for error. In a serious fight you also risk giving the friends of your enemies time to come in as reinforcements."

"But I also delayed my own defeat!" Pradhan averred. "I do believe I am ready to wield the urumi!"

"You are the furthest thing from!" Dhimant seethed. "We have been over this, time and time again, child!"

"My anger, my emotions, my arrogance, yes, I know!" Pradhan grumbled. "But perhaps if I was given a chance then those traits could be rectified!"

"The urumi is the most dangerous sword known to man!" Dhimant barked. "One draw can decapitate armies, and if the user makes an error he can lop off his own head. It is not a weapon for those who are unable to control themselves. I shouldn't have even advanced you this far – you have gained nothing from your years of practice and meditations!"

Pradhan climbed onto his feet and asked "Well, when do you believe I will be ready?"

"That is another one of your problems!" Dhimant sighed as Pradhan rolled his eyes. "You rely too much on me. I am not you, I cannot speak for you. You decide when you are ready. I instruct you further once I recognize that you have made the decision. Not with your mouth, but with your heart. As my American students say - "Get your shit together!"".

Pradhan lowered his head as Dhimant stepped out of the room.

Weeks passed. Pradhan deprived himself of sleep – making up for it with meditation and practicing against other students with the maduvu. These men weren't ignorant of what was happening to the world around them – it had just not reached them yet. They heard news from travelers of how the landscapes of Earth were being devastated. Occasionally their temple would shake. Not from earthquakes – but from gravity shifts as plates of land the size of small countries were tossed across the sky. On clear nights they could watch the moon gradually lose chunks of its surface. The men knew it was only a matter of time before the war would reach them. They wondered which faction would contact them first – assuming their land wouldn't be torn from the

Earth's mantle and used as the next weapon.

One morning a stranger was brought into the temple on a crudely crafted stretcher. He was critically wounded and barely hanging on to life. One of Pradhan's jobs in the temple was to gather and mix medicines. There was nothing that could save the strange man – but it was possible to ease his pain. Dhimant offered to end the man's suffering by executing him – but he declined. Pradhan was summoned to deliver the relieving tonic – unprepared for what he would encounter.

As Pradhan entered the room he immediately noticed something "off" about the stranger. The man appeared human for the most part, but the top – right quarter of his head was that of a dog's! Pradhan nearly dropped the medicine as he trembled. The man accepted the cup as Pradhan offered it to him. He drank the medicine in one gulp then handed the cup back to Pradhan. Pradhan laid the cup on a nearby shelf and asked "What are you?".

The man chuckled and replied "Did you know I understand and speak your language from being told, or did you assume? Judging by your expression I don't believe you were told anything about me beyond my condition."

"What is your language?" Pradhan queried.

"I speak whatever, that is how Kepyet programmed us." The man smiled.

"So you're a Nute?" Pradhan guessed.

"No, no. The Nutes – they are nothing more than broken human souls working for a second chance. I'm...in lack of a better term, a revenant. What I am...my race, we were once animals." The man answered.

"A chimera?" Pradhan drawled.

"A type of one, yes." The revenant confirmed. "We are beyond physical attachment though. Kepyet specifically chose our souls because we were animals that suffered great abuse at the hands of humans. Either as pets or prey that were tortured by psychopathic hunters and farmers. I was a dog, obviously. One of my buddies was a deer that was shot wrong. The hunter just laughed and took several photos of him before digging into his throat with a dull knife – a slow death. Kepyet has an...interesting theory on how to punish people. This human body – it is the body of my owner, the man that abused me. All of us revenants – we share bodies with our abusers. We are the ones in full control, but most of the pain we feel is felt by our host. We only feel enough to know that we have been injured. That is why I decline execution. Your medicine reduced the pain enough so I do not feel it – but the bastard who originally owned this body – he suffers."

Pradhan nodded. "So the war is nearby?"

"I escaped quite a ways, but yes. Full battles aren't in this region yet – but there have been some conflicts between our scouts and the Blessed. There is also some rogue faction calling themselves "The Sons of War" that attack both of us. Judging by my surroundings now – I assume you guys will side with the Blessed?"

"I can't say." Pradhan admitted. "The Blessed pervert the intentions of our gods – but are kept only because the gods need soldiers. The war has gone on for months – we haven't taken a side. How do you think we will be viewed – by both the Blessed and your faction?"

"As an enemy." The revenant chuckled. "When

the war comes here – be an enemy. You humans have so much going for you. You are more than pawns to be used in a game."

The revenant closed his eyes and died. Pradhan looked over the body of the deceased creature – contemplating what was said. He stepped outside of the room only to be startled by his master's approach.

"So, you met the visitor?" Dhimant mumbled.

"Yes...he's dead now." Pradhan lamented.

"It's a miracle he survived as long as he did." Dhimant shrugged. "We will give him a proper funeral. Though his arrival is a grim omen – soon...war will be here."

Pradhan nodded. "I'm prepared to protect the temple."

Dhimant smiled. "We shall see."

Dhimant walked away. Pradhan ventured to his quarters and turned on a TV that was powered by the temple's generator. Although the temple was on the grid there had been no public supply of electricity in months. He stuck an old VHS tape into the device below the TV and watched some urumi training videos. His small room was littered with a diverse selection of books and diagrams on how to use the various weapons of his martial art. He also possessed several cables that he practiced with in secret which had similar weight and flexibility of the urumi.

A couple more months had passed. Pradhan had pushed his body even further than the demands of his sacred exercises. Although his conversation with the strange creature was brief and rather simple – it had impacted his spirit. Pradhan had not realized this yet – but he had discovered a new meaning in life. Wielding the urumi was no longer a concern of his – rather his focus was on becoming the best version of himself.

It was a calm night when the temple shook. Pradhan was resting in his bed when the quakes disturbed his slumber. He had grown used to the shaking – all the men at the temple had. However, this event was different. It was far more intense – as if something had actually struck the temple. Pradhan rolled out of his bed and rushed outside as he heard the battle cries of his fellow students. The sound of gunfire followed.

Pradhan stepped outside to see large chunks of the temple missing and set ablaze. Floating overhead were three Blessed airships. The ground was cluttered with the dead bodies of not only his fellow students but also the temple guard and maintenance crew. Across the smoldering courtyard he saw a demonic creature approaching three of the students. The students were only armed with swords – but the demon was unarmed. Two large, tattooed men smashed through a wall behind the demonic being.

One of the large men shouted at the winged creature. "Quit playing around – Gilgamesh and Enkidu need us to help with the siege!"

The demon shouted back. "I don't believe in leaving tasks unfinished."

The giant roared. "That is an order – Basil!"

The other large man elbowed his companion. "Let's just go – the mummy will catch up."

The giants stumbled through a hole in the crumbling exterior wall of the temple as Basil approached the three students. Two of them charged at Basil with their swords. He folded his wings together and moved them between the warriors. Basil then pulled his wings apart – launching the boys in opposite directions. One was knocked against the nearby wall hard enough for his body to splatter across the bricks. The second wafted past Pradhan and into a nearby fire. Basil grabbed the face of the third student and instantly blazed the flesh from his bones. Basil dropped the skeleton then flew into one of the overhead airships as they began to move away.

Pradhan resisted shock – not knowing what to make of what he had just witnessed. Of the many concerns in his mind only one was significant – his Gurukkal!

Pradhan rushed toward the Kalari. The walls of the primitive gymnasium had all collapsed. The ceiling had crumbled away. Dhimant lay on a large brick in the center of the ruined corridor. His body was covered in burns and bullet wounds – but he clung to life.

"Master!" Pradhan cried as he rushed to his Gurukkal.

"Pradhan..." Dhimant wheezed.

"There has to be a way to heal you! You're alive, that's always a good sign!" Pradhan stuttered.

Dhimant coughed in his attempt to laugh. "Pradhan. You're ready." He coughed some more. "You're ready! The urumi...my belt..."

"Master don't try to talk, save your energy!" Pradhan begged.

"The urumi, mine, take it!" Dhimant coughed more heavily as Pradhan tried to shush him. "You're ready...you're ready."

Dhimant's eyes closed as his head fell back.

Pradhan trembled upon realizing Dhimant was dead – along with everyone else he grew up with at the temple. Pradhan wanted nothing more than to shout in anger – but he knew better. He had to control his rage and channel it into something productive. He reached toward his deceased master's waist and unclipped the urumi. Pradhan gently unraveled it from Dhimant before equipping it on his own person as a belt. The boy grabbed a spear and a sword from what remained of the wall and sprinted in the (hopeful) direction of the two giants.

Pradhan had only ventured a short distance into the blazing forest before he came across a Blessed airship hovering not even a hundred feet above the ground with a rope-ladder dangling from the carriage. It was a dark night with a thick layer of cloud and ash obstructing the star and moonlight. The only light was from the fire of the trees and the same light reflecting off the exterior of the golden zeppelin. Between his rage heightening his senses and having grown accustomed to dimness, this was all the light Pradhan needed to fight.

The two large men were climbing the ladder beneath a couple Blessed troops. A few more Blessed soldiers were on the ground below. Pradhan threw his spear – impaling the blessed soldier above the first giant. As the corpse fell from the ladder the second Blessed soldier climbed into the carriage as the giants and the three Blessed soldiers on the ground faced the student.

"We were peaceful!" Pradhan shouted in English.

"The boy knows English?" The giant on the top

9

of the ladder giggled. "Kill him."

The three Blessed soldiers on the ground aimed their rifles at Pradhan. Pradhan charged toward the soldiers as they opened fire. He lowered himself as he ran just enough so that the bullets wouldn't critically injure or kill him – although his back was sliced by a few that grazed his skin. Pradhan swung his sword across the throats of all three Blessed.

"Who gave the order to attack us?!" Pradhan catechized as he retrieved his spear. "TELL ME!"

The second giant dropped from the ladder. He turned to his companion and boomed "Just get going, Kottos. I'll deal with this!"

Kottos rolled his eyes at his brother. "The Sons of War will be here any minute, Briareos!"

"Then I will crush them too!" Briareos roared. Kottos shook his head as he climbed the ladder. The Blessed airship ascended into the sky.

Pradhan threw his spear at Briareos; it lancinated his flesh and went all the way through the gray mass that was the centimane's torso. Briareos stepped back and tore the object from his chest. He looked at Pradhan and laughed. "Good thing ya missed my heart!"

"Did you feel nothing?!" Pradhan quavered.

"You really are in the dark, aren't you?" Briareos realized. "Let me explain this as simply as I can."

Briareos morphed into a monster similar to what Kottos would become outside of Skyrook years later, except he was several feet taller than Kottos and had larger muscles. The flames had nearly finished consuming the trees and the zeppelin was gone – so Pradhan's vision was even more limited. The light from the dying flames just barely embraced the masses between the folds of Briareos' muscles. Pradhan was thankful this beast's skin was gray.

"I'm a Centimane!" Briareos gasconaded. "I've crushed men, beasts, revenants, undead, fabricants, you name it! I even killed titans!"

Pradhan took a deep breath as he dropped his sword.

"Do you yield, then? I promise to make your death quick!" Briareos offered.

Pradhan removed the urumi from his waist and began whipping it around his body as he charged toward the monster before him. Briareos reached his right main hand toward Pradhan – which was instantly minced by the flexible sword. Briareos screeched as he retracted his hand and stepped toward the boy. Pradhan continued his attack across Briareos' shins. The monster fell onto the ground – catching himself with his hands as Pradhan ran between his foe's legs. As Briareos collapsed his chest and abdomen were shredded by the urumi. Once Pradhan was behind the Centimane he severed both the behemoth's legs at the groin. Briareos reached his back arms toward Pradhan but those two hands were sliced from their wrists in the same attack which removed his legs.

Briareos gyrated and stood on his bottom hands. He struggled to contemplate his surroundings as he was standing within a fog of his own ashes and blood. The powdered monster flesh was equally unpleasant for Pradhan – except he ignored the conditions. His mind was fixated on slaying this otherworldly creature. Pradhan continued his attack – the wind created by the flexible sword helped to reduce the morbid pollutants from the air he breathed. With the urumi he lopped off Briareos' top four arms and the faces on the front of his collar.

Briareos walked backwards – using all the strength in his remaining arms to get away from this warrior. What was this boy? Surely, he couldn't be human! At least that is what Briareos concluded. Regular, mortal weapons aren't supposed to be able to penetrate the skin of a Centimane. Unbeknownst to both combatants the incense of the temple contained special properties that, when burned in bulk, would poison hundred-handers so that their skin would weaken. The goliath had tried to formulate an escape plan – he had to venture into the underworld! There he could heal and regenerate, however if he was slain by this boy then his soul would be sent straight to Tartarus. Although that was the realm of his origin he had no desire to be sent back into that pit. With Hades dead the infernal district of the underworld was eternally sealed, and thanks to Kepyet's early rampage there wasn't much to even return to. Briareos considered banishment to Tartarus, his home, now a fate worse than mortal death. One that was endured by his brother, Gyges. A fate he didn't want to share.

Pradhan approached quicker than Briareos could retreat. The monster had one more trick up his sleeve – fire! He opened his mouth and breathed a stream of fire toward his foe. Pradhan stepped aside and just barely evaded the torrential inferno, but the heat was enough to burn his weapon. The urumi reddened from the heat. Pradhan's hand was scourged by the hot metal – but if he were to let go then he would be defenseless against the monster's next attack. He didn't know aught of Centimanes and assumed that they could regenerate flesh. Was he wrong to make such an assumption? The creature had little reaction to being impaled, and was still very much active despite its injuries. That is when Pradhan realized something! Focusing on the memory of when he initiated this fight he ignored the pain from the heat as best he could and swung his urumi for one, final attack. The blade cut across Briareos' neck – decapitating him. As his head rolled backwards and off his shoulders the torrent of fire ended. With the blade still hot Pradhan swung it down into Briareos' chest. He released his grip on the scorching weapon as the blade fell into Briareos' heart. What remained of the Centimane collapsed into a mound of igneous stones.

Pradhan wasn't entirely sure what killed the creature – the decapitation or the strike to its heart. Perhaps it was both. Regardless, it wasn't entirely relevant to him. If he ever encountered Kottos he would immediately strike him the same way. His hand was pink and blistering from the metal, but other than that he was fine. Pradhan smiled – realizing that he had just slain a mythological creature that's arguably as powerful as a god, and that he did so with an urumi! He knew his mentor would have been proud.

His moment of joy was cut short by another realization – he was now lost. The temple was gone and everyone he knew was dead. Although he had never ventured more than fifty or sixty miles from the temple or the nearby village he had heard from travelers that there wasn't much left of the planet. One traveler had even mentioned that one of the last fertile plots of land was claimed by the Blessed and that a large wall was being erected around it. Where would he go? How could he survive? Is his mastery of the urumi – the weapon he devoted his life to mastering, the conclusion of his story?

The land shook with the thundering roar of an engine. Pradhan turned to gaze into the sky and saw a large, red zeppelin flying overhead. The vehicle slowed to a stop. Several guns protruded from the golden carriage below the balloon and aimed at Pradhan. He grabbed the urumi from the mound of ash. Although the weapon had cooled his palm was still covered in fresh burns. The cold, dirty metal tormented his exposed muscles and blood vessels. He didn't care. If he was to die he wanted to die wielding this urumi. The weapon he devoted his life to becoming worthy to wield, and the object his dying Gurukkal gifted to him.

A man leaped from the carriage of the zeppelin. The boots on his feet glowed as he fell at a reduced speed. He appeared Japanese and wore strange-looking goggles; and had an unusual object on his back which appeared to be some sort of bow. The man landed a couple meters in front of Pradhan.

"Do you recognize this ash?" Pradhan asked in Japanese.

"You speak Japanese?" The man answered, also in Japanese and ignoring Pradhan's question.

"I speak many languages, now answer me – do you recognize this ash?" Pradhan ordered.

The man examined the pile of ash in front of Pradhan. He then glimpsed over the ash which covered the ground between the trees – which were now little more than burning stumps.

"Answer me!" Pradhan shouted.

"Is that the ash of a hundred-hander?" The man marveled. "You killed one?"

"They destroyed my temple! They killed all I knew! I killed this one, I want the others! I want the Blessed! They did this!" Pradhan seethed.

"Where are you planning to go?" The bowman inquired.

"I...I don't know..." Pradhan confessed. "All this happened at once! I don't know where there even is TO go."

The man continued to stare at the pile of ash that was once Briareos. "There may be a place for you. We may have a place for you among us."

"Who are you?" Pradhan asked.

"I'm Hachimanson, one of the leaders of The Sons of War. We look for people such as yourself. People who are driven by something greater than themselves with not only elite, but unique combat skills." Hachimanson replied. "Interested?"

"You will find a place for me?" Pradhan muttered nervously. "I'll join. Take me away from here – far away! And let me kill any Blessed we encounter!"

"There is one condition." Hachimanson warned.

"What is it? I'm not getting rid of this weapon!" Pradhan threatened.

"Not that." Hachimanson said. "Any names you have – forget them. The only name you have now is "Warson." I have a feeling you will ascend our ranks, though. Reach the level of councilman and you will be allowed to name yourself after a deity associated with war."

"Very well." Pradhan accepted. "Take me."

CHAPTER 2

Justice's eyes opened to see the inside of a hospital room. The bright light was disorienting. Strange hands grasped her torso and lifted her into the air. As she was elevated she saw her father sitting on a chair. He appeared to be in his mid-to-late thirties. Lucien had a kind face, although his stringy hair was greasy and it was obvious he skipped a couple days of shaving. The sides of his hair dropped just below his ears while the back was tied into a ponytail. Justice was pulled backwards into the arms of a woman – her mother.

Cooper Thomas stood in the corner the room, watching Justice closely. He was about the same age as her father. His black bangs were evenly trimmed just above his dark eyes. Cooper's hair gradually grew longer as it wrapped behind his head, the hair on the back of his head dropped just below his neck. His upper-lip and chin were both covered by a goatee. An eerie feeling overwhelmed Justice as she watched nurses enter and leave the room without even noticing Cooper.

Lucien stood and approached the hospital bed. He spoke as he knelt down next to Unity. "She looks so healthy!"

"What do you want to name her?" Unity asked.

"You know I'm awful with names." Lucien chuckled. "I'll let you have the honor."

"Hmm..." Unity contemplated. She looked up at the television in the corner of the hospital room. The news was on and currently reporting that a murderer was going to be set free, even though there was irrefutable evidence against him.

"We could half-ass it and open the baby book, too." Lucien suggested.

"I have a name." Unity smirked. "Justice. Because the world needs more."

Lucien nodded. "Justice, I like it."

"Didn't Cooper say he wanted to be here for this?" Unity remembered.

Justice was confused by her mother's question, as she saw Cooper standing in the corner.

"Yeah but, you know how he is. Especially when it comes to our work." Lucien grumbled.

Suddenly, the goddess Nemesis appeared in the room sporting a dress of gold fabric with angelic white wings sprouting from her back. Nemesis wore a white headpiece which covered the top half of her head – including her eyes. Curly red hair dropped from below the cap and down her back. In her right hand was a silver sword. Her weapon had a rather basic shape – however all light that hit it was reflected ten-fold. Time froze as she appeared, with the exception of

Cooper. He directed his attention toward the goddess and glared at her. His eyes radiated with fear. Nemesis swung her sword around the room – slicing the throats of Cooper, Unity, and Lucien. She ended her attack by returning her blade to Cooper – landing it in his chest.

Justice gasped as she woke in her bed. The first thing she saw upon opening her eyes was the terrifying mural of Kepyet on the ceiling. Knocking was heard on her door.

"Hey, Justice, awake yet?" Ellis shouted through the door.

"Awake?" Justice mumbled, somewhat muddled. Her dream was so realistic, as if it wasn't a dream at all. She felt as if she was just snagged from one place and dropped in another. As she learned from Jasper, dreams in Skyrook weren't normal and may have meaning. But what meaning could an altered memory of her birth have? Why was Cooper in the delivery room, and why did Nemesis kill him and her parents? Why was she spared from the goddess' attack? Why did Nemesis strike Cooper twice?

"Yes, awake...are you okay?" Ellis drawled.

"I'm fine! What time is it?" Justice yelped, still sitting in her bed.

"About an hour after you were supposed to be up!" Ellis teased. "Didn't you set an alarm?"

Justice looked at the alarm next to her bed. The screen had a dust-filled crack on the edge and the lights were flickering.

"I think it broke again!" Justice assumed. "Wait, you waited an hour before checking up?"

"I have shit to do in the morning too, kid!" Ellis replied. "Hurry up – the holy folks' tank is about ready."

"Oh! Right!" Justice shouted as she remembered what today's plan was. She threw the covers off her bed and nearly teleported across the room to her dresser. "I'll be ready soon!"

"Sure." Ellis mumbled as his footsteps were heard walking away.

Justice changed out of her pajamas and into her Nute battle uniform as quickly as she could. Although she was thrown off by that odd dream she didn't have the time to meditate on it right now. Three months had passed since she had killed Vritra. Shortly after the beast was slain Jasper had discovered a secret door within Skyrook. Well – he discovered a door had been repurposed. An argument between him and Eric which could only be described as stupid lead to him making the decision to re-enter the ascending labyrinth. However, when Jasper opened the door it led into a massive library rather than the accursed maze. Upon the main lectern was a tome containing encyclopedic information about the devourers. According to that large book the next devourer to appear would be Bakunawa. The more pressing concern though was The Sons of War clan. Earth still had a few weeks before Bakunawa would appear, but The Sons of War had Cooper's alchemy notes for a quarter of a year now and there were already reports of them sending their scouts to investigate the various settlements across the globe.

The Blessed had a subterranean warehouse just outside of Skyrook – another thing they had kept hidden from Justice and her companions! Within the warehouse was a stockpile of machinery and weapon parts. With the assistance of some recruits from New Ur they used the materials in the warehouse to construct a ginormous tank. Their hope was that the tank would be shielded and powerful enough to access the new base of the Warsons and finish them off once and for all.

Justice had finished getting dressed and vacated her room, glancing at the mural of Kepyet on her way out. She entered the ballroom where Teigao, Ellis, Jasper, Eric, and Bruno were standing around the planning table.

Bruno was one of the new recruits. He was in his mid-forties and donned a neatly-trimmed red mustache. His head appeared bald from a distance – but it was gently covered by a thin layer of hair. Bruno carried a long-barreled pistol on each side of his abdomen along with a mace on his back. His mannerisms were those of a military man.

"The what, now?" Teigao strained.

"The monk." Bruno said. "That's the name that's been coming up for the last few months."

"What is going on?" Justice asked as she entered the room.

"Apparently there's some new group going around interrogating people who are old enough to remember details from the war." Ellis explained. "All we know about them is that they're shady and that their leader calls himself "The Monk.""

"Okay, so we have a rogue...historian?" Justice paused. "What's the concern?"

"Apparently they ask a lot of questions about Kepyet." Jasper remarked. "Using his name too – as if too many didn't already know it."

"They might be after his remaining relics." Eric theorized. "Anat was able to find his egregore, there is a possibility he has other shrines that weren't properly desecrated."

"Speaking of her..." Justice turned her attention to Ellis. "Are you prepared to fight her? And you know...get the job done this time?"

"She told me herself." Ellis sighed. "Kaleyla died in our old home. Whoever that fiend is – it isn't the friend I grew up with."

Justice nodded. "Emotions aside – she won't be easy. Heavens know what other upgrades she has done to herself since Jasper shot her."

"I'm a bit concerned about the guy that saved her." Eric admitted. "He survived two airship explosions seemingly unscathed, and your Anat appears to have a LOT of trust placed in him."

"That would be Hanumanson." Bruno clarified. "His youth was devoted to martial arts. Legend has it he killed a Centimane."

"Briareos." Teigao confirmed. "I made the mistake of letting him and Kottos lead a scout mission across South India. Basil was with them. They discovered some remote temple complex the war had not yet reached. Basil noticed them cremating one of Kepyet's revenants. He convinced everyone that the temple was a sleeper cell for Kepyet's army. Briareos lead the attack. Killed everyone there except for one young man. Last report we received was that Briareos attacked him while the others flew to meet us at Kepyet's stronghold. Lost contact with Briareos, about a day after Kepyet was defeated we sent someone over there to investigate. Found nothing but a pile of Centimane ash."

"So...Hanumanson killed him?" Justice

marveled.

"That's what we assume." Teigao said as Eric nodded.

"Well if this tank works then neither him or Anat will be a concern, right?" Ellis blurted.

"Hopefull..." Jasper started before remembering how Justice hates that word. "With any luck...yes." He finished as Justice giggled.

"We are also just assuming they haven't developed any new weapons from Kepyet's research?" Bruno criticized.

"That drive is LOADED with viruses." Teigao reassured. "We couldn't get past the first entry, and that's when we had New Jericho. I doubt our barbaric friends in the mountains have anything better."

A subtle smile formed below Bruno's mustache, almost a laugh, as he nodded. "Right."

At the headquarters of The Sons of War Anat was sleeping in her bed. In her dream she was in a hospital delivery room, although unlike Justice's dream, this delivery room was rather run-down. Gravity was peeling strips of paint from the walls and the majority of the metal pipes and vents were showing signs of rust. The lights on the ceiling were just as bright as in Justice's dream, except the bulbs behind these were flickering. A cacaesthesia overwhelmed Anat's senses as she took notice of the moldered condition of the delivery room.

Across from the hospital bed was her father – an alcoholic man in his forties. His puffy, gray hair circled around a massive bald spot on his bruised head. Some of the bruising appeared recent while there were scars which indicated that he had suffered many head injuries – likely a result of collapses from alcohol intake. Her father wore a tattered flannel shirt with stained jeans. He held a bottle of cheap whiskey in his left hand. The way he swayed in his seat suggested that he was already inebriated.

A feeling of anger filled Anat when she saw her father. He wasn't in her life for long, but she had only bad memories from the time he was. She considers the day of his death as one of the best days of her life – even though she was young when it happened. The sensation was soon replaced with confusion as she noticed a different figure standing in the room. In the corner was a man wearing jet black robes crafted from armored fabric. His face was covered by a black, metal mask which had few features. Was that Kepyet? He wasn't present when she was born. Cooper Thomas was alive then, but he had no connections to her family. Why was Kepyet there?

"I told you it would be a girl!" Her father blurted.

"I never said it wouldn't be one I said I would rather have one!" Her mother screeched. Anat's mother wasn't much better of a parent. Her face was aged from heavy drug use earlier in life, and half of her teeth were missing. Needle scars covered the space between the cheap tattoos on the woman's arms. The majority of the tattoos were warped and severely faded, it was obvious they weren't done by a professional, or so much as someone who simply watched an instructional video.

"Well what are we gonna name it?" Her father shouted.

"I don't know – I kind of like my mom's suggestion – Leah!" The woman shouted back.

"I ain't'in taking a rekkomendshun from that skank!" He slurred. "What about Keah? Key-uh. Kia! "K" is first 'effore "L"!"

"Well if you want her to have a first first name why not something with an "A"?" Anat's mother asked.

"Why?" The man whined. "It's a lazy soundin' letter. All you gotta do to say it is open your face up and exhale! "K" is a nice letter, right in the middle of the alphabet."

"Well what about Kaliyah?" The woman asked. "I had a coworker named that. She was pretty cool."

"Kaleyla?" The man mispronounced. "Yeah we can go with that!"

The doctor, who's facial expression suggested he had already had enough of this couple, handed Anat's father a clipboard and queried "So, you've decided to name her "Kaliyah?" Can you write that down, please?"

Anat's father accepted the clipboard and scribbled the misspelling of her intended name. Time slowed to a stop as he set the pen down. Kepyet stepped into the middle of the room.

"I thought I was rid of you!" Baby Anat shouted in her adult voice.

"Why? Because my egregore dumped itself off below the castle?" Kepyet asked as he grabbed the shoulder of her father. Black flames engulfed the drunkard and disintegrated him.

"So, you left part of it behind?" Anat hissed. "To accomplish what? I am NOT my parents! I am well educated, intelligent, fierce..."

"And still bewildered." Kepyet chuckled as he gently caressed his pointer finger across the cheek of the doctor – reducing him to ash. "I did

not attend your birth, you are correct there."
Kepyet poked Anat's mother's hand – causing the
woman to also degrade into a pile of ash. Anat's
infantile body dropped about six inches onto the
cover of the hospital bed as the arms holding her
crumbled. Kepyet continued, speaking softly.
"That being said – I have been with you your
entire life. Time works in funny ways, and the
human subconscious, especially the
subconscious of an elite soul, operates in even
stranger ways."

"So, is this my subconscious or is there some
pre-programmed message here?" Anat muttered.

"We are in your head...But the mind is
also...quite...large." Kepyet drawled.

Anat woke to the sound of footsteps. The slow
pace of the tapping along the floor suggested the
person walking was orchestrating a failed attempt
at stealth. She tossed the cover off her bed and
stood. The low cut of her undershirt revealed that
she now had a metal plate integrated into her
chest between her breasts – a device to protect
her heart that would also administer an antidote
to almost any poison that would enter her
bloodstream. As she walked the ruckus of her
internal upgrades produced a much softer sound
– implying that her bionics had been improved.

Anat creeped down the hallway – following the
direction of the footsteps. She stepped up the
nearby staircase as the first door in the next
hallway closed. It was the door of the office where
the flash drive with Cooper's notes was stored.
She opened the door and saw a Warson soldier in
front of the computer.

"Excuse me?" Anat hissed, startling the
Warson. "What are you doing?"

"Lady Anat Bellonadaughter!" The Warson quavered as he bowed. "My apologies, I thought I had an idea on how to decode the virus on..."

Anat gave her foot a single, loud tap. The Warson stopped talking, stood, and saluted.

"What do you know of computers?" Anat catechized.

"Well, before my life here, I was a programmer, ma'am..." The man stuttered.

"Were you, now?" Anat smirked. "And I am just now learning of this? After myself and Hanumanson have made the need for an experienced programmer more than obvious?"

"I am new, ma'am. There were other things I had to -" The Warson panicked.

"No." Anat interjected. "You joined...about three months ago? I am fully aware the Blessed posted a bounty for this flash drive the week I stole it. They also have lesser bounties floating around on myself and Hanumanson. I find it rather funny that you joined shortly after the postings."

"Coincidence, ma'am." The Warson assured.

"You think because I am violent I must be ignorant?" Anat growled. "I have watched you, I watch everyone. You do learn our ways well, and you have more than an interest. Your acting though – awful. The other recruits learn because they wish to perform, they wish to execute their orders with precision. They learn as much as they can because they intend to apply it – becoming one of us. You...you learn so you can study. Research."

"I learn faster than anyone else!" The Warson argued.

"Exactly!" Anat laughed. "It's easier to learn

when you learn for the sake of research. The others are slower not because they are dumb, but because they incorporate what they learn into their identity! What they practice is to become a permanent part of who they are."

The man opened his mouth to speak – but Anat grabbed his wrist. She tugged him across the room and to the cement wall. Using the motors of her robotic limb she vibrated her hand as fast as possible – scraping his against the wall. The man screamed in agony as his hand was eroded. Drops of blood splashed onto both his and Anat's arms. Chunks of his skin adhered to the wall. Blood slowly dripped onto the floor from where his hand was being grated. Once the flesh was gone his bones were rubbed against the wall. A subtle, but ear-piercing squeak was produced as the skeleton of his hand was worn away. Anat continued grating his hand until there was nothing left but a small stub at the end of his wrist. The friction produced enough heat to cauterize the wound. Anat released his wrist and he stepped back. His shoes gurgled as their soles absorbed some of the blood on the floor.

"If I see you again, the next thing I'll grind against a wall will be your cock. Get out of here." Anat ordered.

The man held the remnant of the base of his hand and rushed out the door. A moment later Hanumanson entered the room. He was wearing a red undershirt and sweatpants. Silver tattoos covered his arms, the tattoos were writings in Tamil script. He held his adamant urumi in his right hand.

"I heard a shout, what happened..." Hanumanson started speaking as he noticed the bloody footprints leading away from a wall covered in shredded skin and tiny chunks of bone. "...here?" He sighed. "You're going to make another janitor quit."

"If they can't handle the sight of blood then they don't belong here." Anat rolled her eyes.

"That is not what I'm talking about." Hanumanson alleged. "Blood doesn't come out of objects as easily as it does people. Our supply of cleaning chemicals is growing limited. Anyway – who did you torture?"

"Someone the Blessed hired to research us and possibly steal the flash drive." Anat answered as she excavated a handgun from one of the desk drawers.

"And you are just going to let him escape, minus whatever limb you painted the wall with?" Hanumanson deprecated.

"Of course not!" Anat chittered as she approached the window.

The moment Anat reached the window she stuck her hand through it and aimed the gun straight down. She pulled the trigger as the traitor stepped outside the base. The bullet entered the top of his head, passed through his heart, shredded his stomach and intestines, then burst from his crotch before landing in the ground. He fell forward – bleeding from both ends of his body.

Hanumanson looked out the window as Anat stepped away and returned the gun to the drawer. "How is everything you do always so precise?" He quaeritated.

"Half of it is luck." Anat confessed.

"And the other half?" Hanumanson asked.

"I like my fun." Anat giggled.

"Fun for me growing up was sparring with my fellow pupils and mastering our yoga exercises." Hanumanson said. "Before I had my urumis."

"Before killing my fun was..." Anat thought for a moment. "Excluding the trouble Ellis and I got into, my fun moments in life were mostly on the internet. I miss memes."

"Ugh, you too?" Hanumanson shook his head. "Memes sound so stupid, why couldn't you people just come outright and say what you wanted to?"

"Well, we ARE talking about fun, and your suggestion wasn't always fun." Anat smiled. "Wait, you're barely younger than I am! Surely, you remember them as well?"

"I grew up in a temple, remember?" Hanumanson lectured. "Although we did have internet access I only used it to research languages and fighting techniques."

The sun began to rise. Red light from behind the clouds shined into the room.

"I suppose it's time for us to get dressed. Did you collect that program last night?" Anat asked.

"Yes, I'll retrieve the disc from my quarters. It should counteract the viruses on the flash drive and allow us to study the notes." Hanumanson said.

Anat nodded as they vacated the room together.

***

The Blessed airship was hovering just outside of Skyrook with a massive tank parked below. The Blessed tank was roughly twice the size of a double-wide trailer home. There were four armored treads on the sides and fifty metal wheels along the center of the bottom. The bottom edges of the tank contained multiple high-power energy shield generators, and the exterior plating was crafted from diamond-coated adamant. The internal cavity of the tank was split into three rooms. In the front was the main control room with the computers which drove the tank and managed the shields and radar. The rear chamber was primarily a storage room to hold weapons and soldiers. Above and between the two large rooms was a significantly smaller room which controlled the guns. The tank had two small, but armored machine guns up front – one on each side. A large, repeating cannon rested on top near the center. Flamethrowers were built into the fronts of the treads' wheel guards. Several plates of armor on the back of the tank split open as a ramp slid out.

Bruno, Ellis, and Justice ambled out of Skyrook and approached the tank. Jasper stood within the storage room of the monstrous vehicle.

"Hey guys, this thing is FUN!" Jasper blurted. "Slow as hell – but fun!"

"How slow are we talking?" Ellis inquired.

"Slow as in the speedometer is measured in miles." Jasper laughed.

"Damn..." Justice remarked. "Now I understand the need to fly there."

"Still faster than the Exile!" Ellis taunted.

"All it needs now is the engine!" Jasper alleged.

Justice rolled her eyes as Bruno said "This argument again?"

"It needs to be scrapped!" Ellis sneered.

"Really guys? We all know this argument never goes anywhere." Justice pleaded.

"At least my car is dependable when it works!" Jasper yelled. "Unlike the Cannon where you never know when something will go wrong!"

"You mean the vehicle we've lived in and evaded gangs with for eighteen years?" Ellis raised his voice.

"Enough!" Bruno ordered. "Is everything in the tank functional?"

"Sir! Yes, Sir!" Jasper bellowed with a salute as Justice and Ellis shook their heads.

"Good, once we are all inside we are not to leave the tank unless it becomes absolutely necessary for the assault." Bruno announced as he entered the massive vehicle. Ellis, Jasper, and Justice followed. A couple Blessed soldiers and a golem were already sitting inside. Only one of the soldiers had gleaming azure eyes. He was a middle-aged man with several scars on his jaw. The rear hatch closed.

Bruno grabbed an intercom device from the wall and spoke into it. "Alright, Eric. Let's get this show on the road!"

The bottom of the zeppelin's carriage opened as a makeshift claw slowly dropped from the hole. Magnets within the claw activated – lifting the tank into the air. After about a minute the tank was high enough to be secured by the clamps. The claw firmly grasped the tank as the engines of the zeppelin started.

"I'm impressed an airship can carry this thing!" Justice marveled.

The older Blessed soldier smiled and said "Well, Kepyet had us beat in the magic department, so we were kind of forced to maintain a technological advantage."

"Yeah, too bad you folks never picked up after yourselves." Ellis deprecated.

"What are you talking about?" Bruno aggressively muttered.

"After the war they left a shit ton of their military tech behind!" Ellis ranted. "The Sons of War found and repurposed much of it and used the weapons to terrorize the world while the Blessed sat safe in their city."

"We didn't seal ourselves away out of cowardice!" The older soldier alleged. "Do you really think the world would have been better had we remained among the common folk?"

"Ellis..." Justice hissed.

"You had pretty quality lives behind those walls, not to mention REAL food!" Ellis accused.

"We did have resources, yes, but how long do you suppose they would have lasted had we shared?" The soldier asked. "If we took people in – how long do you think they would have appreciated our hospitality before turning on us? Remember – we were hated. There was collateral damage from the war we are guilty of, we had resources bandits desired, and there was the population that supported Kepyet. The Sons of War had a few healthy stockpiles as well. They aren't above destroying the supplies of their foes."

"At least they didn't hide!" Ellis remarked.

"Didn't they?" The soldier riposted. "What do you call occupying the inside of a mountain filled with guns and bombs?"

"To be fair – they often left Underlook." Jasper added.

"What good is arguing about this going to do?" Justice yelled. "Kepyet and his creatures are gone, the Blessed are just about gone, and today we are going to end The Sons of War! No point in arguing over who was right or wrong nearly twenty years ago!"

"I'm just saying..." Ellis instigated.

"Ellis..." Justice repeated.

"If it weren't for Basil that man would be sitting in some castle." Ellis continued.

"Ellis!" Justice raised her voice.

"Eating steak, drinking wine." Ellis persisted.

"Ellis!" Justice nagged.

"While we ate expired canned goods." Ellis rambled.

"ELLIS!" Justice roared. The echo of her voice danced around the chamber – it almost overpowered the ruckus from the airship's engines.

"We can argue later." Bruno said. "Right now let's keep our focus on raiding the Warson headquarters."

The airship rumbled as the Blessed reached their destination. Eric stopped the zeppelin above a clearing just outside the narrow valley The Sons of War occupied. The claw released its grip and powered down the magnets – lowering the tank onto the ground.

Eric's voice came in through the intercom. "Alright guys, we're here. I'll stay back and come in if you need air support – but the tank should be enough to bring a quick end to those bastards. Good   luck!"

CHAPTER 3

Jasper stepped into the front control room as the younger soldier climbed into the artillery room. The tank plowed through the decaying brush and gravel along the narrow path leading to the valley. Jasper made sure that the stealth features were all activated. Metal towers stood on each side of the main gate – with comet rocket cannons for turrets. The gate was roughly fifty feet tall but had little detail beyond its dark color. Its black paint was chipping from the rust. Paint chipped from the towers in a similar fashion, and they were also basic in shape. The towers were simple cylinders with small, pyramid shaped huts sheltering the comet rocket cannons.

As the tank approached the gates Bruno leaned into the corner. He tapped a few buttons on the device covering his wrist.

Within Warson HQ Anat and Hanumanson entered the office, wearing their regular armor. Hanumanson held a CD in his hand. A beeping sound was emitted from Anat's wrist.

"What's that?" Hanumanson asked, startled by the sound.

"Sec." Anat mumbled as she scrutinized a screen on her wrist. A message appeared that read "Special Delivery". Anat smiled upon reading it.

"What?" Hanumanson queried, his curiosity piqued by her sinister grin.

"I got us a gift. Sorry for the secrecy, but I wanted to surprise you." Anat purred.

"I'm confused." Hanumanson admitted. "What have you brought us?"

Anat leaned against the wall as she answered "The end of the Blessed!"

***

Jasper chuckled as they approached. "Sweet! The gate is open!"

As the tank passed through the gate Bruno typed a code into a device on the wall – overriding the stealth system! The turrets immediately aimed at the tank.

"Damn!" Jasper blurted. He grabbed the intercom. "Stealth gone, towers – NOW!"

The gunner rotated the main gun of the tank – firing two massive shots as he did so. Each blast struck one of the towers as the tank continued moving forward.

"What's happening?!" Ellis shouted.

"I don't know!" Jasper squealed. "The stealth system was shut down – now the tank set itself on autopilot and I can't fix it!"

"What do you mean?" Justice consternated.

"We're driving right into their base with no stealth or control!" Jasper panicked.

Bruno quickly unholstered his pistols and shot

the controls of the tank. Jasper was slightly burned from the sparks as the tank stopped moving. Warson snipers gathered atop the nearby mountains and fortress – aiming their rifles at the tank. Several Xports towing comet rocket cannons drove into sight.

The veteran Blessed drew his dagger and swung it as quickly as he could – destroying both of Bruno's guns. "You!" He shouted. "Traitor! I knew we shouldn't have accepted new recruits!"

Bruno laughed as he tossed a small bead into the air. It gave off a magnetic pulse that disabled the main gun.

"Long live the Sons of War!" Bruno shouted as he tore the pin from a grenade on the wall and fell in the opposite direction. The Blessed soldier pushed Ellis and Justice into the control room as the grenade exploded – leaving a hole in the side of the tank.

Bruno stood and rushed outside. Justice attempted to chase him but Ellis grabbed her by the back of the collar.

"What are you doing!" Justice cried. "He's getting away!"

"Every sniper they have probably has their gun aimed at that hole!" Ellis argued as the younger soldier dropped from the artillery room.

"What form of malison has befallen us?" The younger soldier quavered.

"Bruno was working for the Sons of War all along!" Ellis growled. "Brought us right into a trap – we're sitting ducks!"

As Bruno ran outside he threw another bead at the front of the tank – weakening the shields and disabling the machine guns. He laughed maniacally as he approached the main building.

Justice grabbed the intercom from the wall. "Eric! Eric are you okay?"

"Yeah, what's wrong?" Eric drawled.

"Bruno was a Warson!" Justice panted.

"What?!" Eric's voice trembled.

"We need the snipers taken out along with any comet guns you can hit!" Justice begged as the tank began to shake from receiving comet rocket fire.

"Damn! Alright – I'm coming in!" Eric announced.

"How long will these shields hold?" Justice asked the older Blessed.

"Two or three barrages." The soldier answered. "There's a small army here though – we're screwed if we can't get out of this valley soon!"

Hanumanson laughed as he looked out the window.

"See?" Anat effused.

"I see! I see!" Hanumanson cheered. "Congratulations, my lady!"

The Blessed airship appeared between the two mountains at the entrance of the valley.

Hanumanson pouted. "Did you know they brought backup?"

"It wasn't hard to assume." Anat shrugged.

"So, it's a no, then?" Hanumanson sighed.

"It's a "no matter"". Anat uttered as she activated her vocal implants. She shouted so loud that all the Sons of War could hear her. "Keep the rockets on the tank – fire a pulse at the airship!"

The comet rockets began to cool down and reload as two Xports drove by hauling a trailer with a strange-looking tank on the base. The tank was missing its wheels and rather than a gun it carried a device that looked like a flat satellite dish. Eric used the zeppelin's guns to bombard all the snipers and one of the comet rockets before the whimsical device fired a bolt of green lightning at the airship. The Blessed zeppelin rolled onto its side and gently crashed on the top of a nearby mountain.

"Dammit!" Eric shouted over the intercom.

"What's wrong?" Justice panicked.

"They have some weird gun that shut me down! I took out as many as I could but you're still against quite an army!" Eric ranted.

"Golem time." The older soldier stated as he activated the Blessed golem.

Hanumanson growled. "Our snipers!"

"Calm down." Anat ordered. "A necessary sacrifice. We still have the comet rockets and regular soldiers. The Blessed die today!"

Bruno sprinted toward the central building as the Blessed golem stepped through the hole. It fired a long-distance slug as it charged toward the building. The bullet entered Bruno's back and burst from his chest – killing him.

"There goes your spy." Hanumanson remarked.

Anat ignored his comment. Hanumanson correctly postulated that she had planned on killing Bruno anyway. She shouted at her soldiers. "Take out that golem!"

Multiple Sons of War soldiers exited the barracks with their guns. They opened fire on the golem – which ran through the shower of bullets unscathed. The golem was crafted from enchanted metal and ceramics, the occult energies within the fabricant protected it from most weapons. The bullets of the Warsons only scratched the golem's paint.

Inside the tank the younger soldier was

fumbling with the wires of the artillery. A humming sound was heard as he soldered several together. Sparks were emitted from the point where the three wires were linked – but wrapping the sizzling metal wires in electric tape wasn't a pressing nor really a necessary priority.

"Yes!" He cheered. "The big gun is back online!"

"Excellent!" The older soldier exulted. "Shoot the large structure built into the mountainside – then the barracks!"

"Blast that anti-air thing too!" Justice added.

"Got it!" The younger soldier answered as he aimed the gun. He fired the first round.

The blast from the tank landed in the room just above Anat and Hanumanson. Bricks fell from the ceiling as sections of floor collapsed.

"Dammit!" Anat screeched.

"I thought the big gun was disabled?!" Hanumanson barked as the tank blew up the green lightning cannon before beginning to obliterate the other buildings in the base. The golem shot down the majority of the soldiers firing upon it as it neared the main structure.

"It was! Clever little shrews..." Anat hissed.

"Here!" Hanumanson gasped as he tore the flash drive from the computer and handed it to Anat along with the disc.

"What is this?" Anat asked.

"They've leveled the playing field – we can't take any risks. You take these, leave this valley and pay a visit to our founders!" Hanumanson implored.

"That old sleeper cell? We aren't even sure they're still active!" Anat argued. "I'm better off here."

"We can't take the risk!" Hanumanson

shouted. "The Sons of War needs a strong leader, needs you. If we are defeated in this battle then you will win us the war. Take it! Go!"

Anat nodded. "If you kill Ellis – I want his body brought to me."

Hanumanson smiled. "Of course, my lady!"

Anat rushed out the room as Hanumanson gazed back out the window – watching the tank flatten their base.

Anat ran down the stairs. She reached the bottom floor as the golem burst through the wall. Several slugs flew from the golem's arms – taking out all the Warson soldiers in the room. Anat sprinted to the golem before its programming could fixate on her. She grabbed the top of its head and rotated her hand like a drill. The golem's head spun as Anat unscrewed it from the torso. Once the golem's head was removed she crushed the cranium and dropped what remained of the expressionless face and jaw. The golem's body vibrated as it attempted to reconfigure itself. Anat reached into the neck and used her robotic hand to mangle the golem's insides. Magical fog spewed from the golem's husk as it collapsed. Anat turned around and sauntered toward the secret exit in the back of the structure.

The gun on top of the tank overheated as the remaining Warsons approached the tank with their rifles. A loud popping noise filled the air as the energy shields flickered.

"Shit!" Jasper gibbered. "Gun will take a few minutes to cool – what do we do?!"

"Any sign of Anat?" Ellis asked as Jasper panned through the cameras and scopes.

"No..." Jasper mumbled. "But the sword whip guy is in the window up there!"

"I have an idea then!" Ellis announced. "I can challenge him to a duomachy – buy us some time."

"And get yourself killed?" Justice replied.

"I'm a better fighter than you know..." Ellis lectured.

"I have a better idea." The older soldier said. "Let me challenge him. As I fight the kid can come out and ambush him. Then you guys can quickly take out the last few Warsons."

"That might work!" Justice admitted as the younger soldier dropped from the artillery room.

The older soldier stepped through the hole with his hands up. He had to speak fast as the energy shield was growing weak. The man could feel the static electricity as it filled his body. Nervousness overcame him as the shield's steady growls became successive cracks.

"I request to speak with your leader!" The older soldier shouted to the Warsons. The Warson soldiers stopped shooting – but kept their guns focused on the Blessed. Hanumanson couldn't hear what was said, but he correctly assumed what was happening and leaped from the window. His boots slowed his descent.

Hanumanson laughed as he approached. "You can not talk your way out of this. You can not bargain your way out of this. The Blessed die today. My adamant urumi has been hardened. You can not shelter your allies, my weapon can mince your tank."

"I recognize that!" The solder confessed. "I desire only an honorable death."

"I respect your dignity, azure-eyes. But I am not going to waste my time with a formal execution." Hanumanson said sternly as he continued to approach.

"Duomachy!" The Blessed soldier requested.

"Terms?" Hanumanson accepted.

"One on one to the death!" The soldier specified.

"If I win your allies still die." Hanumanson clarified. "I accept."

"This is for myself." The Soldier mumbled.

"So it is..." Hanumanson smirked as he rushed toward the Blessed soldier. The soldier stepped through the tank's shield and drew his sword. It was a simple sword with an average-sized blade attached to a cross-guard with a gold hilt. The soldier sprinted toward Hanumanson as the younger Blessed soldier ran out of the tank with a grenade and a shotgun.

Hanumanson twitched his head – signaling the Warsons to hold their fire as the younger Blessed soldier tossed the grenade into the air. Hanumanson whipped his urumi below the wrist of the older soldier then flicked it up – slicing off the man's hand. As his sword fell the blade of the urumi passed through the cross-guard and sliced the sword in half. Hanumanson continued raising the urumi until it struck the grenade – blowing it up in the air a safe distance from himself but close enough to the Blessed veteran to bombard the back of his skull with shrapnel.

The younger soldier raised his shotgun as the older man fell, but the tip of Hanumanson's urumi extended toward the Blessed recruit and traveled up the barrel of the shotgun – causing it to explode in his hands. Hanumanson flicked his urumi to the side – slicing the recruit's stomach open. He retracted the urumi as the young man fell face-first onto the ground. Hanumanson stepped over the older soldier and chuckled "So much for honor."

Ellis and Justice stepped outside of the tank – knowing that if nobody stepped out the next strike would pierce through their shields and kill them anyway. Jasper climbed into the artillery room as they did so – waiting for the gun to recharge.

"So, you're the ones who have been causing our leader so much trouble, isn't there a third of you?" Hanumanson asked.

"Jasper is on the airship you disabled." Ellis lied.

Hanumanson lashed the urumi into the tank's main gun – ruining it but not cutting deep enough to strike Jasper. Hanumanson smiled. "Can't take any chances. I can respect that you stepped outside to face me. If you desire a clean death I will oblige, otherwise I am open to a duel."

"Well we came here for one reason..." Ellis started.

"To end The Sons of War!" Justice finished as she drew Sal's sword and charged at the Warson soldiers. Ellis drew a sword similar to the one the veteran Blessed soldier used while assailing Hanumanson.

Justice's uniform borrowed shielding from the generators on the tank – protecting her from the bullets the Warsons fired at her. Realizing they couldn't draw her away from the tank, they dropped their guns and attacked her with their swords. While their strikes were disciplined and precise, she spent the majority of the fight evading and blocking their attacks.

Hanumanson whipped his urumi all around Ellis – coming within millimeters of striking him.

The devices on the corners of Hanumanson's eyes glowed as his peripheral vision was improved and more in tune with his reflexes. Ellis raised the sword but Hanumanson's urumi caught on the cross-guard and cut the blade clean off. Ellis dropped the cross-guard and it landed next to the soldier's. The blade also landed near the first Hanumanson severed.

"Well that's cheap!" Ellis blurted as he ran around Hanumanson – just barely out of strike range.

"My Gurukkal taught me to go for the kill rather than drawing out the fight." Hanumanson said as he attempted to strike farther out to hit Ellis.

The tip of the urumi passed less than a millimeter from Ellis' nose. For a moment Ellis believed his face had been cut, as there was a lingering cool spot from the tiny gust of wind. Hanumanson flicked the urumi back toward Ellis, who leaned backward and rolled. A few of Ellis' hairs on the back of his head were sliced by the flexible blade. Ellis wondered about the length of his opponent's weapon – as he was becoming unsure of how much longer he could evade the strikes. Every lash was as silent as it was quick and precise. Ellis somersaulted backwards to evade Hanumanson's next sweep.

"Anat didn't want to murder me herself?" Ellis perplexed while pivoting his body around his elbow to evade yet another lash.

"She trusted me to get the job done." Hanumanson bragged as he continued his assault.

As Ellis rolled out of the way of another urumi strike he pressed a button on the side of his uniform. It released a temporary energy shield. The shield only held for a split-second, but it was strong enough to deflect adamant. Hanumanson's modified alloy allowed his urumi to cut into the energy but when the shield faded the final burst twisted the blade so that it would lash toward its wielder. Hanumanson jumped to avoid being crippled by his own weapon. Ellis used this moment to regain his footing and step closer to his foe. As Hanumanson stepped back and prepared his urumi for another strike Ellis drew his handgun. The gun was similar in design to a flintlock and only carried a single bullet. Ellis fired it before Hanumanson had a chance to comprehend what was happening, striking the Warson in the chest and launching him back. The armor below his garments protected him from being injured, but the force caused him to drop his weapon. Ellis briskly snagged the urumi as he shouted "Now, Jasper!"

The flamethrowers below the tank activated – sending a wave of fire over Hanumanson. Hanumanson casually climbed onto his feet – as if the fires weren't even near him! Ellis debated with himself about the urumi, but thought it best to not risk killing himself with the difficult weapon and threw it into the burning ruins of a nearby structure. Jasper deactivated the flamethrowers – realizing that they had no effect on the Warson. Justice continued to annoy the remaining six Sons of War soldiers as Jasper climbed down from the artillery control room.

"How?!" Ellis stuttered.

"Remember when we first captured your elemental friend?" Hanumanson cackled. "I made sure to fireproof everything of mine."

"But you have exposed skin on your face and hands!" Ellis argued.

"Training." Hanumanson bragged. "When I was young I fought a hundred-hander. I won, I killed it. But it almost beat me with its fire. Since then I meditated with fire every day. I do not feel heat."

Ellis drew his knife. "Well I'm certain you can feel steel!"

"You fight me with a tiny knife?" Hanumanson giggled.

"You are unarmed!" Ellis pointed out.

"I'm armed with exactly what I need." Hanumanson threatened as he removed his shirt – exposing the thin metal plates beneath. The Warson leader then flipped a switch on his armor – causing it to crumble from his body. Hanumanson revealed that he was covered in silver tattoos. He had so many that from a distance it appeared as if he had silver skin on his arms and torso. The tattoos were all writings in Tamil script.

"Please tell me you're keeping your pants on..." Ellis begged – holding his knife in an aggressive stance.

"You're a funny man." Hanumanson growled sarcastically as he reached toward his waist. "It is funny how fate works. Eighteen years ago I watched my Gurukkal die." He lifted a metal handle from inside the waistline of his pants. "He was like a father to me. His final request was for me to take his weapon."

Hanumanson unraveled his belt – revealing it was his original urumi!

"Aww hell!" Ellis moaned as Hanumanson flaunted his weapon.

"He was killed by the Blessed." Hanumanson

lectured. "We were peaceful! Neutral from the war! Kind of like how you were. The Sons of War are not without sin – but the Blessed took my life from me! I was driven here with nothing else. What reason do you have to side with murderers?"

Jasper stepped out of the tank with two handguns. The Warson soldiers were too distracted by Justice to notice him. Jasper opened fire and killed all six.

"About time!" Justice panted.

"Well sorrrrrrrry! I had to try setting whip sword on fire first." Jasper remarked as he and Justice paused to watch Ellis and Hanumanson.

Ellis shouted back at his foe. "Because I'm on the side that is trying to save the world from the devourers! I know your story, the men that lead the attack on your home are all dead!"

"I hear Teigao is still alive and well." Hanumanson seethed. "Although I do thank your young female companion for discarding the trash that was Basil and Kottos."

"Teigao wasn't there when your temple was attacked!" Ellis alleged. "Like I said – I have heard your story."

Hanumanson laughed with a deep, festering rage swelling within his voice. "You don't know about Teigao, do you? No matter – I will kill you, and any who come to your aid. Anat will be pleased when I report the end of the Blessed to her. Then the fiend, the fallen, broken man that is your leader will have no other option than to take his own life or crawl back into his hole."

"You can't blame everyone for what happened to your home!" Justice interjected.

"I don't" Hanumanson assured. "I only blame

the Blessed. You are only enemies because you side with them...well...Anat has some hatred for you. Ellis – you I must kill. You two kids, though...I might be willing to conceal your lives. I do owe you a debt for crumbling Kottos."

"We decline." Jasper and Justice chorused.

"Hey, war-man!" Ellis sighed. "If you just want to talk how about we set up a table and get some coffee?"

Hanumanson began lashing his urumi is preparation for an attack. "Choose your last words wisely!"

Hanumanson charged at Ellis. Ellis began dodging his attacks like before – but then he noticed that this urumi was different than his first. The urumi Hanumanson was now attacking Ellis with was just steel. Ellis focused on gaining his footing. Once he found an opening in Hanumanson's attacks he stood and held out his knife – blocking a swing from the flexible blade. Hanumanson twirled his urumi in for another attack which Ellis also deflected.

"I killed Briareos with this." Hanumanson gasconaded. "The best weapons are those with spirit."

Ellis ignored his foe's remarks and continued to dodge and deflect. Hanumanson became more aggressive in his attacks and nearly surrounded Ellis on three sides with the moving blade of his urumi. Red lines began to appear on Ellis' arms, legs, and face as Hanumanson grazed him with one strike after another. As Hanumanson moved in for an attack Ellis quickly used his knife to strike a spot on his foe's urumi a few inches from the handle. Ellis slid the knife upwards – pushing the urumi blade out of his way. He then reached in and grabbed Hanumanson's right elbow and stepped aside while grappling the Warson forward. Ellis was now standing next to Hanumanson and pulled his knife back down - stabbing Hanumanson in the same elbow he just grabbed. Hanumanson reached his left hand toward Ellis and tried to turn around – but Ellis stomped on Hanumanson's foot and stabbed the palm of his left hand. As Hanumanson retracted his hand from Ellis' knife Ellis slid his left palm along Hanumanson's silver-coated arm and to his hand and grabbed the handle of the urumi. With an exhausting tug Ellis ripped the urumi from Hanumanson's hand and stabbed him in the chest with the knife. Ellis quickly lashed Hanumanson across the shins with the urumi while retracting the knife. He took a few steps back as Hanumanson fell to his knees.

Hanumanson leaned backwards and straightened his legs as he sat in the dirt. Blood dripped from Hanumanson's arm, hand, and chest. However, his legs appeared to have been covered in too much armor for the steel urumi to penetrate.

Ellis took another step back but aimed his knife at Hanumanson, who just laughed before shouting "Long live The Sons of War, long live Anat!".

"What's so funny?" Ellis quaeritated.

"You fight like her." Hanumanson stated. "To a lesser extent but...it's all there!"

"I fight like a man wishing to protect the little he has left." Ellis corrected.

"What little he has left, hah!" Hanumanson coughed. "What is less significant...than nothing?"

Ellis paused for a moment in attempt to figure out what Hanumanson was asking, but Hanumanson passed out right after he spoke.

Jasper and Justice approached.

"Is he dead?" Jasper asked.

"Not ye..." Ellis started to speak as he noticed Hanumanson's breaths stop. "Oh...I guess he is."

"Here he slayed a hundred-hander, and died by a knife wound?" Justice perplexed.

"He was ready to die." Ellis said. "I could see it in his eyes. He realized I was a better combatant pretty early on, he fought to stall us."

"Died for something greater than himself..." Justice muttered, feeling sorry for the deceased warrior at her feet. "To bad he was misguided."

"Was he, though?" Ellis remarked. "The guys we joined up with are far from clean."

"We make a similar sacrifice." Justice stated. "Morality for a chance against the devourers. Part of something greater than ourselves."

"So, what are we going to do with him?" Jasper asked. "I suggest a cremation..."

"You just want the silver he filled his skin with!" Ellis chortled.

"Well deek at it!" Jasper begged suggestively.

"No!" Justice snapped. "This one is a monster of the Blessed's creation. He deserves a bit of dignity."

Ellis' eyes widened as he realized something. "And there's a monster of my creation with Coopyet's research!"

Ellis sprinted toward the main structure – which was beginning to collapse from the mountainside it was carved into.

Jasper continued staring blankly into his distorted reflections within Hanumanson's skin.

The quality of the silver and the almost microbial distance between the tattoos made the brilliant metal exceptionally reflective. The curves of Hanumanson's muscles split the reflections into different planes so that looking at his motionless corpse was tantamount to staring into a hall of mirrors.

Justice smacked Jasper's hand and ordered "Get the Kerosene, and you aren't taking that silver!"

Ellis entered the headquarters of The Sons of War. He nearly tripped over the husk of the golem upon entering. As he continued jogging down the corridor Ellis deduced that the golem was slain by Anat, as nobody else could have so smoothly decapitated the mechanical warrior. Although they had trained and developed their fighting styles together (as Hanumanson noticed) she was more graceful. When Anat engaged her foes her mind focused on the kill and emotions were usually ignored. To Ellis' advantage the style they practiced was strictly offensive, so if he could land a hit the strike would be damaging. He reached the end of the corridor and found himself within a massive chamber.

Flickering artificial lights covered the high ceiling of the room. A couple walkways wrapped almost entirely around the walls. Several Xports were parked haphazardly within the center of the space. Across from Ellis was a large cave opening. A thin layer of water poured over the hole – the remnants of a waterfall which concealed the cave.

Ellis chuckled at the waterfall. "A cave behind a waterfall? Now THAT is pretty damn cliché."

"I said the same thing!" Anat shouted from the walkway above Ellis.

"You haven't left yet – good!" Ellis yelled.

"Well...I was about to but, I had to grab the keys." Anat giggled as she leaped down from the walkway – landing next to one of the Xports. "It's a mess up there." She climbed in as Ellis unholstered his gun.

The Xport started as Ellis fired at it, but the vehicle was protected by bulletproof plating. Ellis stepped back as the Xport levitated into the air and swiveled toward him. Anat fired the Xport's guns at Ellis – barely missing him as he ducked behind a short, but thick, rock wall. She laughed as she rotated the Xport to face the cave exit. Ellis stood and fired a shot into the bottom of the Xport – destroying its levitation technology. The vehicle tilted onto its left as Anat kicked the passenger-side door open and leaped from the car. Ellis aimed his gun at her, but she leaned forward and pulled the trigger on her holstered gun. The bullet tore through the bottom of the holster and struck the handle of Ellis' gun – disarming him.

Anat landed on her feet – but she had to take a few steps forward to avoid falling. Ellis crouched to retrieve his pistol as she turned around and unholstered hers. A loud "SNAP!" followed by a "CLICK!" was heard as the back of Anat's armor flew open. Robotic wings similar to those of a dragonfly spread from the backs of her shoulders. The wings instantly began flapping – lifting Anat into the air as she shot Ellis' pistol – destroying it.

"Dammit!" Ellis whined as he climbed back behind the rocks. Anat snickered as she hovered in place.

"That's new!" Ellis remarked. "So many implants, yet not the fun kind!"

"Still think you're funny, I see." Anat commented. "I have important matters to attend to – I'll spare you this day. But know that next time we meet, and knowing you I'm certain you will be the instigator, I will make up for my previous failure."

"Don't you mean "failures"?" Ellis taunted.

Anat fired a couple bullets at the rock Ellis was ducking behind. She could have grazed him, but intentionally missed. The back of Ellis' head was scratched by the dust which exploded from the points of impact.

"Take it from someone that's known you for thirty-some years." Anat lectured. "Your comebacks suck."

Ellis stood and drew a knife from his belt as Anat flew toward the waterfall. He wished to throw the knife at her – but her buzzing wings carried her with such speed and grace that by the time he could calculate his throw she was already gone.

"Dammit!" Ellis seethed as he threw the knife into the floor. His communication device activated.

Justice spoke through the intercom. "Ellis, everything okay?"

"No." Ellis groaned. "Bitch got away."

"Where to?" Justice asked, speaking quickly. "Eric got the airship back up – we might be able to catch her!"

"No use." Ellis alleged. "She "has wings" now. Can easily hide under our radar."

"What do you mean she has wings now?" Justice perplexed, being caught off-guard by his reply.

"I'll explain later – meet you guys outside."

Ellis moped before turning his device off. With a strenuous tug he removed his knife from the floor and then dragged his feet back toward the front of the building. He was lucky enough to reach Anat before she abandoned the base, but failed to catch her. A sense of shame overcame him as he dreaded the thought of taking partial responsibility for any harm caused as a result of her escaping capture and execution. One wonder did cross his mind though – where is she going? Where is there for her to go now that The Sons of War have been dismantled?

Ellis stepped outside to see the Blessed airship hovering overhead with Jasper and Justice already onboard. A film of dust colored one side of the balloon. The rope ladder was still hanging, allowing Ellis to climb onto it. Hanumanson's corpse had been set ablaze – tattoos intact.

CHAPTER 4

Ronny's ghastly ferry quickly but gently floated along the Styx. The banks of the river were usually an empty gray or red color, and the water was aesthetically closer to fog than liquid. Beyond the banks there was only a dense mist which distorted the silhouettes of the mountains. Shreds of pestilent dark oozes throbbed below the waters' surface. If there was complete silence onboard the ship the crew could hear the subtle, but agonizing moans of the billions of souls claimed by the river. Ronny and Unity stood on the main deck of the ferry.

"So, you are their mother?" Ronny smiled. "You have much to be proud of."

"From what you described – yes. I just wish I could have been the one to kill that beast!" Unity rasped. Whenever she expressed emotion her voice was slightly distorted from the underworld decay. Ronny could tell that she struggled to maintain her sanity.

"Well I hope you are at least a little placated knowing that Justice destroyed the creature." Ronny said. "And with Hades gone – he is forever trapped in Tartarus with his brothers."

"I would rather see them in the Styx!" Unity screeched. Her eyes momentarily filled with a colorful tint.

"Tartarus is a worse fate, from what I've heard Kepyet completely emptied it. They are little more than entities in a field of nothingness." Ronny reassured. "Preserve your mind, we need our wits to find Callum and Sal."

"About that..." Unity started. "What compels you to believe that Sal can be found down here?"

"He died, would he have not landed somewhere along these banks?" Ronny quaeritated.

Unity giggled in an almost sinister tone. "Not elementals...they don't drop near the Styx."

"Well where would his soul be, then?" Ronny snapped.

Unity glared at Ronny for a moment and answered "The Phlegethon."

"The river which feeds the mote of Tartarus?!" Ronny gasped. "That accursed thing is more dangerous than the Styx!"

"Well, that is where the souls of elementals are deposited. I know where the rivers bend in closest proximity to each other – perhaps we could dock there and ask the spirit of Phlegethon about Sal. But I want Callum first." Unity spoke.

"And would you know where we could find him? He wasn't in Charon's passenger logs...but he did enter the underworld relatively close to the gates of the Elysian Fields and the Asphodel Meadows." Ronny said hopefully. "We are nearing those docks."

Unity cackled. "Then my boy will be in for quite the disappointment!"

Ronny's eyes narrowed. "What are you talking about?"

Unity leaned against the wooden support behind the figurehead. "Kepyet didn't want the gods to create beings similar to himself. His orders were to lock the gates of both places – but Pleonex and Gehenna decided to take it a step further. They opened the gates and tipped them toward the Styx."

"Does...does that mean what I think you're implying?" Ronny quavered.

Unity nodded. "The soul of nearly every person that died prior to Kepyet's prime was dumped into this river. My husband included."

"That's...it's just...beyond insane..." Ronny stuttered – realizing the severity of this tragic news.

"That's why this place is so empty." Unity added. "Charon didn't even charge the toll during the war. The gods allowed anyone to enter Asphodel. Any lost souls like myself that found their way back to the Styx were welcomed. Once those places were emptied Charon reinstated the fee, taking those that paid to the gates of Duat. Not that anyone can get in though since Osiris locked it up before leaving."

"So, what happened to the fiends?!" Ronny barked.

"Well...that which calls himself Teigao took some water from the Styx with him and coated his sword with it. Ran it through Gehenna during the war. I believe Basil killed Pleonex as a test of his loyalty to the Blessed." Unity explained. "That last bit is just rumor though."

"Basil is not to be trusted!" Ronny growled. "Wait...what was that you said of Teigao?"

Unity grinned. "I can only explain so much while maintaining my sanity."

"Is Justice in danger?!" Ronny catechized. "Can you answer that?!"

"Calm yourself!" Unity waved her hand. "As long as Kepyet never again steps foot into the mortal realm she will be fine. Now – shall we search for my son?"

Ronny snarled at Unity. "We will search for OUR son, I raised him – remember!"

Ronny tapped the bottom of the oar onto the deck, commanding the ferry to accelerate. Some of the skin around Unity's eyes and lips cracked.

***

Anat buzzed above a body of water nearly the size of the Mediterranean. Her wings were powered by advanced solar technology which was able to keep their batteries full despite the thick clouds. The water below her was festering with the remains of aquatic plants. It was so disgusting that pollutants were more pleasant to examine than the water between them. After a couple hours Anat reached the zone Z4.

Z4 was a wide, open plane. The entire place had no variety in elevation – Z4 was like an ocean of dirt. Anat flew a ways into the zone, keeping her eyes focused on the ground. It lacked so much detail that flying above the region was hypnotic. Eventually Anat spotted a metal circle similar in design to a manhole cover. She landed beside it.

Anat knocked on the metal cover and waited a moment – but there was no response. She knocked again but there was still no response.

With a sigh she grabbed the metal lid with both hands and swung it aside – revealing a dusty spiral stairway. Anat activated the night-vision setting of her eye implants then lurched into the dungeon. She perceived the cushion-like sensation of stepping onto the condensed dust covering each narrow stair. The stairs were carved from stone but each one was secured from erosion by iron carpeting. With grace she maintained her footing as she twisted downward. The spiral stairs lead into a wide hallway. Metal chains with massive cobwebs between them dangled from the ceiling. Stone swords the size of men were lined against the walls. In front of each sword statue was a box similar in design to a coffin. The hallway was several hundred feet long with a throne at the end. There was a locked gate on each side of the throne. Sitting upon the throne was a frightful, slumbering man. The throne itself was decorated to represent the various ages of war. The base was bronze with an iron seat, while the backrest was steel and the armrests were adamant. A thin coating of ruby covered the metal, and the fronts of the armrests bore the symbol of The Sons of War.

The man's skin was white as paper. He had a bald head and clean-shaven face – although there was a hole on each side of his jaw which exposed his molars. The holes in his cheeks appeared to be intentional piercings rather than decay, however the front of his neck actually was rotted off and exposed the muscles and veins of his throat. Below each shoulder there was a massive hole through his chest with finger-like strips of skin crossing over the openings. Glowing, but dim green orbs pulsated within each hole on his chest. They appeared to be linked in some way to his rotting heart, which was barely visible from the corners of the cavities. His arms were muscular, and the veins over the muscles emitted a sickly green aura. The man's legs were covered by dark gray armor below a belt of miniature skulls.

As Anat approached the being's eyes opened. They were round and unusually large. The whites of his eyes were gray and the irises were jet black. He lifted his head and laughed. His voice was surprisingly dulcet, but had some depth to it.

"A visitor...a finder..." He was tardiloquent. "What is your business here, woman?"

"I am Anat Bellonadaughter, leader of -" Anat announced.

"Epp!" The being raised his finger to shush her. "Your name is enough. Logic dictates your arrival here can only mean that Seth's leadership failed. Exactly as I had predicted. I knew he would fail to follow my rhetoric."

Anat remained silent, it wasn't even necessary for her to gesture to inform the creature that his assumptions were correct.

"To think I allowed him to use the name Areseson." The being spoke quickly and moved his hands along with almost everything he said. "I'm sure once you took over things slightly improved but the faction was doomed the day he was appointed. And now the devourers have been set free, and Odinson...Leo...that Blessed idiot failed to preserve Gungnir? Tell me – how many of our organization remain?"

"Just me." Anat answered honestly. She wanted to fear the man before her, but her intuition suggested that it would be unwise.

The man laughed. "Well it is good you knew to come to me!"

"Who exactly are you?" Anat inquired. "We have no records of this branch other than the location."

The being stood. "I am the first Son of War and the true founder and mentor of our clan. The name Areseson was lent to your former leader by me. I was once, and shall again be known as Deimos."

Anat's eyes widened upon hearing the name. "You're a god. The god of fear and battle anxiety."

"FEAR?!" Deimos roared – shaking the cavern with the intensity of his voice. If Anat was anyone else she would have been knocked back by his shout. "Not. Fear." Deimos seethed. "Terror! Fear...it's the inspirational content of amateurs. It's a weak poison...but terror...terror dominates, controls, destroys... Fear does its work and then ends! Terror...terror lingers. The subtle hysteria...it haunts. Once a man experiences terror it remains with him as a stain on the soul."

Anat knelt before Deimos. "First son of Ares. May I ask why you started this faction rather than assisting the gods?"

Deimos sat back upon his throne. "Like the other forgotten children of the major gods they only reached out to me in desperation. I would not have it. Do you see the result? The gods lost and fled. Kepyet was banished and the Nutes died. The Blessed are reduced to what, now? Barely enough members to occupy a blimp? I was right to stay out."

Anat looked up at her new leader. "Are you saying we have more soldiers?"

"We have an army." Deimos assured. He

snapped his fingers and the coffins flew open. They were occupied by heavily armored, sleeping men. The warriors resting within the coffins wore polished crimson armor with blank masks. Their masks didn't even have eye holes – but worked like visors.

Anat briefly panned over the still knights. Even with her night vision active it was difficult to comprehend the details, as if the darkness in the cavern was caused by something other than a shortage of light energy. She turned back to face Deimos. "An army of the dead?"

"Not dead. They were frozen. They will awake when I give the order. Here we have the most elite heroes of The Sons of War. Each has at least a decade of combat experience and is proficient with a greater variety of weapons than imaginable. No soldiers of the Blessed or Kepyet can compare." Deimos explained.

"So, our faction is reborn the day it died?" Anat chuckled as Deimos nodded. "In that case I have a gift – Kepyet's alchemy research."

Anat excavated the flash drive and the CD from a pocket on her belt. She tossed both to Deimos – who caught them with ease. He laid the CD on his armrest and examined the flash drive.

"Hmm...." Deimos smirked. "This is excellent! Cooper's astral travels attracted the attention of a few of us gods long before he eavesdropped on the plans to commence Armageddon. Using his alchemy research we may be able to copy the recipe of the fire used by my uncle Hephaestus."

"The fire used to forge the god's weapons?" Anat marveled. "Such fire...it could win us any battle!"

"The Earth's final decades will be under our

rule!" Deimos declared. "With you as the figurehead, and me in the shadows."

Deimos snapped his fingers and the gates on each side of the throne began to open by elevating into the ceiling.

***

The Blessed zeppelin hovered above Oscar's shop in New Ur. Below the airship a car engine was resting upon a platform with a glowing base. Oscar was standing with Jasper, Justice, Ellis, and Eric holding a remote. When Oscar pressed a button on the remote the platform levitated toward the zeppelin.

Jasper smiled at the piece of machinery and cheered "Once I get that installed she will be up and running again!"

"Until you crash it again." Ellis remarked. Justice hit Ellis with her elbow.

"Try not to wreck this one, kiddos!" Oscar requested.

"What – you don't like doing business with us?" Justice rejoindered.

"Eh, I know better than to answer that question lass." Oscar started. "But these engines are hard to come by! Everyone needs a new engine for their cars, or they take them apart for building other things. I even saw a fella try to eat one before! Though he did have a strain of the syphilis."

A sudden chill overcame the group. As their spines tingled still frames from the most intense moments of their battles flashed before their eyes. They breathed chopping, trembling breaths as it happened. The anomalous anxiety attack only lasted a second, but left an impact on their moods.

"Did anyone else feel that?!" Jasper perplexed. "Please tell me it wasn't just me…"

"I felt something…" Justice confessed.

"You too, kids?" Oscar added.

"Probably just the damn air here!" Ellis theorized as he turned to Oscar. "You can find every damn device invented by man except a purifier!"

Eric just stared into the distance as his eyebrows slowly lowered. Justice noticed his consternated expression.

"Eric?" Justice worried. "Are you okay?"

"Yeah." Eric lied. "Am fine."

Ellis scowled at Eric. "Humph! "Am fine" huh? I'm not buying it."

Eric snapped at Ellis. "Well, aren't you also fine?!"

"Don't play this with me, kid!" Ellis growled. "There's something you aren't telling us! I've just about had it with deceptions, I thought we agreed that you Blessed tell us everything for now on!"

"I don't know what it is!" Eric alleged. "You said it yourself – it could just be the air! Your guess is as good as mine, heaven knows the atmosphere is becoming more defedated by the day."

"I don't buy it!" Ellis shouted as Justice rested her face into her palm. "Tell us your theory, Lancast!"

"I'm honestly not sure what it could be. I just had this weird feeling that something was woken up that shouldn't have been disturbed. But my senses have dulled a bit from spending so much time in that maddening citadel, not to mention that Bakunawa will break into our world any day now." Eric claimed.

"About that..." Oscar interrupted. "I think your guys' book was just a guess-aroo! One of my men reported seeing a large serpent near Geb's Woe."

"Yeah, Jormungand and Vritra were out recently. We killed both." Ellis said.

Oscar shook his head. "This was a few days ago."

Eric showed his teeth. "And you didn't tell us?!"

"Not my job, lad." Oscar winked.

"Considering it wants to eat the world it kind of is everyone's job!" Jasper lectured.

Oscar shrugged. "I was under the impression all magic was gone from the world until Ellis' lady friend went all witch on our airships."

"We should go then!" Eric ordered as he signaled the zeppelin to drop the rope ladder. The engine was already hauled into the airship so Oscar recalled his platform.

Justice acknowledged Oscar before rushing to the ladder with everyone else. "Thanks, Oscar. Kind of...I guess."

Oscar smiled in the corner of his mouth and nodded. Justice climbed onto the airship.

***

Anat stood next to Deimos on a balcony within an underground warehouse. Hundreds of elite Warsons were doing training exercises.

She marveled at the army before her. "All this time we had THIS resource?"

Deimos nodded.

Anat hissed. "Why was it concealed like this?! If we had THIS army the Blessed would already be gone! We would already run the damn world!"

"Quiet, child!" Deimos ordered. Anat stepped back as frames from her battles flashed before her eyes. She smiled and began to laugh – ignoring the visions and focusing her eyes in Deimos' direction.

"Really?!" Anat giggled. "I love the thrill of battle! The adrenaline rush of charging toward someone with my weapons in hand." She took a step toward Deimos. "The devastation in the eyes of those that fall before me." Anat took another step toward Deimos, although she was still blinded by the visions. "The smell of the fires of war, gunpowder, my foes shitting themselves as my swords and bullets tear their organs apart and cripple their muscles!" Deimos stepped back as Anat took another step toward him. "The most pleasing sound in the world is the scream of a dying man, followed by the sobs of his wife, followed up then by the wailing cries of his children! It's just above the sound human flesh makes when sliced apart, bit by freaking bit!"

Anat's flashbacks ended as Deimos grinned. "Completely unaffected by battle, you have made your point. There is logic behind everything I do, reasons incomprehensible to you mortals. Kepyet was a god slayer but the Blessed were also capable deicide. If we emerged sooner we wouldn't be here now, nor in control or able to rise. The events of today were set in motion decades ago, here is our chance to alter fate."

Anat huffed, but knew better than to argue. Although she was immune to Deimos' little trick he was still a god and likely able to kill her. "On a different note – are you ready to read Cooper's notes?" She queried.

"I am." Deimos replied. "Come, I have a computer ready."

Back at Skyrook Ellis, Eric, Jasper, and

Justice were standing around the planning table. Teigao entered the room.

"Well?" Eric asked.

"You read too fast!" Teigao deprecated. "The old miser is correct – the serpent Bakunawa has indeed spawned. The part you read in regards to the time frame are how long it needs to gain full power, at which point it will devour the moon then the Earth. It is imperative we stop it soon!"

"Where is it – then?" Justice inquired. "I'll grab Kepyet's sword and we will head there ASAP."

"N20." Teigao answered, speaking quickly. "I have an errand of my own. I trust you all can handle the beast?"

"Killed the last two without your help." Jasper muttered.

"And the smart one was felled by a Warson, one that was once a member of our faction. Watch your ego." Teigao barked as he vacated the room.

"What's up with him today?" Justice asked.

"Not sure." Ellis sighed as he turned to Eric. "Maybe it has something to do with that trippy anxiety spell?"

"I already told you I know nothing of it!" Eric claimed.

"I believe him." Justice intervened. "And I trust that whatever Teigao is up to is innocent. He's cooped up in here more than the rest of us, probably just needs a break from Kepyet's lingering madness before the real McCoy is brought back."

"I'm with Justice on this." Jasper said. "But seriously – are we going to fight the serpent or what?"

"Please." Justice begged. The others nodded.

Everyone walked out of the room together. Justice made her way down the passage to her quarters to retrieve Kepyet's sword while the others stepped outside to transfer supplies between the zeppelin and the Cannon.

CHAPTER 5

Anat and Deimos stood inside a semi-circular office. The room was lit by artificial lights placed behind the sapphire walls – causing everything to have a blue tint. A lengthy desk rested along the wall with several computers sitting upon it. Anat approached the newest-looking computer while holding the flash drive and virus-blocking disc. As Anat took her seat she noticed Deimos was remaining by the door.

"Not reading the notes with me?" Anat spoke.

"I trust you with the knowledge, Wardaughter." Deimos said. "Something has...come up."

"Do tell." Anat purred.

"It's of no importance, just of interest. Peruse the notes and see if you can extract our fire recipe. I'll return before I'm missed." Deimos explained as he strode through the door.

Anat shrugged before sliding the CD into the tower. Once she heard the disc spinning she thrust the flash drive into the USB port. The document with Cooper's notes opened. The screen flickered for a moment as the software on the CD disabled the multiple viruses encoded into the research document. Once the screen remained stable Anat started reading.

"February 1, 2035

Lucien and I already have our differences. Go figure! His approach is too scientific. A scientific mind is good, that is a certainty. However it can also cross a threshold and into a point where such a mind is closed. Not everything can be explained with science – I have had many experiences which cannot be explained or even described within the boundaries of practical knowledge. This begs the question – what does it mean to be practical?

I am certain the stone is real, and my faith in Lucien is supported by his shared belief. We have decided to start simple and experiment with only the elements and compounds available to the ancient Greeks. I will update this log on a monthly basis, I always considered daily journals to be a sign of insecurity. A trait that is certainly in no short supply.

March 1, 2035

Our research has been going well. Our experiments with open flames, vials of water, dirt, and blowing air have -"

Anat rolled her eyes and stopped reading. She flicked her finger against the wheel of the mouse in frustration as she skimmed the journal. Many of these entries came off as childish to her, and that it should have been easy to predict they would fail. Anat chuckled at the entries which mentioned Justice's birth. She continued skimming until she reached the end of the journal – but something caught her attention. Cooper's writing seemed different, as if he was going mad, but one entry in particular appeared useful.

"August 1, 20threeonepastsix

Alchemy alchemy oh alchemy. To Egypt my mind went! But it was different, and not the fun part – thank Alex and the Persians! Bastard enablers of Cleopatra! Zosimos of Panopolis said words to me, words, words. For the stone it is a blood we need! I told Lucien elemental or god descendant, but half-truths they are! A life elemental may resurrect but even that is weak – and god blood may empower other elements but no stone there. Purity is need! Is must! Even god blood impure, the elements though. Water...mercury. Vaporized philosophorum – only with laser! Vapor with the mercury is the water, purest of! And its foil – the flame. Laser vaporized philosophorum too, but with sulfur. Air and Earth are lost, perhaps carbon for Earth? Needless though. None of four make a stone. Care should I of legacy? I'm already destined to be immortal! I returned to my body. I saw sights on the way oh way the sights be saw! An island, a secret one with a castle and her grave. A gray swamp kingdom where her heartbeat is offered. Am I haunted? Lots of hands, even more blood. A castle in the sky doomed to sink. I returned to my body, but not after seeing a door I should not have seen. I will open it in the coming days.

Orichalcum is a strange substance. With lightning it alters. Vapors of all elements, but what takes the next step? The Egyptians did have a fondness for gold.

August 18, 2037

Door I did a go through, the godsthey havelost theirdamnminds! Destroy and remake?! I can't allow it! We as a species must protest!"

The file ended there. Anat read over the final entries carefully – contemplating what Cooper was trying to say. Her subconscious understood his words perfectly – even to the point of comprehending details left out of the journal entries. Her surface conscious, however, struggled with the word salads.

***

The cannon flew toward N20 from Skyrook, less moisture than usual appeared in the air content analysis on the dashboard.

"That's peculiar." Jasper stated – observing the readings.

"What, now?" Ellis responded.

"The moisture reading is low." Jasper pointed at the dash. Justice and Eric peeked at it from the back seats.

"Be grateful that's the only oddity." Eric said. "Moisture is the first thing the serpent devours. If we can kill it in these early stages then we buy ourselves extra time before Bakasura emerges. With the sword only good for this one use, time is a valuable resource."

Justice sighed as she gazed down upon the accursed blade. "Is summoning Kepyet truly our only option?"

"Having doubts?" Ellis inquired.

"I don't even know." Justice confessed. "What will happen to the world with him back? Obviously it's better than falling into Apep's belly...but will Kepyet be reasonable after the snake is slain?"

"Probably not." Eric chuckled. "We defeated him once, though. There is always a way."

Everything shook as the Cannon neared Geb's Woe. The gravity shifts hadn't gotten any better. Ellis gently steered the Cannon to drive along the rim of the large hole.

"Keep your eyes peeled." Ellis suggested. "Somewhere below us there should be a serpent."

***

V28 was a massive crater as wide as a small country and as deep as an ocean. The dirt within the crater was a burgundy color. A green fog oozed from the dirt like incense smoke. Thick, stoic clouds of the same color floated near the top of the crater just barely below the surface. The metal casings of bombs and missiles littered the interior walls of the depression. V28 was a dumping ground for nuclear weapons during the early days of the war. The radiation in the zone was so potent that any human that inhaled the air would instantly collapse and mutate into little more than an amalgamation of suppurating, cancerous, tumors.

Deimos stood near the center of the crater. His health was unaffected by the radiation, but the glowing orbs within the wounds of his chest appeared to shine happily in response to the toxic environment. A silhouette appeared behind the smoke and approached.

"It's been a while." Deimos commented as the other figure neared.

"That is has." The figure answered as he revealed himself to be Teigao. The glow of his azure eyes appeared red through the chemicals in the air. "I was wrong to have assumed you perished."

"Not every god died, how many of your kin walk among the humans?" Deimos catechized.

Teigao smirked. "Only I earned redemption."

"So, you are free. Why do you continue to lead the Blessed?" Deimos wondered.

"It's the only place I can maintain some control over the flow of events. You are familiar with how I feel about the captivity I shared with my brothers and sisters. I would rather not return – so playing human works to my advantage. As does maintaining my loyalties." Teigao explained.

Deimos burst out in laughter. "You're one to speak of loyalties! Shall we rewind to your days in the last war?"

Deimos raised his right hand and pointed at Teigao, who collapsed onto his knees. Visions of an ancient war conquered Teigao's mind. The skin around Teigao's eyes turned scaly and red, and his eyebrows receded into his face and were replaced by several tiny bumps with even smaller horns protruding through them.

"Pathetic!" Deimos disparaged. "And you're a chosen leader? The second war ended eighteen years ago. You're free "Teigao"."

"And?" Teigao whimpered – struggling to hold himself up.

"We don't have to engage each other, you can go off and be your own person, no longer a scapegoat! Leave me to my games, do keep in mind that us with stable divine blood are still superior." Deimos offered as he released his grip on Teigao's fears.

Teigao slowly regained his footing. "I don't do what I do out of obligation, I do it because it is right! I have seen the error of my ways in the past and redeemed myself. My job now is a protector. I will guide my followers to victory over the devourers, and to victory over yourself."

Deimos shook his head. "You know that's a falsehood as well as I do. All your pets have seen battle. How do you suppose they would fare upon challenging me? I rest a strict glare upon my soldiers. I've played this game before and won. Have you played at all – or were you just a pawn? Pardon! A knight?"

"I know not how you've endured this long or what strain of cowardice acted to hide you away all these years..." Teigao started. "But, I will ensure the Earth will be safe from you!"

Deimos chuckled. "The ailment I spread across the Earth infected nearly every human and was passed down through hundreds of generations. Think back on what you've accomplished. You are one to speak of cowardice, "Teigao", having hidden within a walled city for nearly two decades."

Deimos vanished. Teigao bellowed an unearthly roar as his face regained a human appearance.

***

N20 was one of the zones near Geb's woe, but the mountains in this region were covered in black ash. The Cannon parked on a ledge overlooking a slumbering Bakunawa.

Bakunawa was a massive serpent – similar in size to Jormungand. His scales had the appearance of glistening sapphires with a gray fog flowing within the gems. Several sharp dorsal fins ran along his back, and equally sharp fins extended from the sides below each dorsal. The ominous devourer ooze sprayed from Bakunawa's gills, and his head was twice the size of

Jormungand's.

"So, this is the moon eater?" Ellis observed. "It's asleep, will it stay asleep or is this dragon round two?"

"So, you finally admit Vritra was a dragon?!" Jasper cheered.

Eric groaned. "What I would give for more variety in your arguments."

"Where do I stab it?" Justice asked as she excavated Kepyet's sword.

"I assume the head." Eric stated. "I have some flarebursts ready to load into the Cannon's guns should things get tricky."

"Well...here goes nothing!" Justice said as she leaped from the edge of the cliff. Her plunge was retarded by her boots. She landed on the center of Bakunawa's cranium, but the beast remained asleep.

After a deep breathe Justice raised Kepyet's sword above her head and thrust it into Bakunawa's skull. The beast's eyes flew open as he began to squirm. Justice managed to retrieve the accursed sword from the monster's flesh but lost her footing and rolled off his head. She hurt her back and bruised her limbs upon landing – but she ignored the pain and crawled away from the writhing devourer. Once she felt secure enough to spare a second Justice climbed onto her feet and ran as far away as she could. The steep wall of the cliff obstructed her path – but she knelt down and rested against the wall, knowing she was a safe distance from the dying fiend.

The ominous ooze sprayed from the monster's wound and gills as Justice crawled away. He writhed more violently as sections of his body caved in. The monster quickly shriveled into nothing but a puddle of dark ooze with a cloud of noxious mist floating above. As the puddle began to atomize the sapphires leftover from Bakunawa's scales were uncovered and sparkled.

Ellis looked over the edge of the cliff and shouted "Justice! Are you alright down there?!"

"Yeah, I'm fine!" Justice answered. "Just a little bruised, I'll launch myself back up once that black fog stuff clears!"

Jasper focused his goggles on the puddles of devourer ooze. "Hey guys, look! Its...blood...stuff, residue? I'll go with blood...anyway, the pool is filled with sapphires!"

Eric turned his attention to the puddles as well. "When defeated their soul and organs lose power, and the void within their bellies close. Not unusual for whatever their external anatomy is comprised of to remain behind."

"So, can we loot them?" Jasper queried.

"Really?" Eric groaned.

"I'm with the kid on this one." Ellis admitted. "Look at how many there are!"

Eric shook his head. "Well I don't see why you can't, just wait until the ooze has cleared."

Justice examined the sword in her hand. When she fell Bakunawa she sensed the extreme drain on the sword's power. Wielding the weapon was no longer a strain on her soul. She wondered if any magic remained within the blade, beyond whatever enchantment was needed to summon Kepyet that is. Holding the sword still gave her feelings of unease, but she was unsure if the cause was magic within the blade itself or just her mind playing tricks on her based on what she knew of the sword. Regardless of the lost magic –

it was still a good sword. The weapon was lightweight despite its density, and the guard above the hilt was secure. Its blade was also exceptionally well-crafted. The edges were sharper than a katana's ha, and the point was like that of a rapier.

"Justice – look out!" Eric blurted as the remaining ooze of the devourer cleared. On the opposite end of the pile of sapphires was a tall figure. It looked like a man, except a large buck-like horn protruded from the left side of his head. The top-left quadrant of his face was concealed by a ceramic mask painted to mimic the creamy color of his skin. His face was clean-shaven and he appeared to be in his early forties. The strange man was dressed in orange leather armor.

Justice climbed onto her feet as she held her sword in a defensive stance. Ellis, Eric, and Jasper made their way down the cliff.

"Who are you?!" Justice catechized as the man approached.

"I came for that sword." The being replied. "It is among the relics we were ordered to track down."

"Ordered by who?" Justice quaeritated.

"The Monk." He responded. "I see that the sword's power is gone, it is no longer of use to you."

"What use do you have for it, then?" Justice asked.

"That's classified." The being answered. "I mean you no harm – I only desire the sword. However, my intentions are subject to change if you act to engage me."

"Stay away from him, Justice!" Eric ordered and he and the other two men dropped near her. Eric and Ellis unholstered their pistols as Jasper wrapped his palm around the handle of the miniature flamethrower on his belt.

Justice questioned Eric. "Who is he?"

"That's a revenant!" Eric divulged. "They were thought to be extinct!"

"We nearly were." The revenant growled. "Your men killed almost all of us. Myself and a few of my kin survived though."

"Revenant?" Justice asked.

"I'll explain later." Eric said. "How did you survive?!"

"Funny story." The revenant started. "Myself and several others of my kin were ordered to recover some orichalcum from a newly formed cave. There was a small tribe of humans which had found refuge within the corridors. Well – the entrance of the cave was lined with a rare, fast-acting toxin. The antidote is radiation – which the people that moved into the caverns were already poisoned by, making them immune to the substance around the mouth of the cave. The Blessed searched the cave first but their soldiers dropped dead only meters beyond the entrance. Kepyet ordered a few Nutes to search the caverns once he discovered the new cave, and they weren't able to survive much better than the Blessed were. The superstitious people hiding within assumed they were being protected by a deity. They invented a goddess and a whole religion around it over the month they hid! Ironic, isn't it? Here a group of humans were protected by a goddess that didn't even exist! My group was then sent in to investigate and we were able to smell the toxin before entering lethal range. We scanned the area and found the nearby radiation weakened the toxin. Equipped ourselves with hazmat suits, carried a few bricks of plutonium, and passed into the cave without trouble."

"Then what?" Jasper interjected as the revenant took a breath.

"Getting there." The revenant growled. "What we found was a group of people covered in sores – cowering in the corners of the cave. They refused to join us and be cured, out of loyalty to their goddess, so we were ordered to put them out of their misery. No sooner we entered the cavern collapsed. Our reinforcements were forced to respond to a more pressing matter at Kepyet's stronghold. We dug ourselves out, but learned that Kepyet had been slain. We made our way to a secret mountain and took refuge there, then several months ago this ceramic man appeared calling himself "The Monk". He gave us purpose again."

"Tell us more about this "Monk" fellow." Ellis requested.

"How about we trade?" The revenant offered. "Information in exchange for that sword."

"We refuse." Justice and her companions chorused.

"Then I take it by force!" The revenant shrieked as he drew two knives from his belt. A concealed alarm on his neck buzzed. "Uh..." The revenant took a step back as Justice and her companions exchanged confused expressions. "Hold on! I gotta take this."

The revenant pressed a button on his collar. "What?"

"Do not engage!" An elderly voice with a peculiar dialect spoke through the device.

"I wasn't going to..." The revenant lied.

"You aren't the only of your kin I have out

there, dude." The voice said.

"...Did his boss just say "dude"?" Justice giggled to her companions.

"What about the sword?!" The revenant barked.

"Leave it." The voice answered. "In good time it will be brought to us. Return to me."

The revenant sighed and addressed to Justice. "You are a fortunate one!"

Justice shouted at the revenant as he turned around. "Wait!"

"What?" He snapped with his back facing her.

"Why does your superior want us spared?" Justice perplexed.

"Ask him yourself. You're bound to meet eventually, assuming he doesn't change his mind about sparing you." The revenant responded as he ran away. He vanished when Justice and her companions blinked.

"What was that about?" Justice inquired. "Who were the revenants?"

"I'll explain on the way back to Skyrook." Eric assured. "With the sword emptied we need to collect the other relics."

Jasper and Ellis retrieved and unfolded bags from their pockets which they hastily filled with Bakunawa's sapphires.

***

Deimos entered his laboratory. Anat was sitting at the desk wearing upgraded armor. Her new uniform looked similar to her old one – only this one was a tighter fit and more lightweight. She also wore a gold cape with the symbol of The Sons of War painted in blood on the center.

"Anything for me?" Deimos asked.

"Perhaps." Anat returned. "Much of the notes

were boring, more a neglected journal than anything. He must have lost his mind when writing the last few entries, but among them were a few phrases which may be of interest to us. Where have you been?"

"Meeting with an old friend." Deimos smirked. "No mortal business. The notes – what did they say?"

Anat's eyes narrowed at Deimos – wondering what he was hiding from her and if it may be more relevant than he leads on. "We may have a recipe for stronger fire and water. Water is difficult to harness but I think the fire could easily be used with artillery. Perhaps it is the recipe used by your uncle. We need sulfur, though. I don't suppose your storehouse here contains any?"

"No. That worthless substance – really?" Deimos groused.

Anat opened the page on the computer and pointed at the screen. "See for yourself."

Deimos leaned over the Wardaughter and examined the screen. "Well then..." He mumbled as he stepped back. "Go get some."

"Excuse me?" Anat hissed. "Don't you have a few hundred toys out there that could run the errand?"

"Yes but I don't desire the chore half-assed." Deimos retorted.

"Care to explain how buying one thing can be half-assed?" Anat carped.

"Just do it, that is an order!" Deimos growled. "I'm certain you can find some in New Ur or C9."

"Because I am so welcome in both places?" Anat argued.

"I said to "get" some, I don't care how. Trade

for it fairly or go on a killing spree until there's nobody to stop you from taking it. It's up to you – just make sure you bring us a plentiful supply! Besides – with the other Sons of War gone knowledge and concern of your past deeds are surely evanescent." Deimos elaborated.

Anat stood and raised her middle finger to Deimos as she marched toward the exit.

"Respect your god!" Deimos advised.

Anat paused for a moment and turned her head over her shoulder. "You say that to an officer of a group you yourself founded in protest of the gods. If I had the means to slay you I would, and you know that. So, save yourself from looking the fool with hypocritical orders."

CHAPTER 6

Teigao sat at the head of the planning table shaking his head. Ellis, Eric, Jasper, and Justice stood across from him.

"If he knew you had the sword then surely he knows where to find the other relics." Teigao griped. "My concern now is WHAT he is."

"Could he be a god?" Ellis wondered. "I mean there are rumors that not every god was accounted for after the war. Back when it was just me and Kaleyla we had a few encounters where we suspected our client was one of them."

"Unlikely." Teigao asserted. "When the gods disguise themselves they pretend to be regular people or turn into animals. Cryptically hiding behind a pretense like "The Monk" would be counter-productive to whatever reason they have to hide."

"A Nute, perhaps?" Justice suggested.

Teigao shook his head. "No, the underlings all perished and Basil was the last living general. I killed Gehenna myself, and Basil killed Pleonex. If Kepyet shared his power with a fourth Nute we would know."

"Because you are so great at always being on top of things?" Ellis razzed.

Jasper remembered something and raised his voice as a means to avoid interruption. "Wait! The voice over the speaker – it called the revenant "dude". Isn't it unusual that some powerful, wise, old being would use that word?"

Teigao nodded. "Yes, but in order to narrow down our list of suspects we actually need some to begin with. I am not as concerned about The Monk's identity as much as I am his search for Kepyet's relics. The revenants aren't the most trustworthy group either, if they obtain Kepyet's power they could easily abuse it."

"So, what do we do?" Justice asked.

"Make haste and retrieve the ring and whatever remains of the mask." Teigao ordered. "Split up. Two of you travel to the atoll in F2, the mask should be somewhere among the ruins of Kepyet's stronghold. The other pair is to venture to J15, among the ruins of Atlantis there should still be a working portal to the base on the moon where Kepyet's ring was stored."

"Why would his ring be on the moon?" Jasper groaned.

"That's where it was last reported." Teigao sighed. "How it got there I don't know, or care. You need not worry about such trivial matters either – just get it!"

"No need to get snippy!" Ellis barked. "It isn't the kid's fault you lost track of a precious artifact."

"Just go get them!" Teigao said as he slammed

his fist on the table.

Ellis shook his head as he and the others left the room.

As they entered the central chamber of Skyrook Jasper asked "So, who is going where?"

"I've always wanted to check out the ruins at the atoll." Justice expressed.

Eric nodded and added "I've been there, I know it well so I should accompany her."

Ellis turned to Jasper and smiled. "Well kid it looks like we're on moon duty!"

Jasper looked up at Ellis and mumbled "Last time I was on moon duty it involved pulling my pants down."

Ellis smacked Jasper aside the head with his knuckles.

"Owch!" Jasper yelped as Justice rolled her eyes into turning away. Eric followed her through the exit.

Jasper rubbed the sore spot on his cranium and quaeritated "So, who is taking what vehicle?"

"They're taking the airship." Ellis stated. "It seems we have the Cannon to ourselves for a day or two. It will be just like the old days!"

"Minus Kaleyla." Jasper corrected.

Ellis' smile retreated into a blank expression. "She is never to set foot in my truck again."

"Just a meaningless comment – chill." Jasper argued as Ellis started to stroll toward the exit.

***

Anat drove a rusty Xport into C9 and landed in a crumbling parking lot. The moment she stepped out of the vehicle several people instantly recognized her and tried to run away. She unholstered one of her pistols and shot each fleeing civilian in the occipital knob. The bones crunched as the lead bullets crushed through them. The faces of her victims exploded from their skulls as the powerful projectiles passed through their heads.

With a sinister smile Anat sashayed toward what remained of the town square. Her cape bounced back and forth with each step, and her new leggings insulated the rough noises produced by her implants. She paused upon entering a dark alley.

"I know you're there." She threatened. "I cannot be killed by a coward. It's been attempted in the past. Many times, actually."

A loud, but soft gunshot was heard – the whirl of a sniper's bullet. A bullet twirled in the air from behind her and clanked as it ricocheted off her right shoulder. As it bounced she raised her right hand and caught the bullet between her pointer and middle fingers. Anat slowly turned around as she bent her robotic fingers inwards and flicked the bullet away like a booger.

A fit man descended from the window of a nearby building. He wore a leather vest and blue jeans, and appeared to be around her age. The man's scalp was shaven with multiple, jingling rings pierced into the back of his head. A sniper rifle was strapped to his back and he held a titanium bat in his hands.

Anat smiled at her attempted assassin. She admired the piercings on the back of his skull and correctly assumed they were a record of successful kills. "There you are."

"You call me a coward..." The man taunted. "You're the one with universally magnetic spaulders and robotic hands!"

"The hands weren't by choice." Anat shrugged.

"As for my armor, well...what can I say? People like shooting at me!"

"Yeah..well..." The man started. "I'm here to collect the bounty on your head!"

"Are you?" Anat smiled to one side of her mouth. "Which one? Alive...dead – or, or the one for the flash drive which I don't even carry?"

"Your corpse fetches the prettiest price!" The bounty hunter answered as he assailed her with his bat.

Anat reached and caught the bat in her left hand as she tilted her head to her right. The man swung a punch with his brass knuckles toward her kidney – but she caught his fist with her right hand.

"Not too bright, are you?" Anat said softly. "This will be quick, but that doesn't mean it won't be excruciating."

The man leaned back and howled as Anat crushed his fist. She closed her other hand as well – breaking the bat in half. As the man lowered his right arm and released his grip on the bat she reached across his arm and grabbed his right shoulder. The man stumbled backward and shrieked again as Anat closed her hand over his shoulder – breaking his right arm off. What remained of his left hand was ripped from his body as he pulled his other arm from her fist.

"Why can't you fight like a man?!" The bounty hunter cried.

"Well...for one, I am female. And second – the point of a fight is to win." Anat replied.

The bounty hunter pressed his bleeding wrist against the open wound that was once his shoulder. "You fight with no honor!"

"That's why I'm still alive." Anat cackled as she

unsheathed one of her swords and swung it across the man's mouth – slicing his upper-gums open. "It is ironic though, you tried to snipe me. I prefer the intimacy of blades." His screams became more blood curdling as his teeth fell from his upper-jaw. Anat then aimed her left knuckles toward the man's face as she sprayed kerosene from her hand. The man turned around as his bottom teeth were covered in the fluid. When he attempted to run Anat grabbed his collar and pulled him back toward her. He fell onto his rump as Anat stepped around him. "Fire is fun too...almost as personal! What was that about honor?" With a flick of her finger a spark was produced that landed on his lips. His lips and bottom teeth were instantly ignited. A rapid, popping sound could be heard as the blood pouring from his upper-gums boiled. Anat ended the man's misery by kicking his face in with her boot. The splash of blood extinguished the flame.

Anat began walking away – but her foot was lodged within the man's skull. His body dragged with each step as she attempted to shake the corpse from her sabaton. She sighed as she pulled her free foot toward the corpse's head and crushed the left half of his face – opening the skull enough so that she could free her other leg.

As Anat approached the town square she noticed that almost nothing had been repaired since her previous visit. The center of the town was still a massive, charred crater from Am-Heh's lava surrounded by scorched building debris. She ambulated toward the drug market – hoping to locate someone who makes methamphetamine.

***

Eric and Justice occupied the cockpit of the

Blessed airship as it soared toward the F2 atoll.

Justice watched the somber clouds darken as they raced the sunset. She had never been to F2 before, but although Eric made her feel strange because of that it wasn't as unusual as the Blessed would believe. Even though it was an easy zone to access for anyone with a means to get off the ground the atoll had little sentimental meaning. All it stood for was the end of the war and the final nail in society's coffin. F2 was where Gilgamesh and Enkidu sacrificed not only themselves but the remainder of the gods' supreme powers to banish Kepyet. Albeit Kepyet's initial intent was to be a savior his forces caused almost as much damage to the planet as the divine's, and took just as many casualties. To most people F2 was was little more than a reminder of their poor quality of life following the war.

"It's nice having some quiet for once – huh?" Eric remarked.

"What do you mean?" Justice asked.

"Well it seems like with Ellis and Jasper we have to listen to one fracas after another." Eric explained.

Justice shrugged. "I don't mind, sometimes it's entertaining."

"When the time is appropriate." Eric added as the airship began to descend.

***

Ellis and Jasper neared the ruins of Atlantis.

"Did you remember to reload our weapons?" Ellis inquired.

"Yeah." Jasper answered. "We should be fine, but do you really think we will encounter anything?"

"Who knows." Ellis murmured. "My only concern would be coming across The Monk's goons again."

"They won't hurt us, though." Jasper claimed.

"They won't hurt Justice." Ellis corrected. "Plus they're revenants. I doubt they appreciate our association with the Blessed."

"Well you upbraid the Blessed so much those revenants can probably be convinced we aren't among them." Jasper theorized.

"Yeah, well.." Ellis thought for a moment. "We're still working with them against The Monk's interests. Whatever his interests may be."

Atlantis, now known as J15, was a crater about three-quarters the size of New York City. The ground surrounding the crater was distorted and bore the appearance of oceanic waves slithering toward the depression. J15 was also surrounded by debris which floated in the air – unmoving, frozen in time. The stoic objects ranged in size everywhere between specs of dust to vehicle-sized boulders. Ellis drove the cannon through the dream-like wasteland.

"Wow!" Jasper gasped. "How is everything just floating...still, like that?"

"The synthetic gravite bomb, it left a permanent disturbance in gravity around this area." Ellis explained.

The Cannon drove into the crater and parked on the first flat surface. Atlantis, the once great city, was now something straight out of a nightmare. The walls of the crater were lined with petrified windows and doorways. Each one was intricately carved, and no two were alike. Although only stone casts were left behind the details of each object remained in pristine condition. Charred obelisks twisted into springs stood throughout the region. Ashen casts of multiple buildings stood, but stretched and shrunk into microscopic points toward the center of the city. The foundations of various homes and temples levitated above the ruins, each with a trail of stoic dust dripping toward the middle of the crater.

Ellis and Jasper were immediately distracted by the gentle, slow flickers of light that sparked throughout the city like a field of fireflies. The lights ranged in size from a couple millimeters to the size of headlights. Gravity is what held the light energy in place, and also what reduced their intensity. The "ghost" of a headlight wasn't much brighter than the flame of a candle from more than a couple meters away.

Also floating throughout the region were long, spaghetti-like blue lights which slowly flickered and faded no differently than the other lights within the ruined metropolis. These strands of lights were what remained of Atlantis' power grid. Gravity had frozen some of the electrical energy in place sans the wires which once encased it. A hole roughly the diameter of a corn silo occupied the center of the city.

"None of this makes sense!" Jasper stuttered. "I get that magic is real and whatnot, but – this place defies the laws of physics!"

Ellis snickered. "Does it? Synthetic gravite, kid. The governments of the past kept its existence secret and in short supply. Kepyet took almost all of it right away, kind of gave him an upper hand in the war for a while. The material was produced sub rosa for a reason. What you see before you...that'...this is the reason."

Jasper, awe-struck, marveled at his surroundings. "And all this time I thought this place was only ruins!"

Ellis glared askance at Jasper. "What do you call this, then?"

"You know what I mean!" Jasper whined.

Ellis looked down and shook his head. "Well, the teleporter to the moon should be in the ruins of the undercity down that hole there."

"Did the gravite destroy that area, too?" Jasper quaeritated.

"Most of it." Ellis answered. "The foundation of the main city was constructed to be nearly indestructible, but the black hole bomb sucked what it could through the one passageway between the two layers of the city. Honestly I don't know what compels Teigao to believe that the teleporter would still remain intact."

As Ellis and Jasper prowled through the ruins of Atlantis they became minorly disturbed by yet another detail. Not only was light frozen – but sound energy was as well! The men would occasionally pass through points where they could hear the dying screams of the Atlantean citizens as the bomb landed. Sometimes the screams sounded distant and distorted, and other times the shouts were clear as if the people producing the screams had wrapped their mouths around Ellis and Jasper's ears. The heavy, rough sounds of incomplete explosions were also audible and could be mistaken for the roar of a lava flow.

The list of disturbances within the crater seemed endless. Some spots were affected by a heavy wind, while in others the air was stoic. Other places were torrid, yet others frigid.

Pulsating flickers of light surrounded the hole in the center of the city. They were cloudy and colorful – like the Northern Lights. The men stopped for a breath as they neared their destination.

"What's that, then?" Jasper panted as he pointed toward the light show.

"Hell if I know." Ellis returned. "Probably frozen magnetic energy of some sort. Almost everything can be affected by gravity, black holes, and worm holes."

"How did the bomb not destroy the rest of the planet?" Jasper asked.

"Synthetic gravite doesn't hold its power for very long when on its own." Ellis answered. "Kepyet probably calculated the exact amount for the carnage to be contained within the limits of the city. He could have also used his own power to suppress it. Nobody knows exactly how powerful that freak was. Ready to continue helping him come back?"

"No." Jasper muttered. "But...I get that we must."

Ellis chuckled as the men strolled into the colorful fog. The magnetic lights became overwhelming and for a moment both men were blinded. As Jasper stepped out of the strange energy he discovered that he was now alone.

The landscape had changed as well. Jasper was no longer inside a large crater. This new region was flat with no apparent end. The magnetic lights had vanished. Jasper's heart began to race as he contemplated his surroundings. The sky was clear with no cloud in sight, and the ground was nothing but ash and salt. Breathing became arduous due to the lack of oxygen.

A person in shining white armor appeared before Jasper and raised their hand – magically surrounding Jasper with oxygen-rich air. The person's armor appeared lightweight, but was mostly covered by a bulky, white cloak. Gold trim shined from the joints. They wore an expressionless white mask – similar to Kepyet's. Their mask enveloped their head just as Kepyet's did, and their eyes shined the same piercing crimson as Kepyet's.

Jasper stepped back from the being and shouted "Who are you?!"

The corners of the mask's mouth cracked upwards just barely enough to visibly smile as the voice of an older woman was heard. "Saved your life, is who."

"Umm...thank-you? But why? Who are you besides that? Where is Ellis – and where am I?!" Jasper panicked.

The being stood still as she examined Jasper. "I knew one who would have appreciated this moment. You are lost, what year do you think it is?"

"Oh no, you don't!" Jasper barked. "Answer my questions first!"

The woman's voice racketed through her mask as she laughed. "I am reminded of what I missed. Be calm, this must be Atlantis for you?"

"What else would it be?" Jasper remarked. "Where is Ellis, and how do I return to...wherever?!"

"Gravity affects time, the bomb in Atlantis created multiple wormholes. Be grateful you are here where I am, as I am not here in all futures, or available in any past." The sparkling entity explained. "This is one future of many, and I will say it is a future you do not want."

"Is this where the devourers won or something?" Jasper queried. "Am I to learn some heartfelt lesson here?"

The woman laughed again. "No, no. You are here by chance...but also by good fortune. This was not the devourers, I may disrupt the balance of things if I explain too much, which is also why I conceal my identity. I can send you back to the moment you stepped into this future. Heed my words, though, please."

Jasper crossed his arms. "Alright, lady...if you actually are a lady. I'm listening."

The being tilted her head back and groaned, almost as if she was annoyed. "There may be a child. A boy."

"Stop there." Jasper sniggered. "A child? Not possible. Nobody on Earth is fertile."

"Circumstance lead to a single exception." The being explained. "The child, the boy. When...if...he comes. Believe him."

"When will this happen?" Jasper catechized.

"It might not." The woman shrugged.

"So, why tell me?" Jasper whined.

"Just in case." She answered as she waved her hand.

Jasper fell forward and started ranting as he climbed onto his feet. "What kind of bullshit is..."

Ellis stood above Jasper with his hand over his mouth – chuckling. Jasper's eyes widened as he processed his surroundings. He was back in Atlantis and standing barely a hundred feet from the hole. The magnetic lights surrounded the area and Ellis stood next to him.

"Are you alright?" Ellis teased.

"What happened?" Jasper stuttered.

"OH, come on!" Ellis drawled mockingly. "Don't be such a baby!"

"You're back! Well...I'm back!" Jasper cheered.

"What are you talking about?" Ellis asked.

"When we walked into the fog...I was taken into this other universe! I think a future, and there was this weird lady thing there." Jasper began to explain.

"Quite a story." Ellis snickered. "Clever cover story for tripping on a pebble and eating shit."

"It really did happen, though!" Jasper alleged. "Gravity can affect time, I stepped into such a phenomena!"

"Right." Ellis commented – still skeptical. "Ready to climb into the sub-city, or are you in another fantasy land?"

Jasper shook his head. "Let's just get the damn   ring."

CHAPTER 7

The war was in its final months. Unity sat in her cave gazing upon her infant son, Callum. Their cave was little more than a grotto in the side of a mountain, only a few hundred square feet. Most of the space was occupied by hoarded supplies. Her bed was a tattered mattress with several sheets and a pillow crinkled on one side. Callum's cradle was iron and eroded where Unity filed down the once sharp edges. Curtains colored to match the stone face of the cliff concealed the entrance to the cave. The room was illuminated with the dim, cloud-filtered light from the tarnished full moon.

Unity heard a whooshing sound outside – like a gust of wind. No other sounds accompanied the whoosh, not even the usual sound of crumbling leaves scraping against the rocks. The cave became even darker than it already was. She grabbed her shotgun and peeped through a hole in the curtain. The outside was as dark as her grotto – all she could make out was an ominous figure standing between the dead trees below an eclipse. Unity instantly recognized the grim individual as Kepyet. She knew she couldn't fight him, and that he could see her. Hopelessly she rested her shotgun against the wall and stepped outside.

Unity approached Kepyet and noticed that he was alone. She quavered "Kepyet, I presume? You come alone?"

"My army exists not for security nor power. It's a symbol, an ever-growing symbol of both redemption and rebellion." Kepyet answered. His hauntingly melodious, crisp voice echoed through his mask.

"So, this war is a game to you?" Unity cried. "You destroy the planet for a symbol?!"

"It's a play within a game initiated by the gods long before my time. Their tyranny is the cause of this desecration, and their defeat is the only hope mortals may have of recovery." Kepyet explained. "I offer true protection and liberty, and have the means to better the world once the divine are gone. My powers are limitless, surely there is something you desire? Ahh...there is. Desire flaunts its radiance within your heart."

"I've learned better than to take up offers from anyone." Unity argued. "Why are you here, shouldn't you be off winning the game?"

"Because there is something I more than desire. A necessity for the success of my goals. I need a philosopher's stone, and I know you have an understanding of alchemy much deeper than even your husband was aware of." Kepyet spoke.

"Forget it!" Unity growled. "Wait...What do you mean "was"?"

"He's dead, but restrain your panicked heart! Your daughter is fine." Kepyet confessed. "I have been exclusively straightforward with you. Information has always been the most valued bargaining currency."

"You come to tell me Lucien is dead, without specifics about the safety of my daughter!" Unity sobbed. "Your words aren't reassuring, they're poison! You're little more than a snake, and I won't take your apple!"

"Perhaps you would address my offer with less hostility if you knew I once went by the name "Cooper Thomas"?" Kepyet asked. "I sense your skepticism but I also see that you know I speak only truths. You're also unable to hide your grief over Lucien. His soul wanders the underworld, I can resurrect him with no hassle. But for such a favor – I need one in return."

"You lie!" Unity yelped.

"Do I?" Kepyet chuckled. "You are reacting, knowing I speak no falsehoods."

"Cooper wouldn't have conditions for something like that! He was a close family friend, to both of us!" Unity alleged.

"That much is true." Kepyet confessed. "But Cooper is no more. My soul was corrupted from my damnation. I have set most biases aside. There is great weight to the favor I request, but the reward is greater. A rock in exchange for the resurrection of your love...and godhood. For both of you."

"Why would a creature like you even need the stone?" Unity catechized. "You're already beyond the power of a god."

"I can still die." Kepyet snapped. "My resurrections are instant, but I still die. The stone would solve that predicament. I do what I can with baetylus, but it isn't a perfect solution."

"Baetylus...you have some?!" Unity stuttered.

"What do you suppose the base mineral for my armor and most my body is?" Kepyet replied. "Baetylus replaces that which doesn't heal. Will you contemplate my offer?"

"I need clarity." Unity panted. "Remove your mask. Show me your face."

"The face of a dead man?" Kepyet sniggered. "Very well."

Kepyet reached toward the sides of his head and pulled his hood down. His head was entirely concealed by the grainy, black metal. Three small horns crowned the top of his scalp. The horns retracted into the metal as Kepyet pressed against his temples. A click was heard as he separated his mask from the rest of his headgear.

Kepyet's skin had become the stereotypical pale white as other villains within pop culture. His goatee was a spectrum of black and light silver. The dark color of his eyes hid behind the red light from within his semi-demonic soul. Discolored bags rippled below each eye – blending into the faint, but noticeable wrinkles skipping down his cheeks. His lips were gruesomely chapped. Kepyet's human teeth had all been replaced with the corrupted baetylus alloy which the majority of his mortal form was comprised of, and struggled to conceal his partially decayed tongue. The top of his nose had become corrupted baetylus, and there were ramate streaks of the material crawling from his temples toward the corners of his eyes.

Although his transition into Kepyet had disfigured him, Unity still recognized the man as

Cooper. With a sigh, she nodded and said "So...you really are Cooper..."

"Somewhere in time." Kepyet smirked.

"I should have known, you probably believe a part of me did know." Unity shook her head. "Alright...I am considering your offer, but I would like input as well."

Kepyet cackled as he reattached his mask. "Elaborate." Without the mask to filter the sound waves, his voice was distorted and weak from the material coating his vocal chords.

"I need an upfront payment before I even begin researching the stone again." Unity asserted.

"You dare speak as if you possess the authority to modify my offer?" Kepyet roared.

"You spoke earlier of symbols." Unity paused for a moment. "You are a symbol of defying authority. Your soldiers follow you for the promise of redemption and a better world, but you also inspire them. You were at one point just a man, yet you challenged the gods. Even after they damned you you continued to rebel, and here you are... So yes, as a mortal human...the very same, weak, flawed creature you once were...I bargain with you, a god...of sorts."

Kepyet fell into a fit of laughter. "You misinterpret what I represent, but your bravery and stubbornness are both admirable. I shall give ear to your plea, but I am not one to accept or even consider any deal or terms without knowledge of every detail."

"I demand a guarantee that my children will remain healthy." Unity chattered at an almost unintelligible speed.

Kepyet gently tilted his head to the side. "A mortal woman's request if I ever did hear one. It is...within acceptable parameters of the extents I am willing to compromise. I can not guarantee your children will survive the consequences of their behaviors as they grow and mature. It is health you want – and health your son now receives!"

"Not enough!" Unity seethed. "What about Justice?"

Kepyet crossed his arms. "Your daughter's health was never susceptible to decline."

"What are you talking about?" Unity's voice trembled.

"Nothing need you feel anxious about." Kepyet assured. "My response will become clear in time, given the threads of fate remain loyal to their weave."

Unity groaned. "And I thought you spoke like a madman before. My children are and will remain healthy, then?"

Kepyet lowered his head and waved his arm in a fashion comparable to a bow. "Yes. Have I not always been a man of my word?"

Unity tapped her foot. "Did you not just tell me that Cooper is a dead man?"

Kepyet and Unity's eyes pierced each others' souls for a moment. Kepyet drawled "And what kind of man doesn't take his principles to the grave?"

"The kind that would force his best friend's wife to bargain for the resurrection of her husband and the safety of their children." Unity trembled.

"Did you truly love Lucien?" Kepyet queried.

"I DO love him, something an empty-hearted fiend like yourself wouldn't ever understand." Unity said brusquely.

The mouth of Kepyet's mask cracked with his subtle smile. "Then I would hurry."

Unity blinked and Kepyet was gone. The all-embracing darkness weakened as the object blocking the moon's light squirmed away. A single, pink rose grew from the ground where Kepyet had stood. Unity took a step toward the rose and interpreted it as a sign that Cooper still resided within the foul shell of stone and metal. He had never divulged to her the significance of roses, but her intuition suggested that this one was a sign of sincerity. The news of her husband's passing troubled her – but she had no time to mourn. She had to use her grief as fuel to complete Kepyet's task.

CHAPTER 8

Eric and Justice dropped from the rope-ladder and onto the atoll. The fog was so thick that the duo constantly felt as if they were being sprayed. Unusual warmth from the liquid prevented the sensation from being refreshing. They had to watch where they landed each step as the terrain was covered in shredded metal and crumbled stone. Occasionally they would find mangled bones between the debris.

Justice felt dizzy as they approached the center of the atoll. She took long, deep breaths and sat on a brick. Eric shifted attention to her and asked "What's wrong?"

"I don't know..." Justice gasped. "I just feel weak...and sickly. It worsens as we near the water."

"This is a dreadful place." Eric commented. "Although I think it's just all in your head. The air here is less polluted than much of the rest of the world."

"I don't know..." Justice mumbled as she held her stomach and hunched forward. "It's like...I feel the pain of those that perished here."

"There must be a hex somewhere." Eric theorized.

Justice leaned too far and fell forward off her seat. As she landed on her side she raised her hands and grabbed her head. The fog slowly twirled around her.

Eric growled as he deeked at the air's behavior, knowing what was likely causing the phenomenon. "I'll be back!" Eric promised as he ran away.

Justice didn't notice he left. Her vision had blurred and all she heard was an intense, ringing sound as her head throbbed. Justice passed out, and her dream took her back in time.

***

F2 was a beautiful, circular island surrounded by mountains. A palace similar to Skyrook stood on the northernmost end of the valley. The area in front of the citadel was protected by a curtain wall the height of the outermost towers which wrapped around the interior of the valley. Its white crystals sparkled with shades of green reflecting the flora which blanketed the mountains. A stoic eclipse rested between the clouds, and the circle of sunlight shined directly upon the wall. The center of the fortress was an enormous, circular stage with Kepyet's symbol carved into it. Three sentries hovered behind the citadel as an army of Blessed soldiers approached from the southern mountain tops. Kepyet stood in the center of his symbol – anticipating the attack. He held a sword similar to the one discovered in Skyrook, but this one lacked many of his other sword's powers. The center wave of soldiers on the front line were Amazoness warriors armed with heavy wooden bows.

The engines of the sentries lit up as they prepared to move ahead, but Kepyet gestured his hand – ordering them to hold back. Camulus, Enyo, Hachiman, Mixcoatl, Montu, and Ullr appeared around Kepyet.

Camulus was a muscular man with bronze skin. He was bare chested and wore only iron spaulders and a metal guard over his groin. His jaw was covered by a beard the exact color of his skin. The deity carried a large sword with both hands. Camulus' weapon was crafted with little detail, however it was also the color of his flesh.

Enyo wore a Spartan-style helmet. A shining strip of angelic white fabric was crudely wrapped around her body just barely enough to cover her breasts and hips. In her right hand was a bloodied rod with a blowtorch-style flame at the end. The blaze projected an orange aura onto her cloud-white skin, and caused the tiny gemstones in her wrappings to scintillate.

Hachiman bore the appearance of an older Asian man. He wore a brown-colored suit of Samurai armor and carried a Katana. Otherworldly flames roared from between the cracks of his armor, and lava flowed along the flats of his sword.

Mixcoatl was a brown-skinned man with a short, bright red beard and dreadlocks. His armor was jade green with golden chains holding the plates together. The god's helmet and cape were covered in green feathers. His eyes were concealed by a black mask and white, candy cane style tattoos wrapped around his arms and legs.

He carried two ostentatious, red maces forged in the shape of dragon heads.

Montu was a dark-skinned man with the head of a falcon, but as he looked at Kepyet his eyes reddened and his head transformed into that of a bull. His chest was bare, and his legs were covered by a golden shendyt. The Egyptian god carried a simple spear in each hand.

Ullr was slightly shorter than the other gods and carried a bow crafted from an alloy of gold and orichalcum. His skin was white with a blonde goatee and long blonde hair. The Norse god wore a vest of bear fur and stood on skis.

Enyo pointed her torch at Kepyet. "Enough of this war!"

"More hackneyed suggestions I surrender?" Kepyet chuckled. "Or have you grown jaded of losing?"

Montu directed his spears toward Kepyet. "You have evoked our wrath. Tartarus was a mistake, you should have been fed to Apophis!"

Mixcoatl stomped his foot and bellowed "No more talk!"

Kepyet teleported behind Mixcoatl – running his sword through the god's neck as he appeared. Kepyet whispered in Mixcoatl's ear "I agree."

Mixcoatl forced himself forward and slid off Kepyet's weapon. He gyrated to swing his maces – but Kepyet teleported back to his original position and clapped his hands. Two more Kepyets appeared beside him. The wound on Mixcoatl's neck healed.

Ullr prepared to fire an arrow at the Kepyet in the center but all three teleported around the god and lunged their swords into his neck. Montu charged toward Ullr but Kepyet teleported back to his original spot before Montu could land a hit. Ullr collapsed as Kepyet's clones vanished. The Norse god held his throat – attempting to heal it, but this time Kepyet had channeled a spiritual toxin into his swords.

Mixcoatl took a step forward, but Kepyet swung his fist toward the god. As Kepyet punched the reality around his fist cracked. The air condensed into an umbrella shape over his fist with black lightning sparking around it. A flash of shadow struck Mixcoatl – launching him backward and through the southern wall. Kepyet raised his free hand – teleporting Mixcoatl into his grip. The Aztec god squirmed as Kepyet instantly siphoned the deity's life force. Kepyet's other foes backed in fear as he released his grip on Mixcoatl's corpse.

Kepyet clapped his hands again, but this time black lightning fell from the sky and into the bodies of his divine contenders. The gods fell to their knees in confusion.

Camulus quavered as he struggled to lift his sword. "What is this?"

"You're mortals now." Kepyet answered. "You know what that means."

Kepyet snapped his fingers – killing the five remaining gods.

Artemis teleported in front of the Amazon warriors as the army reached the top of the mountain. Her hair was braided and gray, and she covered herself with a jeweled, golden toga. The moment she appeared she drew back the string on her hardwood bow with orichalcum spikes. Ten arrows materialized along the string as she released her grip and angled toward Kepyet.

Ten Nutes appeared in the air above Kepyet and fell along the path of the arrows. Every arrow landed within a falling Nute. Kepyet raised his fist into the air - resurrecting his meat shields. When he opened his hand their bodies crumbled as their souls swirled toward Artemis. Those damaged souls of Kepyet's soldiers conquered the goddess' body before she could react. The Amazons and soldiers turned their backs and ducked as Artemis' flesh exploded from her body in a flash of blue light.

As Artemis' skeleton fell from the cliff the Amazoness women aimed their bows at Kepyet. They drew their strings back along the lengths of their arms and against the scars on their chests from where their right breasts were removed. As the women aimed their bows the other soldiers cocked their rifles and prepared to fire upon the demon.

Kepyet snapped his fingers. Arrows haphazardly flew across the sky and into the front lines – killing the Amazons and the soldiers near them. The deaths of the front-line soldiers caused an avalanche of bodies and guns to roll down the mountainside. Every surviving soldier climbed over the remaining bodies to reach the edge of the cliff – ready to take aim.

Kepyet opened his wings and flew into the sky. The wraith hovered in place as he examined the army attempting to siege his fortress. Skyrook was barely visible for a moment as it passed through the sky toward the Southeast.

"Have the Blessed truly manipulated so many of you?" Kepyet's voice was amplified loud enough to be heard by the entire army. "Decaying below are some of the pantheons' greatest warriors!

Your gods fall before me like insects. What does that make you?"

Several Blessed zeppelins appeared in the distance. As they flew toward Kepyet the sentries behind powered their engines and started moving ahead.

A flash of light from behind the army stunned Kepyet. His armor and mask cracked upon his landing, but repaired itself as he struggled onto his feet. A large creature descended from the sky and landed in front of Kepyet. The being's body was crafted from a mix of clay and metal. Its head had two mouths – each with long, sharp, golden teeth. Four silver eyes with an azure gleam were placed in a row along the forehead. The creature's long black hair had streaks of red. A glowing ring like that of a planet gently rotated along its neck. Lightning dropped from the ring and struck the creature's white spaulders. The muscular arms were crafted from a mysterious, dense gold alloy. Covering the being's back was a cape as dark as the night sky, filled with shooting stars. The golden armor covering its body was trimmed with a similar design as the cape – with the shooting stars barely visible. In the center of its chest was a symbol of the Blessed crafted from sapphire. A crimson cloth with sapphire-colored trims covered its armored legs. The creature spoke in two voices – each with a heavy Middle-Eastern accent.

"No more...Kep...Yet...." The golem drawled.

Kepyet's eyes gleamed as he analyzed the golem's souls.

Kepyet smiled under his mask. "Gilgamesh and Enkidu. The gods weren't generous enough to allow you each your own vessel?" Gilgamesh and Enkidu manifested a sword similar to Kepyet's in their right hand as their foe continued. "You should have called out to me, instead you now waste the body you've been allowed to share."

"You're more of a mortal than we were." The golem taunted. "You fight with stolen power."

"Power that was purloined prior my acquisition, the strongest argument against theft is the victim. My victims are dead, and weren't even worthy of what they owned." Kepyet argued.

"Who are you to speak of worth?" The golem growled.

Kepyet pointed his sword at the tip of the golem's and sniggered "More of a mortal than you were."

***

Justice's eyes flew open as she heard a loud, screeching shatter. Eric stood in the distance near the water – holding two halves of a skeleton. He dropped the remains as Justice stood and anxiously contemplated her surroundings.

Eric sighed with relief as he approached her and yelled "Feeling better?"

"What happened?!" Justice gasped. "And yes, thank-you."

"I guess you were affected by a curse." Eric theorized. "I had heard some gods tried to record what transpired here."

"All the gods I saw died before you broke the curse though." Justice perplexed.

"Yeah, it's a strange spell." Eric explained. "You know the egregore Kepyet left behind – the one that haunted the Wardaughter?" Justice nodded as Eric elaborated. "Well, it's kind of like a weaker version of that. Just a pinch of spiritual energy, soul essence. It lingers wherever it's placed and records, but it remains linked to the deity that placed it. Usually only they can view the recording – but if they die then it can be viewed by anyone with divine energy in them."

"Wait!" Justice stuttered. "But I don't have divine energy in me. You do though but how come it didn't affect you?"

Eric shrugged. "Well, I used up most of mine against that parasitic shade in the labyrinth. Not sure how you picked up on it, I'm guessing Kepyet's sword may have attracted the curse? You also carried the relic from Ra's spear around with you for a while."

Justice inclined. "It must be the sword, especially since when the curse took over my mind it did so aggressively. How did you break it?"

Eric pointed at the mangled skeleton by the water. "I desecrated the corpse of the deity that placed the curse. That over there is the skeleton of Artemis. A miracle her bones remained intact when the island was obliterated."

Justice stared at the skeleton. Seeing the bones of a once powerful goddess would have normally struck her heart with sadness, but right now she was irritated by the vision which had possessed her. She strongly prefers reading history as opposed to experiencing it. Was Kepyet's sword the true reason the curse affected her, though? Was Artemis' recording spell really dumb enough to be beckoned by her slayer?

Justice took a deep breath. "So, where are we going?"

Eric tilted his head toward the water. "The mask is likely under the water. Our luck under a pile of bricks. Are the diving features on your uniform functional?"

"Kind of." Justice answered. "They work – but not for that long. I'll have to surface to reload the oxygen every ten minutes or so."

"Good enough." Eric said. "Let's dive in and get started!"

Justice and Eric both pressed a button on their neck. A leather-like mask flipped out from Justice's collar and covered the bottom half of her face like a bandanna. A pair of goggles extended from the mask and sealed themselves over her eyes. On Eric's outfit the diving gear was a strip of metal which slithered along the back of his head until it dropped from his forehead. Once between his eyes a pair of goggles flipped out from the thick wire. A different strip of metal crawled from the front of his collar and into the corner of his mouth.

The duo slugged into the murky water. The Adam's ale was the exact same temperature as the air on the surface. Large rocks, bricks, and metal debris filled the lake. Justice noticed a piece of metal that was glowing orange and causing the water around it to boil.

"What's that?" Justice panicked to Eric.

"Nothing." Eric assured. "When Gilgamesh defeated Kepyet there was so much energy in the burst that a few scraps were unnaturally super heated. Even after eighteen years that debris hasn't cooled, and it may be another eighteen years before it's depleted of energy."

"How come the metal didn't just vaporize though, if it really does have THAT much heat in it?" Justice wondered.

Eric giggled "Well, this is one of those instances where we can just go with the cheap and easy answer humans have for everything they can't explain – magic!"

Justice rolled her eyes. "I would have rather learned how exactly this works rather than watched Kepyet kill a handful of gods and hundreds of people."

"Maybe Artemis meant for one of us to see the recording." Eric hypothesized. "A warning to not bring him back."

"The cons significantly outweigh the pros of bringing him back." Justice admitted. "Other than the fact he might be able to kill the devourers I don't see what good can come of this."

"I agree." Eric groaned. "It's already obvious that we are already playing along with his agenda. An agenda that we have only scratched the surface of."

"We wouldn't even be in this mess if it wasn't for Teigao's misplaced trust in Kepyet's general." Justice blurted, instantly regretting how much she sounded like Ellis when making that statement.

"Perhaps not." Eric thought for a moment. "But perhaps we would also be exactly where we are now. He would have found another way, and more than likely he had not only one but a ridiculous list of equally viable back-up plans."

Justice pouted, but as much as she desired to argue she knew that Eric was correct. There was likely no way around this scenario and any attempted detour would eventually lead right back into the mess. The realization that Kepyet could manipulate the world in such a way that everything falls into line exactly how he desires brought her an even greater sense of unease about resurrecting him. Justice dreaded to think what the next stage in Kepyet's plan was. She could almost see him clearly when she imagined him sitting in his personal realm – patiently awaiting the moment when the Blessed, his enemies, reluctantly accite him out of desperation. It would be humorous if it wasn't so cruel.

As the two swam nearer the center of the lake the amount of searing metal increased. Eric and Justice had to navigate what was almost a maze of dangerously hot bubbles. They reached the remains of the large platform where Kepyet stood in his final moments. The topmost layers of the platform were eroded, his symbol with them. What remained was crumbled and slightly conclave. Bits of Gilgamesh / Enkidu's armor rested upon many of the bricks – each piece not even a square inch in size. Naught remained of Kepyet's armor. Justice swam toward the surface to refill her oxygen – having remained submerged longer than she thought her suit allowed. Eric followed.

Justice gasped as her head burst from the water. Her uniform produced a subtle humming noise as it refilled. Eric emerged beside her.

Justice took deep breaths for a moment before saying "How are we supposed to find his mask in that mess?"

"The sword isn't helping?" Eric perplexed.

"No." Justice replied. "It didn't react to the egregore either."

"You'd think the fiend would want this task to be easier on us!" Eric remarked.

"I'm not sure he had much say in the matter." Justice guessed. "I'm concerned that his mask may not have even survived. Did you see what I saw before we surfaced?"

"A crater of bricks within a bigger crater of bricks?" Eric chuckled.

"No." Justice squeaked. "The flakes all over the ground down there! I recognize them from Artemis' hex! That's the armor the Gilgamesh golem wore."

"What about it?" Eric asked. "It's just powerless metal at this point."

"That's all there is, though." Justice drawled. "There's nothing down there that looks like it belonged to Kepyet. That's why I'm concerned about the mask."

"Well – most of what Kepyet wore was baetylus. It wasn't just his armor – much of it was his body! There were other materials forged into it but almost his entire getup was connected directly to his soul. When his soul left his armor followed." Eric explained. "His mask was crafted from a slightly different alloy, though. It still contained and synchronized with baetylus and became a part of him when worn – but unlike the rest of his armor it wasn't a part of his spirit."

"So, why would it have been spared the detonation here?" Justice wondered.

"We can only assume it was crafted from alloys stronger than what we are familiar with – or enchanted to remain intact." Eric guessed.

A loud splash was heard. Justice and Eric watched the direction the sound originated – they barely distinguished a pile of debris protruding from the water a few hundred feet away. The two looked at each other then dove back underwater – prepared to draw their weapons.

Eric and Justice had to squint to make out the other visitor – but it was swimming too fast for them to distinguish details beyond his ichthyoid swimming ability. The two swam as fast as they could – but the mysterious figure had already lifted and searched under several bricks. As they approached the figure pushed a large brick aside – revealing a small grotto within the remains of a wall.

"See the way he swims?" Eric asked.

"Yeah." Justice answered. "What about it?"

"It's not normal. Even with technology. I have a feeling that we're facing another revenant." Eric complained. "Likely after the mask!"

"Probably a member of the monk's galère." Justice added.

When Eric and Justice were forty or fifty feet from the grotto the revenant emerged from the shadowy hole – with Kepyet's haunting mask in hand. The revenant wore a basic diving suit sans an oxygen tank. He had the appearance of a boy in his mid-to-late teens with short, black hair and a deep-black eyebrow above his human eye. One of the top quarters of his face was that of an old turtle.

Eric drew one of his pistols as Justice rested her palm around Kepyet's sword.

The revenant hissed. "The mask is ours! We will come for that sword – soon as The Monk allows! He feels the world, he is very intuitive."

"If his intuition was wise he would know better than to challenge us!" Eric growled.

"He knows your threat!" The revenant confirmed. "The two devourers, their deaths surf upon rumors. And the Centimane – that's impressive. You may need to return to wielding the Pyroguard's blade once that sword is relinquished!"

"How do you know those things?!" Justice

stuttered.

"The Monk is wise!" The revenant alleged. "He is ancient, well-informed, knows where to dig for information. Pray he maintains his desire to meet you – lest we are permitted to kill you."

The revenant scratched the forehead of Kepyet's mask – releasing a discombobulating flash of darkness. When Eric and Justice's vision restored the revenant was nowhere to be seen.

"Dammit!" Eric shouted.

"He couldn't have gotten far!" Justice hoped.

"It's no use. He's long-gone." Eric alleged. "The Monk's revenants are freaking ninjas."

"Well we have to do SOMETHING!" Justice begged.

"I'm thinking!" Eric yelped. "They are after the sword – eventually they will come for it, or lure us somewhere. We must remain on our guard. When they try to take the sword we will have an opportunity to learn more about The Monk, who he is, and most importantly WHERE he is. He can't be more dangerous than foes we have felled in the past."

"I'm not too concerned about finding him or retrieving the other relics." Justice snapped. "Well I technically am, but my concern is recovering the relics in time! Bakasura approaches our world, and we don't have a way to thwart him!"

"Well let's get going back to Skyrook then!" Eric suggested. "Retrieve the life elemental's heart from the subterranean labyrinth and see if there's any information about The Monk in the library we can use to get a step ahead!"

Justice gestured in agreement.

***

Ellis and Jasper stood above the hole in the

center of Atlantis. A mountain of debris rested beneath them – with its peak at the center of the hole. The men leaped from the edge onto the debris and slid down the side into the undercity of Atlantis. A long cloud filled with lightning wrapped around the outer-wall of the cave – illuminating the entire area. The undercity wasn't in as good of condition as the duo had hoped – most of it was pulled toward the center and the diameter of the region was only a couple thousand feet. It was once almost as large as the above-ground section of the city – but the black hole bomb sucked most of the underground toward the center where it bent upwards and jammed together – forming the walls which now surround the central debris welter. The debris walls themselves were void of all color – now only a dusty, lifeless gray. Ellis and Jasper examined the ground – noticing that the brick road was oddly intact. Even some of the blue and gold colors within the bricks were still distinguishable.

Jasper pouted as he realized the undercity was just as ruined as the surface. "Well...this place was destroyed too."

"You don't say?" Ellis blurted.

Jasper turned to Ellis. "You know, your churlishness gets frustrating."

"What?" Ellis muttered.

"You know what I said!" Jasper argued.

"Should I care though?" Ellis instigated.

"You should care that this place is destroyed!" Jasper shouted.

"Not really." Ellis confessed. "I mean I saw it coming – physically a black hole bomb wouldn't obey the barriers of a metal and stone...er...barrier. Our way to the moon may be gone, but if Kepyet could find it in him to do THIS who's to say he would even be in the mood to spare anyone?"

"He's our only shot at slaying the devourers though!" Jasper reminded his companion.

"Yeah – being eaten may not be so bad at this point." Ellis alleged. "Imagine what sort of torment Kepyet may put us through if he decides he doesn't like us. Or what if the gods come back? They would probably torture us for reviving their pest!"

"Well – I would rather take my chances with Kepyet!" Jasper declared. "It's our shot at survival. And that is what humans do, it's actually the purpose of all life. To survive."

"Only long enough to breed!" Ellis corrected. "And let's see here – no human is able to do that anymore! Also - with people it never really was JUST survival. We weren't as great as the Atlanteans, but we did build some pretty great cities and invent a lot of neat stuff!"

"Yeah, well..." Jasper started. "Those are the highlights. There was that one year when teenagers snorted condoms and ate laundry detergent."

"Didn't you eat laundry detergent before though?" Ellis criticized.

"It was just soap!" Jasper yelled. "White bar soap that YOU kept in a cream cheese wrapper!"

"How the hell would there be cheese a decade after they stopped making cheese?" Ellis deprecated.

"I was twelve!" Jasper whined.

"Why would I keep cheese with bathing supplies?" Ellis continued.

"Maybe you like snacking in the shower!"

Jasper chattered. "I don't know – I was twelve!"

"A dumb twelve." Ellis said as Jasper seethed. "Anyway what do you want to do here – look around for a moon teleporter or just return to Skyrook with the bum news?"

A clanking sound was heard from the outer-wall near the men. They glared at what they identified as a hole in the wall. A woman with wavy brown hair wearing dust-covered clothing crawled out of the hole and dropped near Ellis and Jasper.

"Umm – hello?" Jasper stuttered.

"Hey now!" Ellis flirted. "What's a fox like you doing he-"

The woman tossed her hair out of her face – revealing that that top quadrant of her visage was that of a spider's!

Ellis and Jasper jumped back and yelped as they drew their pistols. The woman leered at the men with her five eyes as she excavated a ring from her pocket. Ellis and Jasper tried to pull the triggers on their guns but an unknown force prevented them from moving.

With a smile, the woman charged toward the men. She leaped over their heads and onto the junk pile. The men were freed from the strange paralysis, but the revenant reached the top of the mound and escaped before they could even look up.

Jasper gazed at the hole in the wall and said "Well, I guess there was a portal here. Not that it matters now – that's probs the ring we need."

"And now we have to explain this to the others! Dammit. DAMMIT!" Ellis pulled the trigger on his gun – blasting a few holes into the ground.

Jasper took a step back from Ellis before they

approached the mountain of junk. They began climbing.

"Hey Ellis." Jasper vocalized.

"What?" Ellis groused.

"You said that lady was a fox..." Jasper mumbled. "She was actually a spider."

"Just   climb."   Ellis   snarled.

CHAPTER 9

Anat stood outside the entrance of a slowly crumbling building. She knocked on the door. As she knocked a cracking sound was heard alongside several squeaks – almost as if the wooden frame and rusted metal hinges were ready to break at any moment.

A shaky man with greasy hair stood by a desk inside the structure. It was all one room and filled with chemistry equipment and vats of various toxic substances. An electric generator lay on its side in one corner of the room a few feet from a stained toilet. A grinding sound echoed through the room as the generator powered several devices on the man's desk. He heard the knock.

"What do you want?!" He shouted.

"I'm in the market for some sulfur." Anat replied.

"I'm closed!" The man shrieked.

"Don't care." Anat muttered as she kicked the door down.

The man snarled as Anat stormed into the room. She drew her pistol and aimed it at him as he grabbed a shotgun from under the desk. His eyes widened as he saw her.

"Sulfur. Now." Anat ordered.

"You look familiar..." The man mumbled as he lowered his shotgun.

"And you look like the typical tweaker." Anat replied.

The man growled through his remaining teeth as he lifted his shotgun back toward her. "I know you! Kaleyla?! That's you – right?"

Anat tightened her grip on her pistol, it cracked from the strength of her robotic hand. "Carter." She replied. "Back from the dead, then?"

"What are you talking about?!" Carter asked, with doubt below his words.

"Right after you left me you had me believe you died." Anat stated. "Something about a car crash. I mourned you, and here you are?"

"My memory from then is a tad fuzzy!" Carter quavered.

"Yes, you've fried your brain with drugs." Anat pointed out. "Drugs that contain sulfur, which I need. Where do you keep it?"

Carter pulled the trigger and fired bird shot. All the pellets swerved into Anat's spaulders, but one grazed her chin along the way – leaving a small cut. Anat shot a bullet down the barrel of the shotgun – destroying it. Carter stepped back and nearly tripped over his desk as he dropped his weapon.

Carter's whole body shook like a jackhammer. "You're a freaking sociopath!" He cried. "I had to get away from you somehow!"

"THE SULFUR!" Anat seethed.

"It's in one of the boxes out back!" Carter said reluctantly. "It's in one of the small ones, yellow tags. You're still a psycho!"

"You don't know the half of it." Anat smiled.

Anat shot Carter five times in his chest. As he collapsed she threw a knife into the center of his forehead – damaging his brain so that his biological death switch was disabled. Carter now sat on the ground in great agony, unable to die – the exact torture Anat used against Lyth and Vlad several months ago.

Anat stepped toward Carter and squatted in front of him to make eye contact. "I'm also damn good with knives. Always was...so I'm leaving you one to remember me by...right up there!" Anat tapped his forehead. "Where memories are made and stored."

Anat used a razor at the end of her pointer finger to cut his eyes open then stood back up and tipped a vial on the counter onto its side. A thick, slow-moving acid fell from the mouth of the vial and spread across the surface. The acid reached the edge of the table above Carter and began dripping onto the left side of his body. Carter remained alive as the acid corroded him, feeling not only that pain but also the agony of his eyes and bullet wounds. He would remain alive until the knife in his head slipped from its position. Carter heard Anat's footsteps as she vacated his shack.

***

Ronny slowed the ferry as he and Unity approached the docks of the Asphodel Meadows and the Elysian Fields. The actual docks were gone, and the two gates were across the Styx from each other. The sky in this part of the underworld was a bloodied gold color, with fast-moving clouds slithering across the sky. Each gate was on a cement platform and tipped toward the river. The gates were large, stone hoops with seven circular depressions around the opening. There was nothing beyond the openings, if someone were to walk through they would find themselves on the other side of the gate against the mountains along the river. The fourteen depressions appeared to be keyholes of some kind. Ronny halted the ferry as it reached the two gates.

"I don't sense anybody." Ronny announced.

"Me neither." Unity pouted – losing a few skin cells to decay as she did so.

"He may have wandered. That boy did enjoy exploring." Ronny said. "By the way – how are these gates activated?"

"Keys." Unity replied. Her tongue vibrated with the "s" sound. "Kepyet's goons just left them in. They may have fallen out."

Ronny thought for a moment then dripped the end of his oar into the Styx. A whistling sound was emitted from the oar as it gently shook within the water. Fourteen orbs crafted from a glass-like substance rose to the surface and floated toward the oar. Ronny and Unity grabbed the orbs and set them on the deck of the ferry.

"They all just fell into the river." Ronny observed. "I think it best we don't open the gates until we find the boys and repair the platforms."

"Yes." Unity agreed. "Where do you suppose Callum is now, though?"

"Once someone refuses the toll they are lost from the Ferryman's radar." Ronny sighed. "I only found you because you were walking along my route."

"So, he could be anywhere in this wasteland?" Unity hissed as her eyes fogged.

"Unfortunately, but if we can locate Sal he may be able to track Callum. Elementals have exceptional senses – especially when they aren't limited by a human form." Ronny suggested.
Unity nodded. "Let's find him. Continue ahead, I can navigate us to where the Styx and Phlegethon bend toward each other."

Ronny tapped the oar and the ferry was propelled down the river.

***

Teigao, Justice, and Ellis stood around the planning table. Ellis had just finished speaking when Teigao slammed his fists on the surface.

"So you just left?!" Teigao growled.

"Well...yeah!" Ellis shrugged. "She already snagged the ring, moved way too fast for us to catch her."

"There are many rings in this world." Teigao lectured.

"Obviously." Ellis stated. "But the revenants work for The Monk, and The Monk is also hunting the relics. They snagged the mask before Eric and Justice could grab it, pretty sure the ring they stole as Jasper and I arrived was Kepyet's."

Teigao tightened his fists and said "Well, you better hope that the creature below is the only life elemental, and that we can figure out where the hell this Monk character is storing the relics!"

Justice raised her hand. "I still would like to know why he's collecting them. Are they not worthless to everyone except us?"

"They may wish to resurrect him as well."

Teigao explained. "The revenants were among Kepyet's elite soldiers, after all. One concern I have, though, is that they may desire to destroy the relics. It's a difficult task, but not impossible."

"Right!" Ellis blurted. "So they can just let the world be devoured. Sure the revenants weren't on your side?"

Teigao interjected. "Not like us, at all! The Blessed supported a remake – much different than desiring it expunged."

"Could they be working for the devourers?" Justice worried.

"Unlikely." Teigao reassured. "The devourers would never trust or assign any beings outside their circle to a task. In fact – they barely trust each other. Apophis himself was driven mad by the neglect and aggression of his creators. Tiamat was betrayed by the pantheon she created. If they need agents they program leviathans."

"Aren't those all dead, though?" Ellis asked.

Teigao shook his head. "Nay. There's an army of them, lurking just behind the veils of shadow. Dormant, awaiting the day their programmers deploy them."

"Could Tiamat be reasoned with?" Justice suggested. "If she was indeed once a goddess – perhaps she could be sympathetic to us."

Teigao laughed. "Her mind and soul have become pure devourer at this point. The gods have warred before, there are pantheons that have fallen. Some erased from history completely, others labeled as demons. Tiamat may be a struggle for even Kepyet, and Apophis is even stronger than her."

"It might be worth considering, at least." Justice nagged.

Teigao sighed. "Perhaps showing is easier than telling."

Teigao snapped his fingers and the doors of the ballroom locked. He then stepped back from the table while stretching his left thumb and pointer finger as far apart from each other as possible. A hellish red flame ignited between the fingers.

"Speak nothing of this." Teigao ordered. Justice noticed his shadow didn't quite match the figure of his body – it was proportioned slightly larger than it should be. She decided it was best not to inquire, as right now she needed Teigao. Ellis had his doubts but Justice was certain that Teigao was on their side.

The fire between Teigao's fingers swirled and grew. He pulled his hand back – dropping the swirling flames onto the ground. Ellis rested his palm on the handle of his gun as Justice just watched the fire open a portal. A heavy cloud of black smoke creeped from the flames and condensed into a demonic creature.

Teigao's summoned beast had a canine body with the wings of a griffin. The feathers appeared to be rusted iron, with blood dripping from the crevices between them. Its fur was short and black, and many of the hairs were ignited like miniature wicks. The beast's puffy tail was bloody smoke, and its razor-like claws appeared to have once been gold but have since converted to lead. Its ears flopped like that of a puppy. Ellis and Justice were more than unsettled by the creature's face. What they saw before them would haunt them for weeks to come – nightmares while they slept, and momentary terror whenever they closed their eyes. The face of the creature was mostly canine, except the eyes were perfectly round and slightly larger than they should have been. Its scleras were the dark color of decayed blood, with pupils almost too diminutive for the naked eye to see. Gently glowing circles of red rippled from the pupils – growing in size then disappearing as they reached the eyelids. If Ellis wasn't so horrified he would have cracked a joke about how the creature's hypnotic eyes were like targets. The eyebrows were thick and similar to a human's – floating separate from the beast's forehead above the eyes. A humanoid, ear-to-ear, smile filled with teeth not much different from those of an angler fish completed the creature's terrifying visage. Teigao's ring of fire surrounded the creature, and shackles attached to searing black chains dangled from the monster's legs.

"What the..." Ellis muttered.

"Fear not." Teigao shouted. "This beast is bound!"

The creature slowly motioned toward Teigao and attempted to say something – but Teigao pressed his thumb and pointer fingers together which appeared to torment the fiend.

"Silence!" Teigao ordered.

"What is going on?!" Justice shrieked. "What's this thing?! Who even are you?!"

"This fiend..." Teigao started. "His name is President Glasya-Labolas. He was a god once, original name lost upon falling. This beast once commanded legions of demons, he programmed manslaughter and bloodshed into the hearts of man. The early humans summoned him to hypnotize their enemies into loving each other...to the point they became possessive and eventually homicidal. He even granted some men invisibility.

This demon – he can see into time, and share what he views. It is unwise to deek at the futures presented by demons though – context is never shared, that is if the images shown are even accurate. The past, however, is unchanging."

"So, this dog thing. It's going to tell us a story?" Ellis perplexed.

Glasya-Labolas tilted its head and panted into a cackle as Teigao replied "Not quite. He is going to show you why Tiamat is beyond a lost cause, why she isn't a cause. If you can see what he sees – then there's no concern that you will do anything stupid." Teigao paused for a moment. "Glasya-Labolas! President and Earl to authors of Hell, present to my allies the fall of Tiamat!"

Glasya-Labolas panted as his eyes swirled. His pants transitioned into a howl as Justice and Ellis became entranced by the demonic gaze.

***

The year was unknown, but it was some time in the very distant, forgotten past. Trees the height of mountains filled the landscape. Many of them appeared ill and were infested with vines and fungi. Rivers flowed between the branches of the massive trees and waterfalls descended from holes on the sides of the trunks and branches. The wind roared as it passed between the excessively large flora. A city of stone temples similar to ziggurats sat within the forest. The platforms and roofs of each building were decorated with smaller trees and flowers. A line of debris (Earth's ring) crossed the sky.

The Mesopotamian gods all stood in front of the city. As they looked into the sky it began to darken.

Marduk, a tall man wearing a gold crown

embellished with rubies and emeralds, narrowed his great eyes. His long, thick beard was black onyx and he wore a gold-plated robe decorated with the same jewels as his crown. He carried a weapon which appeared to be a spear with a sword-like head.

"She comes." Marduk warned in a lost language. "Make yourselves secure. This challenge is mine."

The other gods bowed in relief and accord, and retreated into the city. Marduk watched the sky as it was emptied of color. A massive, blurry dragon the size of a town appeared in the distance. The trees and temples cracked from the intensity of her roar. As the dragon neared it shrank and transformed into a human-like figure. Tiamat approached Marduk. She had the figure of a woman, but her skin was scaly and gray. Her flesh glistened from the diamonds embedded between her scales. Tiamat wore a sleeveless shirt of woven gold threads over her chest. Various gemstones dangled from the shining threads. Her waist was covered by a skirt crafted in a similar fashion. Draconic wings extended from her back, and her talons dug into the ground with each step. Her eyes bore the appearance of portals into space, and lightning sparked from her vampire-like incisors. Smoke of various colors slipped out from between the scales on her scalp.

"Jusssssssst you?" Tiamat cackled.

"I am all that is worthy to reunite you with Abzu." Marduk taunted.

Tiamat screeched as she rushed toward Marduk. The god lowered his spear and stepped to his side as he swung it down. Tiamat collapsed as a draconic tail sprouted from the ground behind her – with a bloody end. Marduk kicked the tail into the sky as it began to expand into a white cloud filled with stars.

Tiamat knocked the spear from Marduk's hand. As she swung her claws for a second strike he conjured a net and tossed it over the dragon woman. She hissed as she struggled to cut herself free from the entanglement. Marduk then conjured a wooden club and pummeled Tiamat as she struggled with the net. Her tears grew in size and began to flood the ground – rushing into the nearest crevices and cutting rivers into the landscape. Marduk raised the club to deliver a fatal blow – but Tiamat liberated herself from the net and tore the club from Marduk's hand.

Marduk clapped his hands together – as if he had predicted Tiamat would disarm him. A gust of wind forced Tiamat onto the ground, then as she attempted to stand the wind condensed into arrows and filled her back. Tiamat roared with enough force to break the wind as Marduk reclaimed his spear and assailed the goddess. As Tiamat stood Marduk cut her in half. Tiamat opened a portal into the underworld – saving herself from death.

"Not this time!" Marduk barked as he followed Tiamat into the Stygian valley.

The underworld was colored with green and blue plants. The Styx flowed like a regular river, but still contained some screaming souls. Tiamat landed in the Styx but swam to the banks before the top half of her body was consumed by the river. Marduk landed on the opposite bank and aimed his spear at her.

"No escape for you, dragon!" Marduk shouted as a bright light filled the area. Marduk and

Tiamat directed their attention to the top of a nearby mountain. Ra stood upon the peak. He was only the silhouette of a man – cloaked by the brilliant solar disk hovering above his falcon-like head.

"Actually, Marduk..." Ra corrected. "She is in my jurisdiction now."

A thick darkness filled the areas untouched by Ra's light as a red-eyed figure appeared on the peak of the mountain opposite of Ra.

A deep voice lectured "Actually she is in mine."

"Set..." Ra grumbled. "You know I bring light to the underworld at this time."

"That doesn't change the fact that we are in my domain!" Set opined.

"Tiamat is mine!" Marduk roared. "She has only caused strife!"

"Well..." Set drawled. "She is a being of primordial chaos."

Tiamat began etching symbols into the dirt as the gods squabbled.

"Indeed she is!" Marduk confessed. "And a being of creation in times gone! The chaos now, you are obliged to agree must be vanquished! Need I remind of the primordial chaos which foiled the both of you time and time again?"

The underworld shook as massive fissures appeared above the river. A heavy wind blew into the fissures, and many of the plants were torn from their roots and sucked into the cracks.

Tiamat laughed as her legs slowly regenerated. She climbed onto her feet as the three gods aimed their spears at the rift.

"See now, what I mean?!" Marduk seethed. "While you senselessly challenged my agenda, she committed the unthinkable!"

Tiamat spread her arms and raised her chest toward the rift. "Great serpent Apep – Come to me!"

"She called Apophis?!" Set stuttered.

"How did she summon the snake?!" Ra growled.

"Desperation!" Marduk replied. "I will end this now!" Marduk threw his spear toward Tiamat – and it landed in her back. Tiamat collapsed to her knees. The rift weakened as her life force drifted into the Styx.

Ra and Set combined their powers, light and shadow, to further weaken the rift.

"Time remains..." A quaking voice echoed from beyond the rift. "You, too, are chaos..."

Tiamat struggled to retain consciousness. "I...fallen..." She muttered.

"Chaos...consume..." The wheezing voice from the rift thundered.

"Close the damn thing!" Marduk screeched.

"I'm trying!" Ra and Set chorused.

Tiamat launched herself back into a standing position and roared with such intensity that the three gods were pushed onto their backs. She turned to face the portal she opened from Earth and inhaled. All plant life in the underworld was siphoned into her body, and on Earth the great trees and the rivers they carried fell into the portal and were also absorbed into Tiamat. The gods regained their footing and prepared to strike. Tiamat leaped through the rift – closing it as she passed through.

Marduk threw his spear into the underworld's sky – through the portal to Earth.

"Dammit!" Marduk bellowed. "This mess, it is

on the two of you!"

Marduk flew through the portal and back to Earth before the Egyptian gods could respond. The portal closed as he reemerged back on the Earth's surface. Earth was now void of all plant life. The remaining water had condensed to ice and the ground was slowly freezing. Marduk shook his head, gazed at the Earth's ring in the sky, and snarled as he slowly froze with the rest of the planet – not knowing how many thousands of years will pass before the world would thaw. As the frost claimed his eyes he examined the vast new galaxy which had spawned from Tiamat's tail.

***

Ellis and Justice caught themselves as they gently fell back. Glasya-Labolas cackled like a hyena as his body crumbled to dust.

Teigao hummed. "Now, do you see?"

Ellis rubbed his eyes. "Still blurry from your dog's spell."

Justice groaned. "Not what he meant..."

"I get what he meant!" Ellis bantered. "I do see...Tiamat is a psychotic bitch. Not exactly an unfamiliar archetype in my life."

"This isn't even comparable to your Wardaughter friend!" Teigao barked.

"She gave into the chaos..." Justice quavered. "She cared not for the world she helped create?"

Teigao nodded. "Tiamat was an elder goddess. Younger, and not nearly as powerful as the others...but the power she did possess surpassed most other deities. Marduk embarked on a journey not too different from Kepyet's to challenge her, many other gods were killed in the war against the dragon. She can not be reasoned with. I even wonder if Kepyet will be able to defeat those two devourers."

Ellis realized something as he cleared his mind. "Wait, in that vision there was a ring in the sky. Where was this?"

"Earth." Teigao answered. "Tens of millions of years ago, when Earth had its second ring. This planet is more interesting than many humans are aware. I do, and always did agree with Kepyet that Earth should be saved. We just have differences in the philosophies of accomplishing that."

"Tiamat is still a goddess." Justice shifted the conversation back to the original topic. "Kepyet kills gods and goddesses like nothing. I witnessed it first hand in F2."

"Tiamat has also incubated within the primordial chaos and the shadows for a multitude of timelines." Teigao argued. "Time beyond the veil works differently than it does here. The devourers exist in many different dimensions simultaneously, trapped in each one knowing nothing but chaos. Kepyet's knowledge is still limited to the divine."

"Wait a minute!" Ellis interjected. "The divine still held the devourers at bay. Including Apophis, I mean wasn't he permanently banished and nearly killed by that cat goddess?"

"In a time he was already held back by a pantheon and a solar deity not far below elder status himself." Teigao explained. "There's another concern. Kepyet's origin as Cooper Thomas. What he is dates back prior to when he was smitten. Not the beast on the surface, but the seeds of vecordy that sprouted into his ability to slay gods."

"What do you mean?" Justice quaeritated.

"New Jericho had a library of encyclopedias." Teigao started. "Among them records of every person. Legal records, journals, social media posts, etc. Cooper's records...they had some warped pages. Some partially erased, and some that were missing altogether. There were also pages that referenced records of people and things that there were no known records of. I thought nothing of it at the time, I didn't imagine he would reach such a point of desperation as to have Basil accite the devourers. The concern now is that there is...was...something significant to him that no longer exists. Apophis knows all that does not exist, sees all that does not exist, and is believed to have the ability to conjure what does not exist. Tiamat may mimic such power."

"So, we're worried about blackmail?" Ellis inquired.

"Bribery." Teigao corrected. "Apophis may wield something more important to Kepyet than success. Tiamat may as well."

"And you believe he would abandon his values so easily?" Justice snapped.

"Part of him...somewhere...is still human." Teigao alleged.

"And humans with strict goals and values aren't so easily turned!" Justice opined.

"Eh." Ellis whined.

"What?" Justice queried.

"I wouldn't be so sure." Ellis drawled. "There was this bounty hunter Kaleyla and I once knew. Great guy. He had a pretty strict moral code. He wouldn't harm an innocent, or any child. Man oh man was he true to that – he even allowed several of his marks to get away because he didn't want to risk people being injured in crossfire. He also had a wife who he loved very much. Well one day his wife fell ill. I forget her condition – it was something hard as hell to pronounce. Anyway, it was curable, but the cure was difficult to mix. One doctor knew the recipe."

"So, he beat it out of him?" Justice guessed.

"Worse." Ellis paused for a breath. "He served him. The doctor had a feud with this other man. He wouldn't go into detail but it was something about being financially screwed by this guy prior to the war. The doctor wanted revenge, and his creativity needed a spark. My friend encountered the doctor on his search to find a cure for his wife. The doctor offered him a deal. Revenge in exchange for a cure. The doctor's rival wasn't to die though, he was to suffer, and the doctor was pretty specific about how. The doctor asked the bounty hunter to kill his rival's family. A wife and three kids, none older than twelve. My friend...his moral code was to never take an innocent life or the life of a child. Well – so much for all that. He killed all four with no hesitation, his wife was important. His values were abandoned to accommodate for an unexpected turn of events – his own wife's illness."

"Did he at least receive a cure?" Justice asked.

"He did." Ellis frowned. "But her conditioned worsened and she died before he could administer it. The guy became a monster after that – taking any mark he saw posted and caring not for casualties until a bounty was placed on his own head. Kaleyla accepted that mark. Though she is another example of what we are talking about herself! Always swore she wouldn't join the Sons of War and that their philosophy had more holes than a sponge. Now she leads them."

"Thus is the flaw of humanity." Teigao concluded. "Sudden changes in priorities. Kepyet is no exception. He could have challenged the gods without an all out war, leaving the planet in better condition. His ego though...he focused more on the message and pageantry than the original goal. What we are doing...we must tread carefully."

***

Anat entered the First Sons' base carrying the box of sulfur. Five men were bowing before Deimos – who sat upon his throne.

"Just in time!" Deimos laughed as Anat approached.

"For what?" Anat snarled as her eyes glanced over the men. "I think I recognize a couple of these guys, what's going on?"

"They tracked you!" Deimos smiled as he pressed his fingertips together. "They're bounty hunters – skilled ones. Not after the fortune to be claimed by your corpse, they actually wish to join us!"

Anat set the sulfur on the floor beside the throne as she stood next to Deimos. "Oh?"

"Tell me, Bellonadaughter, did Seth accept applicants?" Deimos catechized as his large eyes focused on the five men.

"If they possessed desirable talents." Anat replied honestly.

"Well..." Deimos pressed his teeth together. "I will take this opportunity to refresh our policy regarding applicants!"

Deimos snapped his fingers and the five men

instantly became haunted by images of battles they had experienced. Two of them died from heart attacks as the terror struck their souls. Those two men were the fortunate ones, as the others screamed uncontrollably. They screamed even after their breath was depleted. Their lungs strained and inverted, and blood began to spray from the men's mouths as they twitched and contorted on the ground. Anat cringed at the pool of blood forming below her – the blood was nearing her boots which she had just sanitized before entering the complex.

"These men were great warriors!" Anat yelled at Deimos as the other three men died.

"Perhaps they were." Deimos confessed. "But they came here. Seth was lenient, but I enforce our policy regarding denying ALL applicants. People join factions because they believe they are better off as a member, that being in a group will make them stronger and improve their chances of survival. Even outside of survival scenarios – joining something relinquishes independence. These men feared us, figured they would be safer and better off as Warsons than they are as bounty hunters – despite having had independently survived on Earth for so long. It's weakness, is weakness worth your time? It certainly isn't worth mine. We exclusively recruit. We decide who is worthy."

"Same logic, though." Anat taunted. "When you recruit you think you'll be better off with the person being recruited, that you aren't as strong without them."

"As you should know our goal isn't individual strengths." Deimos hissed. "It's a stronger world, consisting of the strongest people. Expendables, but strong. Those we recruit are simply a part of my dreams and goals of a stronger human race."

"I'm still not seeing the difference." Anat admitted.

"Because you are human!" Deimos reacted.

"I was also possessed by part of Kepyet!" Anat lectured. "I have experienced the thoughts of the greater being."

Deimos laughed as he stood up from his throne. "When a computer gets a virus, does it then receive and access every file stored on the device the virus was created on? You were a taxi for his egregore. Nothing more. You're no goddess, no deity. Just a human."

"A human immune to your powers." Anat mumbled.

"The world's most efficient sociopath!" Deimos cheered. "PTSD torments those with it, and those that experience the exacerbated symptoms I can manifest. You enjoy traumatic flashbacks of physical battles. I could play the images of your father hitting you, or your mother blacking out between beatings by her various partners. You would laugh at all that though, wouldn't you? An awful childhood you're grateful for – after all it is what made you a fighter, trained your reflexes, solidified your interests in martial arts..."

"So, you admit you have no power over me, hah!" Anat blurted. "Stalemated by a human."

"Oh, I'm not done!" Deimos wheezed as he raised his hand toward Anat. Her vision became clouded. "Everyone has my favorite resource, terror is embedded into human DNA as is the need to battle. As a young child you stopped caring about things at an early age – but then as you grew up you babysat for money, you babysat that Ellis character and constructed quite the friendship. In your late teens he was your salvation."

Anat snarled as she took a step back and hunched.

"There it is!" Deimos bellowed menacingly. "There it is. Ellis is your trigger...the good old days, the good memories!"

Visions of Anat and Ellis' childhood flashed through her eyes between visions of their bounty hunting days together.

"This is wrong!" Anat cried. "Illusions! You're a god of terror, I fear nothing here! A god of battle anxiety – there are no battles in these memories!"

"Internal battle." Deimos sniggered. "You want...need...to kill him. Your past though begs you not to."

Anat screamed as she lashed her right arm forward. Her robotic grip claimed Deimos' decaying neck as she stepped toward her left – slamming the god against the wall. She pressed him into the stone as visions continued to taunt her.

Anat struggled to maintain a proper breathing pattern. "I am...who...I...need...to...be, the past is gone! Irrelevant! You are nothing but illusions – I am Anat Bellonadaughter! Leader of the Sons of War, you are only the founder but you are no leader! No, no no no not at all! I am the leader, and you will NOT dethrone me!"

Anat raised her hand – slamming the top of Deimos' head into the ceiling as he began to laugh.

"Yes!" Deimos effused. "Excellent! I found your weakness but even while it's being used against you you STILL don't lose track of what is important!"

Deimos released Anat's mind. She continued to hold him against the wall in her attempt to strangle him. He kicked her in the chest – and the force of the kick launched her across the room. However, her robotic grip remained strong and Deimos was dragged through the air with her. Anat opened her wings – which cut into Deimos's sides as she landed on her feet and slammed the god into one of the empty stone coffins. Anat released her grip on Deimos.

"Very good!" Deimos laughed as he stood. Anat fell to her knees – gasping. "Shame though." Deimos continued. "The air down here is so thin, a strain on the stamina...even for someone like you."

Anat's wings retracted back into her armor as she whimpered "You wanted this..."

"Yes." Deimos confessed. "A test of your reactions. I trust my faction with you. Hate me, fear me, do as you must. But without me the Sons of War are dead. Remember that."

Anat sighed. "Are we going to experiment with the sulfur I stole or not?"

A small smile slithered across Deimos' face. "Now that you understand your place – yes."

Anat leered at Deimos as he strolled past her toward the laboratory. She needed another moment before she could stand. Anat hated her new "master". Seth was a fool – but manageable and transparent. Deimos' intentions weren't entirely clear to her, and she questioned how effective his policies actually were. Did he truly underestimate their foes as much as she suspected, or did he have a few other tricks up his sleeve to combat the Blessed? Even when

Anat lured her foes into a trap they still triumphed over the Sons of War. Is Deimos certain of the advantage of his divine blood and upcoming access to pure fire?

CHAPTER 10

Eric, Jasper, and Justice stood within the basement of Skyrook near the door to the underground labyrinth.

"Ellis really has no interest?" Eric perplexed.

Jasper shrugged. "He thinks he's more useful above ground. Helping guard if we get attacked again. He's probably doing research on the devourers too."

Eric raised an eyebrow. "Doesn't come off as the research type to me."

"Well..." Justice started. "It's more or less about survival. If this quest of recovering the relics fails we do need a back-up plan."

Eric nodded. "Well, are you two prepared for whatever nightmares lie ahead?"

The other two nodded. Eric pushed the large, ominous door open.

"No locks?" Jasper remarked.

"Basil." Eric snickered. "He opened this door a while back...couldn't get far in the labyrinth though."

"Reassuring." Justice said sarcastically as the trio stepped into the darkness.

The door slammed behind them as a dim, source-less light filled the corridors. This labyrinth's ceiling consisted of mismatched bricks arranged in optical illusions which mirrored the artwork on the carpet. The design tricked the eyes into seeing the room shake, twist, and narrow. In addition to the other headache – causing trickery the floor also appeared wavy despite being perfectly level.

The labyrinth's walls were constructed from odd statues which were flawlessly arranged into lines and identical to each other. A strip of dull, navy blue covered most of the statues' featureless faces. Bloody scarlet paint decorated the scalps and jaws. The statues' shoulders were painted the same dull blue, and their torsos a rusty orange. Their arms crossed over their chests like a corpse, and displayed few features beyond the scarlet color of the building material. The bodies gently narrowed into an upside-down rocket shape with the curve just above the floor. Two gray feet protruded from the wall on each side of the curve and faced forward. A singular, gold eye with a gleaming emerald iris rested between the hands and neck. The wall between the statues was a matching bloodied scarlet color.

Jasper and Justice leaned against the walls outside the door.

"I think I'm going to be sick..." Jasper squirmed.

"Where do we even begin here?" Justice asked.

"This maze is one, big illusion." Eric explained. "According to Basil we just need to find our way through…but if we take too many wrong turns we may end up in a dream-like scenario."

"How do we find our way?" Jasper whined. "I'm not sure I'm willing to play trial and error navigating this mess.

Justice scrutinized the statues near the door and noticed something.

"Hey guys…" Justice started. "The paint on these statues, it looks like it's more cured on some than others. I think the paints may even be mixed differently!"

"They look the same to me." Jasper contended.

"They're the exact same colors, but I think an ingredient was added to the paints of some of these statues but not to others, one that doesn't affect the colors." Justice explained. "It's difficult to tell what parts were painted with the special concoction, but I believe that may be the key to navigating this place."

"So, we have to take a magnifying glass to each part of each statue to find our way around?" Eric groaned. "That's a lot of time wasted on something we aren't sure of the relevance of."

"There might be something that makes it easier." Justice hoped. "Let's play the guessing game for now – see if we come across any clues on what to look for."

"If there are any." Jasper grumbled. "This may just be a maze with no guide, wouldn't put it past Kepyet to pull such a trick."

"He also wants us to find our way through." Justice argued. "There's a trick to this place, we just need to figure out what it is."

"Let's get walking then, I guess." Eric uttered.

The three began walking down the hall. Although their legs moved along the floor as if they were walking they didn't seem to move. The floor remained still, despite giving the sensation of walking on a treadmill. They tried walking faster but still remained in place. Eventually the three found themselves running – but still unmoving. Jasper opened his mouth to say something when the trio suddenly appeared at the end of the corridor and rammed into the wall. They moaned in pain as they fell backwards onto the ground with bruises on their knuckles and faces.

"What the hell was that?" Jasper whimpered.

Eric rubbed the bruises on his forehead. "I hate this place already."

Justice rubbed the top of her forehead then inspected her fingertips – checking for blood. "Well, at least we reached the end of the hall."

"Is every hall going to be like this?" Jasper worried. "Because if so I'm so not down for risking any dead ends!"

"It's alright!" Eric remarked sarcastically. "Justice here believes there are clues to help us through! Like in the last labyrinth."

Jasper blinked in confusion. "But the other labyrinth didn't have any clues. No good ones anyway."

"Exactly." Eric confirmed as Justice rolled her eyes. "Which way now, left or right?"

"Who's left and right?" Jasper quaeritated.

Justice regarded each direction. She noticed that the optical illusions along each route were different. The path toward the entrance was hilly but the end of the hall appeared to be even with where they were standing. The path to their right appeared ascending while the opposite route appeared to descend.

"Guys, look at the paths!" Justice ordered. "This way goes up and that way down."

"They both hurt my eyes." Jasper blurted.

"So, we go this way, then?" Eric suggested as he pointed toward the descending path.

"I don't think so." Justice argued. "That's too obvious. The labyrinth descends but knowing how the illusions work up might be down...or at least the direction where we will discover any clues on how to navigate this mess."

"Or Kepyet is using counter-logic." Eric commented. "Maybe he believes we would suspect that, and the proper path is the descending one."

"Or!" Jasper interjected. "None of these paths is the right one and we actually walk on the walls and onto the ceiling. Notice it matches the floor?"

"Kepyet wants us to resurrect him." Justice alleged. "He wouldn't over complicate things by THAT much. I don't think he would anyway."

"I think down makes the most sense, here." Eric asserted.

"I really don't think so." Justice stated. "Kepyet likes to repeat things. Assuming he did plan this all out and see the future to a great extent – consider all this. There were two god weapons left and Basil destroyed both. We fought Basil twice. He had two significant castles, each with a relic for summoning him. The sword had two uses against devourers. The doors into the original labyrinth worked twice – once for the labyrinth and once for the library. There were two high shades in the first labyrinth. Two of us were killed and we both were resurrected by two friends that were killed. I will also point out that Lyth and Ronny were killed around the same time. The first labyrinth we traveled up, I think at the start of this one we are to travel up again."

"That's complicated though!" Jasper shouted.

"Agreed." Eric nodded. "Didn't you just say he wanted to be summoned and wouldn't use such a convoluted plan?"

"I guess I did...but..." Justice paused. "I don't think it would be straightforward either. I meant I don't believe he would leave us completely lost and in the dark. We can probably use trial and error to navigate this place, but with the extra effort and cleverness of figuring out the clues I believe we will be rewarded with an easier adventure through here. I'm going up, and I would rather us not separate."

Eric and Jasper exchanged glares before returning their attention to Justice.

"Alright..." Eric drawled. "Lead the way."

Justice took several steps "upward". As she did the optical illusion made the floor appear as if it became steeper and she collapsed. Eric and Jasper collapsed behind her and began to crawl along the floor as if they were climbing.

"Guys..." Justice nagged.

"What?" The boys chorused.

"What are you doing?" Justice inquired as she regained her footing.

"Uhh...climbing?" Jasper drawled. "How are you standing?"

Eric blushed as he stood back up. "Illusions."

"How is THIS an illusion?!" Jasper yelped. "I FELT the gravity shift on me!"

"It's advanced." Justice theorized. "It's so perfect that it not only tricks our vision but also our Equilibrioception."

Jasper blinked in confusion. "That sounds like something lotion or pills can fix."

Justice sighed. "It's your sense of balance and perception of gravity. It's so perfectly designed that your brain...your sense of feel...and your internal gyroscopes trick you into believing you're falling."

"So, that's established." Eric interjected. "It's all subconscious, now how do we get past the illusion? Being aware of it doesn't change the fact that our bodies will automatically collapse after the first step or two. Even now I'm feeling the faux tug of gravity behind me."

"Oooh! I know!" Jasper shouted, expressing excitement like that of a puppy in anticipation of a bacon treat. "We close our eyes!"

"That's dumb." Eric deprecated.

"Well..." Justice spoke through her teeth. "It might work."

"It's too easy." Eric argued as Jasper walked down the corridor with his eyes closed and arms spread apart – occasionally bouncing side to side to tap the walls for navigation.

Justice crossed her arms and smiled at Eric.

"Okay..." Eric paused. "Well, I've been wrong about worse things and right about better things."

Justice giggled as she and Eric closed their eyes and followed Jasper down the hall.

Jasper suddenly turned into the wall and fell. He rolled back a couple meters – tripping his companions.

"Owch!" Everyone cried simultaneously.

"What the hell?" Eric grumbled.

"It's not my fault!" Jasper claimed. "I was walking just fine...but then the echoes from my footsteps changed directions around me! It got really loud and confusing!"

"Couldn't ignore it and continue using the wall as support?" Eric asked.

"The ears assist with balance." Justice explained. "I can kind of see how that would have knocked him off his course...though Jasper, you DO have a tendency to exaggerate things."

"I was right though!" Eric cheered.

"I was too at first!" Jasper opined as Justice melted her face into her hands.

"At first!" Eric chuckled. "Yeah...I was more right. I knew it wouldn't be so easy as just keeping our eyes closed. Can't expect simplicity when it comes to Kepyet's facinorous mind games. This labyrinth is meant to be a strain. I've given it thought – he wants to be resurrected but also certainty that whoever brings him back can be trusted, is devoted enough, and clever enough to serve him."

"We aren't serving him though? Are we?" Jasper worried.

"Enough!" Justice screamed as she raised her head from her hands. "All this arguing is getting old. We can't waste time. As we speak the devourers gain power and the Monk hunts us. He is likely to send his goons here to retrieve the sword soon. Not to mention that Anat could attack again at any moment."

"The Sons of War are gone, though." Jasper posited.

"Yes, but she's dangerous enough alone." Justice pointed out.

The eyes of the statues began to glow as a dusty smoke sprayed from their necks. Beams of fire danced between the statues behind the trio.

"Dammit!" Eric panicked.

The three began to run away from the rays of

fire which bounced statue to statue behind them. At the end of the hallway was a wooden door. Justice twisted the knob aggressively – expecting it to be locked. To her surprise the door opened into a blinding flash of light.

As the trio fell into the next room the door slammed behind them. The floor was a damp, gray stone with little texture. In the center of the room was an altar with a strange torch resting upon it. Dust covered the simple torch, which was black in color with a weathered orichalcum rim around the bowl. The blank gray ceiling was supported by a series of stone pillars. Windows surrounded the room and the only wall was the one leading back into the labyrinth. Justice noticed that the outside appeared familiar. The thick, white mist made it difficult to comprehend the environment outside of the room – but Justice was certain that they were outside the labyrinth below Skyrook. The cliff opposite the chasm was the right distance away.

Eric rubbed his head. "What was all that about?"

"We got past the trippy hallway!" Jasper cheered. "How?"

"Fear." Justice hypothesized. "Terror...actually. Escaping the fire took priority over contemplating the illusions. We're outside the labyrinth now...under Skyrook. Eric – do you know what that thing is?"

She pointed at the torch as Eric rubbed his chin.

"It's divine." Eric noticed. "Not a weapon, too weak for combat. There's also mortal stain on its aura."

"It looks like a torch." Jasper observed.

"Greek."

"A significant Greek torch?" Justice repeated. "Sounds allusive to the Olympics."

"Prometheus!" Eric realized. "This is the torch of Prometheus! The torch that carried a spark from the flame of Olympus and introduced man to fire!"

"It must be the key to the labyrinth!" Justice guessed. "The torches flame might reflect off the different paints and guide us through that mess."

"What about the fires though?" Jasper worried.

"Let's hope the fire traps is just a time limit thing." Eric said. "Kepyet had similar traps in his old bases according to my father. That's one of the reasons why the Blessed could never properly infiltrate his army."

Jasper nodded.

A squishy "smack" sound was heard in the corner of the room. The group was startled as they turned to face the direction it came from. A large, bloody liver throbbed on the ground. Several more livers manifested from the ceiling and fell around the room. Each liver was identical and not significantly, but distinguishably larger than a human's. Drops of long-stale blood splashed from each impact. The room was filled with the rancid stench of the meaty organs.

"What the...?" Jasper panicked as Justice grabbed the torch.

"Let's get out of here!" Justice ordered as the room rained bloody livers.

As the trio ran toward the door they were drenched in blood. They struggled not to slip on any of the livers which now covered the floor. Eric pulled the door open then they stepped through. The door slammed behind them and the blood covering their clothing cracked to dust as they fell into the hallway.

"What was with the livers?" Jasper growled. "Why livers?"

Justice held her free hand over her chest as she attempted to regain her breath.

Eric smiled to the side of his face. "Kepyet's sick sense of humor." He explained. "In the story of Prometheus Zeus punished him for sharing fire with the mortals by chaining him to a stone where a bird would peck out his liver each day, only for it to grow back each night."

"And we're really summoning this guy?!" Jasper blurted.

"Trying to!" Justice giggled. "Honestly though, Kepyet feels safer in this scenario."

"Explain yourself." Eric ordered.

"Who would you rather work with?" Justice quaeritated. "The man who ordered another's liver to be devoured each day – or the guy who simply joked about it?"

"If you want to play this game..." Eric began speaking. "Would you rather the man who tortured another for a few moments each day, or the one that restored millions of mangled livers then programmed them into a trap?"

"You...have a point there." Justice confessed.

Jasper rubbed his abdomen. "I hope I get to keep my liver after all this is over."

***

Anat and Deimos stood on opposite ends of the laboratory. Between them was a forge-like device. A simple cross shape was carved into the ground with a bowl filled with sulfur in the center. Each fissure of the crossing was encased in metal walls with reflective screens on the interior sides. The edges of each wall nearest the bowl contained clear gemstones which hummed with an electrical charge. Directly above the forge was a mirror crafted from polished adamant.

"Deimos..." Anat grumbled. "All the sulfur? Supply of this element isn't in uberty, what if this fails?"

"We're staying accurate to the theory." Deimos argued. "A laser forge with sulfur...the bottom of the bowl is orichalcum."

"It will melt." Anat alleged. "And what in the world is with the stones? Another deviation from my design!"

"Lightning encased in perfect diamond!" Deimos answered with a flavor of pride behind his words. "Perfect crystal structure, both conductive and insulated. The energy is trapped – trying desperately to escape its scintillating prison!"

"Why, though?" Anat whined.

"When heated the energies will communicate with each other through the philosophorum vapors, acting to stabilize the flame while preventing outside contaminants." Deimos replied. "I'm counting on the orichalcum melting, because when it does it will cool the philosophorum before it burns into plasma. At which point the sulfur should already be ignited and suspended by the vapors and the electricity."

Anat crossed her arms. "Well, I obtained the sulfur and would rather not be responsible for it being wasted if this fails."

"Do you have a better plan?" Deimos hissed.

"Yes, THE ORIGNAL ONE!" Anat screamed.

"The one that would have caused the sulfur to instantly vaporize with nothing to hold a flame?" Deimos deplored. "As you stated yourself, we cannot afford to waste the little sulfur we have."

"Just start the damn forge then." Anat growled.

Deimos snarled as he motioned his hand to activate the device. A powerful laser shined from the cross in the floor and reflected from the mirror back onto the bowl. Electricity burst from the diamonds and swirled around the laser beam like water. Anat's eye implants protected her vision from being damaged by the intensity of the light. A hissing noise ravaged her ears as the philosophorum was vaporized. Melted orichalcum dripped from the bottom of the bowl as the sulfur began to carry a blue flame, which gradually turned lighter and lighter.

"It seems to be working." Deimos bragged.

"You say that as if I had hoped it wouldn't." Anat remarked.

"Was I wrong? You seemed so certain this would fail." Deimos argued.

"And I was." Anat confessed. "But believing something will fail isn't the same as wishing that to be the case."

"What of acting on said belief?" Deimos inquired. "Believing that something would fail so taking a different course, one that may also fail?"

"My alternative wouldn't have risked our full sulfur supply, I like leaving room to experiment." Anat explained. "Is this plan not you doing just what you accuse me of? Is the world not as it is because you gods believed humanity would fail to the point it wasn't even worth giving us a chance or another session of guidance?"

"You make some points." Deimos admitted. "Do not rule me in with the others, though!" He warned. "Human terror is the sweetest. Unlike Earth's fauna, humans understand terror and comprehend exactly why they feel it. I wouldn't vote to completely exterminate my favorite toys."

The sulfur's flame had become almost blindingly intense and nearly white as the last of the orichalcum started to melt. Electricity had begun to pass beneath the sulfur – helping it levitate.

"Toys..." Anat sniggered. "Myself included?"

"Not quite..." Deimos paused for a moment. "You have a more professional, practical purpose. I consider you a tool."

Anat burst out in laughter. "You aren't entirely fluent in human culture and linguistics yet, are you? Unless you meant that as an insult."

"It's a compliment, you have purpose." Deimos wheezed. "Albeit minor."

"Calling someone a "tool" is an insult, a more masculine one at that." Anat explained, resisting the temptation to accurately apply the insult to Deimos because of his error.

The orichalcum had fully melted and the sulfur was reduced to a white, levitating orb. All the electrical energy had formed a ring around the glowing object. Deimos flapped his hand to shut down the forge. The laser instantly deactivated as the overhead mirror shattered – disintegrating before any part reached the floor.

"It worked." Deimos said calmly, with a nearly measurable weight of pleasure in his voice. "Pure fire, smokeless, still, independent from its surroundings."

Anat grabbed a modified rifle from a nearby counter. "Let's test its destructive power."

She grabbed a wooden shaft from the same counter then approached the pure flame. Anat gently poked the orb with the shaft and a small, white flame attached itself to the tip of the shaft. Despite the intense heat and brightness the flame didn't seem to damage the stick.

"It doesn't burn?" Anat questioned.

"Pure fire does as it is commanded to, test what it does under direction." Deimos suggested. "Continue with the experiment."

Anat faced the cave wall farthest away. The wall was stone, with no decorations. She aimed the rifle toward the wall and slowly tipped the shaft toward the opening in the start of the gun's barrel. The instant the flame licked the gunpowder the rifle exploded in Anat's robotic hand. Although the rifle had been destroyed the bullet had fired successfully – leaving a gargantuan crater in the wall several meters deep. Anat's artificial skin had been seared from the palm – but her non-cosmetic parts remained intact.

"Excellent." Deimos marveled. "Now imagine that in larger doses."

"Another test is necessary..." Anat mumbled as she grabbed another rifle from the counter.

"And what would that be?" Deimos catechized as Anat snagged another shaft and approached the flame. She used the shaft to grab another dab of fire.

"Let's see how it fares against important targets. Considering that our use of it in an encounter against the Blessed is inevitable." Anat said as she aimed the rifle at Deimos.

The god growled as Anat tapped the barrel with the flame and fired the rifle. Deimos was launched across the room and crashed into some shelving. Most of his torso and bottom jaw were incinerated by the blast. The little that remained of his torso was carved by the broken glass and metal as acidic chemicals eroded his scalp.

Anat hummed as she dropped the crumbling gun. To her disappointment Deimos climbed onto his feet and his body instantly regenerated. The deity bellowed with laughter.

"Of the many attempts on my life that has to have been the most entertaining!" Deimos praised.

"I have no idea what you are talking about." Anat teased in dismay.

"It's alright." Deimos reassured. "Imagine what that will do to humans, imagine what it will do to anyone that isn't a god."

"Exactly what we need it to." Anat answered.

"I want our comet rocket cannons modified, their firing mechanisms are to be activated by the introduction of the pure fire." Deimos ordered. "We will use this to siege. Our first target is New Ur!"

"And not our threats?" Anat contended. "We can obliterate bums and merchants with our regular weapons."

"If I remember correctly..." Deimos hissed. "Your assault on Skyrook was canceled by a merchant."

"It wasn't "canceled", he had an airship not much different than the Grand Admiral." Anat claimed.

"Yes, and if it wasn't for that ship the Blessed would be gone!" Deimos seethed. "The only reason you entered the citadel was because Kepyet himself wished it!"

"The Blessed are still the greater threat." Anat attested.

"Save your aggression for where it is actually

useful!" Deimos lectured. "We will destroy half of New Ur, and keep the other half under siege. The Blessed, under the guidance of your old friends, will come to the rescue. If my soldiers aren't enough to end them then we will use the fire. With the Blessed finished off in view of New Ur the city will bow before us. We use their fear and pleads for their lives to obtain all the sulfur. Once it is ours we finish off the city."

"And then what?" Anat asked. "Blessed gone, over half of the remaining human population gone. What's your endgame? The devourers are still coming. Do you have a plan for them?"

"With enough of the pure fire I can fight them." Deimos said. "I can forge a divine weapon with it – their weakness."

"And become god of a dead planet and an infertile species that won't even last a century." Anat sniggered.

"The other issues will be worked out in good time, but do you protest our immediate plans?" Deimos queried.

"Get those cannons modified." Anat purred.

CHAPTER 11

Justice studied the torch in her hands. She retrieved a lighter from her pocket and attempted to ignite the end.

Eric watched as Justice tried over and over again. "Flame not catching?"

"Maybe it needs fuel?" Jasper theorized. "Or a different type of fire...Olympian maybe?"

"A torch is a torch...I think so anyway." Justice replied as she continued to rotate the lighter's flame around the end of the ancient relic. "I think it is just damp...that room was rather moist, and the blood from the livers didn't help."

Jasper held back laughter and mumbled to Eric "She said "moist"".

"You're older than me!" Justice groaned at Jasper, having heard his remark.

"Let me see that!" Jasper changed the subject as he snatched the torch from Justice's hands.

Justice and Eric crossed their arms as Jasper examined the artifact. He gently caressed the sides of the old tool.

"Well?" Eric nagged. "In your expert opinion – how does this thing work? I'll remind you both that we may not have much time before the walls spit a lattice of fire again."

Jasper slammed the torch against the wall and the outside material crumbled to dust.

"What the hell! Trying to imitate Basil or something?!" Justice reacted as a cloud of dust fluttered away from Jasper's hands.

"Calm!" Jasper ordered as he flapped his free hand to blow the dust away. When the aerial debris cleared Jasper's discovery was revealed. In his other hand he held a shiny, orichalcum torch. "It was in a case." Jasper explained as he pressed a button on the side. A brown foam-like substance filled the bowl at the end of the shaft. Jasper handed the torch back to a blushing Justice. "Try now."

Justice accepted the torch and flicked her lighter back on. The brown substance in the bowl was instantly conflagrated. The light from the torch disrupted the designs along the floor and ceiling – disabling the optical illusions. The paint along several of the statues reflected the ardent torchlight.

Eric nodded in approval. "You were right, Justice. Some of the paints are different! Let's follow the paths that reflect the light, then?"

"You're welcome!" Jasper whined. "You know, for figuring out how the torch works."

"Thank-you, Jasper." Justice sighed. "It looks like each wall has a reflective side and a dull side. I think solving this labyrinth requires a tad more wit."

"What do you mean?" Eric inquired.

"Clichés." Justice said. "Following the light, that's too cliché. Kepyet is a dark being, perhaps we should follow the darkness instead?"

"Makes sense to -" Eric started before Jasper interrupted.

"Wait!" Jasper raised his pointer finger. "Consider the objective! We aren't looking for Kepyet. We're looking for the bottom floor of Skyrook, where the life elemental is imprisoned. We're technically in a tunnel – to get out of a bad situation, like this maze, you're supposed to look for the light at the end of the tunnel! Also – Kepyet is a being of death. We're looking for a "life" elemental, but we have to kill it for the heart. We kill a life elemental for its heart to summon Kepyet – a being of death!"

"Get to the point." Eric requested.

"Yeah, yeah." Jasper gibbered. "If you're having a near death experience, or are suffering – they say go toward the light. The light is where death resides. The death being..."

Justice finished Jasper's sentence "...the killing of the life elemental and the next step in summoning Kepyet."

"Exactly!" Jasper confirmed.

The group ambled through the labyrinth – Justice walked in the lead holding Prometheus' torch – keeping the illusions disabled and the path revealed. They walked for what felt like hours. Although the scenery never changed they knew they were progressing as the air gradually became thinner, and their senses suggested that they were deeper underground. Skyrook's subterranean labyrinth was so silent that the group could hear their own heartbeats and blood flow.

Eventually the labyrinth led to a sliding door. Dead vines pressed themselves against the wall opposite the door's handle. The door was crafted from a single slab of an unidentified dark metal.

"Is this it?" Jasper quaeritated.

"I believe so..." Justice replied.

Eric approached the door and tugged on the handle, but it wouldn't even budge. He then stepped to the other side of the handle and attempted to push the door – but still nothing.

"Dammit!" Eric growled. "The door's locked...can't just blow it up otherwise we risk the room collapsing on us or angering the statues."

Jasper carefully felt and inspected the dead vines. Behind the largest vine was a silver, upside-down skull embedded into the wall. "I think these vines and this thing have something to do with it." He mentioned.

Justice raised the torch to the door, the light exposed engraved text. The writing was in a language that Justice didn't recognize. Eric balled his fist upon noticing the mysterious writing.

"Eric." Justice said. "Know what language this is?"

"A better question is how is it written here?!" Eric quavered. "I know it. It's a code that the Blessed developed during the war in the event any of our few written messages were intercepted. I suppose it can be referred to as a language as well. Every Blessed was required to learn it, although the only time it has been used since the war is in Teigao's name. "Teigao" translates to his code name "Titan Goat." which he prefers to his real name. This is a language Kepyet isn't supposed to have known..."

"Perhaps Basil leaked it?" Justice hypothesized.

"What is Teigao's real name?" Jasper inquired. "Because "Titan Goat" sounds allusive to Satan."

"He isn't Satan." Eric confirmed with a chuckle. "His real name is known only to the gods, his old identity was sacrificed to the gods as part of the ceremony to lead the Blessed."

"Back to what's relevant..." Justice spoke. "What does the text here say?"

Eric stood next to Justice and squinted his eyes – struggling to read the shallow etchings.

"The value of life is praised here." Eric began reading aloud. "The value of human life is exaggerated elsewhere. These vines are one plant, its strength unmatched. A turn of the skull seals the deal. Lend life, borrow strength."

"It sounds like a lesser form of a sacrifice..." Justice realized.

"I'll do it." Jasper volunteered.

"You're going to die." Eric pointed out. "We don't know how temporary the deal is, or if the text is even honest."

"Well then I trust you two to find a way to bring me back!" Jasper argued. "You're the fighters, I'm still next to useless in combat unless you need something shot or blown up."

"Jasper, there might be subtext we are missing..." Justice said.

Jasper grabbed the skull. "Let's hope not!"

Jasper twisted the skull upright. A flash of black light burst from his eyes and mouth. His body collapsed as white smoke poured from his mouth before being absorbed by the vines.

"Jasper!" Justice screeched as the vines slowly regained their bright green color.

Eric grabbed Justice's shoulders and pulled her back as the vines squirmed in place, their movements became increasingly erratic, as if they were relearning how to move. The vines reached across the door and wrapped their ends around the handle then slowly pulled the door open. Eric and Justice stood back as the room shook from the force. Once the door was open the vines reached around the door to hold it in place. The next room was dark, but the sound of dripping water was audible.

Justice knelt over Jasper's corpse. "What are we going to do with him?"

"Leave him." Eric suggested. "Nobody else is going to come down here, and we don't know if moving him from place will mess anything up or not."

Justice sadly lowered her face as she stood. Eric appeared calm, and she wished she could be. She was torn enough when Ellis was believed to be dead, so seeing Jasper's corpse was nothing less than terrifying. The door did say that his life was only being "borrowed" but knowing Kepyet's trickery she was concerned about the room for misinterpreting the message. When the life is returned would it still be Jasper? Where exactly is Jasper's soul? She held the torch and lead the duo into the next room.

***

The ferry approached a wide bend in the Styx. Unity sat on the rail near the figurehead.

"Up here!" Unity shouted. "Stop!"

Ronny tapped the oar and the boat drifted to the left side of the river. The ramp extended from the ferry and onto the bank. Unity lifted herself from the rail and followed Ronny to the ramp.

"You are sure this is the place?" Ronny asked.

"I am." Unity answered. "The Phlegethon is just over that hill."

The landscape of the underworld was difficult to comprehend. Gray and red fog filled the region, but Ronny was able to distinguish the silhouette of the large hill Unity spoke of. It was less than a mile away and just barely below the height of a small mountain. Several figures climbed out from below deck and stared at Ronny with consternation.

Ronny nodded at the souls. "Don't worry, I will be back. I take the oar with me, as long as I hold it you are safe and nobody else may board."

The concerned spirits felt reassured and returned to their cabins as Ronny and Unity began their journey toward the Phlegethon, hoping that the spirit of the flaming river will know Sal's whereabouts.

Outside the First Sons' base in Z4 the Warsons were preparing a fleet of tanks armed with comet rockets. Engineers tinkered with the guns to modify them for pure fire. A section of the ground near the manhole was open – exposing the secret vehicle storage unit of the base. A gargantuan red cargo plane rested within the hole. Anat and Deimos stood near the massive airplane.

"You're certain it still flies?" Anat asked.

"It's in perfect condition." Deimos replied.

"Parts can decay with age." Anat spoke. "I want to be sure that the giant piece of metal we're going to ride will remain airborne until properly landed."

"I'll be onboard too, for good faith." Deimos assured.

"You're also a god." Anat snapped.

"Fear not, child." Deimos snarled. "In the event of a crash you'll be teleported out as well."

"Right." Anat mumbled in semi-disbelief.

A Warson approached the couple and saluted. The soldier's mask distorted his voice, and he spoke in an unrecognizable accent. "The engineers say the tanks are nearly ready to use the fire. All other functions are fully operational!"

"Good." Deimos replied. "Open the plane and begin loading the tanks. Plot a course where we are least likely to be seen or heard as well. To my knowledge this is the last surviving airplane."

"Lord Deimos, where will we land?" The soldier inquired.

"A couple miles south of the city." Deimos answered. "We will attack New Ur from the same point Seth did last year."

The solider saluted again then marched away. Anat watched the soldier for a moment then eyed Deimos.

"Where did you get these men from?" Anat queried. "Their accents aren't any I have ever heard."

"Various places." Deimos spoke. "They've been frozen for nearly two decades. It's a speech impediment from relearning to talk."

"As long as you are sure of their competence." Anat muttered.

"Completely." Deimos assured.

CHAPTER 12

As Justice and Eric entered the next room the torch was extinguished by the water dripping above the entrance. Justice prepared to activate the lights on her chest but the room's lights turned on automatically. They were dim, but provided all the light the pair needed to explore. Justice strapped the torch onto her back.

The room was a semi-circle constructed from pale, brownish-gray bricks. Dim, amber lights were built into the ceiling. A few rotting wooden tables stood in the room, it was miraculous that none of them had collapsed yet. The dusty floor was littered with broken glass from various vials and beakers. Occult and scientific textbooks black from mold lay about the floor as well. The wall opposite the entrance was a row of bars – like a prison cell. A metal door hung open in the center.

Eric and Justice explored the first room, taking caution not to step on any broken glass. Their circumspection was mostly instinctual as their boots would fully protect their feet if they stepped on debris.

"What was this place?" Justice queried. "It looks like some sort of lab..."

"Yeah..." Eric said. "There were many rumors that Skyrook was used for experiments. Vulcan's shade did tell us his transformation took place down here as well."

Justice opened the metal door. The top hinge broke as she did, the crack startled her and she jumped back as she released her grip. Eric stepped back as well when he heard the hinge break. The door tipped on its side – breaking free from the bottom hinge, and slamming onto the ground. Eric and Justice leaped toward the center of the room as the tables collapsed from the quake caused by the door.

The duo entered the next chamber. An enclosure of broken glass filled the right half of the room – a prison during its prime. A long desk with broken computers rested along the opposite wall. The next door lead to a stairway. A loud, eerie heartbeat was heard from below.

"Hear that?" Justice asked.

"Yes." Eric replied. "I'm guessing that's our life elemental downstairs."

"The last of its kind..." Justice pouted. "And we are forced to slay it."

"Captured, experimented on, and left alone in its prison. It likely went mad ages ago." Eric reassured. "And if not...well...we give it an easy death."

"It still feels wrong..." Justice uttered.

"A sin committed for a greater good. Likely to resurrect Jasper, too." Eric added. "As is the nature of Kepyet's cruel games."

***

Ellis was sitting at a desk within the Skyrook library. The enormous room was circular and several stories in height. Its walls were covered in books. Stacks of tomes also littered the floor. Many of the books were occult grimoires and treatises on arcane subjects. Several curved desks were against the walls with writing utensils and notepads built into their corners. In the center of the room was a massive lectern with a miniature set of spiral stairs leading to the top of it. An adjustable, steel rolling ladder rested against one of the bookshelves.

A buzzing sound was heard from a device on Ellis' wrist as he studied a book on divine weapons. He pressed a button on an object near his ear.

"Yeah?" Ellis greeted.

"This thing working? Check check...A...B...C..."

"What do you want, Oscar?" Ellis grunted.

"...D...E...F...G..." Oscar continued.

"OSCAR!" Ellis shouted.

"Oh! You can hear me?" Oscar rambled.

"Yes, I can hear you. What do you wa...wait...how did you get my number?" Ellis answered.

"I don't remember..." Oscar replied. "The signal clear?"

Ellis rolled his eyes. "Yes, it's clear...what do you want?"

"Ahh, good! Good! Well – no good is why I'm calling." Oscar said.

"Get to the point, I'm busy." Ellis badgered.

"Well do you remember airplanes? Ya know – big metal tubers with wings..." Oscar inquired.

175

"Yes, what about...oh no, I'm NOT helping you dig one out!" Ellis stated.

"There's one in the air, lad!" Oscar elaborated. "Big, big red one! Reckon it's carryin' cargoes. Heading to New Ur..."

"Okay, why are you telling me? So someone found a functional airplane?" Ellis quaeritated.

"Well ya see..." Oscar paused. "It looks like it's a Sons of War plane. Big guns under the wings too – probably some shielding and whatnot...not sure my airship could take it out."

"Impossible – the only Warson left is Anat, and she's no pilot!" Ellis alleged.

"Well...this thing is in their style and colors...seem to be preparin' to land where they attacked the city before. I'm having my men pack up the shop and we're getting out of the city." Oscar said. "Wait! They're in range of my scanners now...ohh boy, it's loaded with tanks! There's something onboard too – looks kind of like a flame but far too hot to be a regular fire. New Ur could use a hero if you kids are interested – but I'll be long gone by the time those tanks are unloaded!"

The transmission ended. Ellis slammed his fist on the table and kicked his chair away as he absquatulated the library.

Teigao was passing through the ballroom as Ellis entered.

"Ellis?" Teigao breathed. "What's so urgent?"

"We need to get to New Ur!" Ellis demanded. "NOW!"

"What's in New Ur?" Teigao asked.

"The Sons of War are preparing to attack the city again!" Ellis stated. "They apparently found an airplane and loaded it with tanks!"

"Though unfortunate, New Ur isn't our responsibility." Teigao opined.

"Most of the remaining human population resides there!" Ellis lectured. "And the Sons of War remain a formidable opponent! There can't be many of them left – this our chance to end them!"

"And leave Skyrook undefended?" Teigao interjected. "Our companions remain underground. Thwarting the devourers is our top priority."

"That is just like you Blessed..." Ellis seethed. "Caring nothing for the regular people!"

Teigao stomped toward Ellis and raised his finger. "You know nothing of what I did for "regular people", the gods had just about abandoned their destructive plans when they commissioned me to lead the Blessed. Without the devourers slain there will be no humanity to save – and the endgame of the Sons of War isn't total annihilation."

"With the chaos they preach it may as well be!" Ellis contended.

"We will address the Sons of War after we resurrect Kepyet!" Teigao roared. "You are to remain here while we wait for the others."

Ellis raised his middle finger to Teigao as he returned to the library.

***

Eric and Justice lurched down the stairs. They found themselves in a heart-shaped room half the size of a football field. The ceiling was a hundred feet high. Black wires nearly surrounded the room. In the center of the white, crystal floor was a pool of blood. Occasional bolts of static would burst from the wires and into the sanguineous puddle.

Justice approached the puddle. "The heartbeat...it's coming from here. I don't trust that electrical charge though. Ideas?"

"Can't figure this one out?" Eric remarked.

"Well...my friend who is like a brother to me is dead, and I'm not sure what the process of getting him back is...so you could say I'm emotionally distracted." Justice stressed.

"Fair..." Eric started. "I don't know what to do here either...but we can possibly do something about the charge."

Eric drew one of his pistols and shot part of the wired wall. A crackling sound echoed throughout the room as all the wires vibrated and hissed with steam. In one final "pop" the electrical charge came to its end. The blood in the center of the room bubbled as the puddle shrank and condensed.

Eric and Justice sprinted backwards to the door as the blood transformed into a being the size of a Centimane. The life elemental took the shape of two athletic, naked people merged at the back halves of their bodies. One side was a man and the other was a woman. Its skin was blood red. The joints were all double-jointed so that neither side was the front or back. It was the male side that faced Justice and Eric.

Justice marveled at the being before her. "Life elemental! You are free, how long have you resided here?"

"Free?" The life elemental chorused in two androgynous voices. "Humans...you lie! My fate is still imprisoned by the will of the captor, a will...that...you seek to enforce! No!"

The beast raised its hand and several vines

dropped from the ceiling and attempted to grab Justice and Eric. Justice quickly armed herself with the Pyroguard's blade and cut the tips of the vines as Eric unholstered his second pistol and shot at the plants. Carnivorous mushrooms crawling on vines appeared along the walls and ran to Justice and Eric as the life elemental stepped back.

Justice used her sword to slay the aggressive fungi as Eric filled them with bullets.

"Looks like the training has been paying off!" Eric cheered as he watched Justice fight.

"Yeah, just need a less insane foe." Justice giggled.

The life elemental gyrated so that the female side faced its enemies. She waved her hand and three bloody bulls appeared on the ground. They charged toward Justice and Eric. Eric shot down two of them before they could reach the duo and Justice slid across the ground beneath the third and lopped it in half with her sword. Swarms of ants crawled between the pair and the life elemental. Justice retrieved an upgraded version of the multipurpose gun from her bag and sprayed fire at the insects. Eric used his feet to crush as many of the red bugs as possible.

"They fight well..." The life elemental mumbled. "You fools! I will make children of you..."

"Say what?" Eric stuttered as he and Justice continued fighting the seemingly endless army of ants. The life elemental squatted and a blood-clone of Eric dropped from between its legs, followed by a blood-clone of Justice.

"Nasty!" Justice gagged.

"Now that's just wrong..." Eric moaned.

The clones charged at Justice and Eric. Eric

shot the blood clones but they seemed to be unaffected by the bullets. Justice sprayed a torrent of fire at the clones – but although they caught on fire it appeared as if they weren't being burned.

Justice equipped the Pyroguard's blade posthaste and swung it at her clone. The blood Justice was injured by the sword, but rapidly healed. Justice began to butcher the clone as Eric wrestled with his. He saw that melee weapons affected the clones so he drew one of his guns and slashed it back and forth across his foe.

The life elemental pivoted so that the male side faced the duo. It stomped its foot and the blood clones collapsed into puddles. Vines dropped from the ceiling again and grabbed both Justice and Eric. Justice activated her rocket boots and flew toward the life elemental – the force caused the vines to tear and release their grip. Justice prepared to stab the life elemental, but it grabbed her with its right hand and threw her across the room. Justice re-balanced herself only a couple meters from the wall and flew back toward the life elemental. It swung its body around so that the female side faced its enemies – swinging the female's right arm as it did so. The back of the hand smacked Justice and launched her across the room. She contorted herself so that she wouldn't hit the wall – but the vines grabbed her again and deactivated her boots – holding them so that they couldn't be turned back on.

Eric wrestled himself free from the vines and shot the ones above his head as he fell. Upon landing he blasted the vines holding Justice – releasing her. The life elemental screeched as a giant bear was conjured between it and the humans.

Justice excavated a grenade from her satchel and tossed it at the bear – blowing the beast up.

The life elemental twisted so that the male side was facing forward. It attempted to manifest another blood monster but collapsed onto its knees.

"Weak!" The life elemental cried. "No...no!"

The life elemental's skin hardened into wood. Ivy leaves and toxic flowers of various colors covered the elemental's body.

Justice blasted the elemental with her flamethrower – burning away the plants. The elemental stood and growled as the wood began to burn. Once Justice had a clear shot of its face she reset her gun to squirt compressed water. She fired several aquatic pellets at the life elemental – drenching it and extinguishing the flames.

The life elemental chuckled as it regained its footing – believing that dousing the flames was accidental. Justice set her gun to its lightning setting and struck the elemental with an electrical charge. The water carried the current throughout its body – causing the wood to disintegrate and its body to be stunned. The life elemental fell face-first onto the ground. The female side watched Justice as she sprinted toward the monster's head with her sword. She leaped over the elemental's face and slashed her sword across its neck – decapitating it. Eric kept his guns aimed at the neck in case of regeneration as Justice carved into the elemental's torso. She reached into its chest and tore out a fist-sized wooden sphere covered in thin vines. Once the object was removed the life elemental's body collapsed into a powder.

Eric and Justice panted as they put their weapons away. Justice marveled at the object in her hand.

"So, that's it..." Eric commented. "The heart of a life elemental."

Justice turned to face the powdery outline of the monster. "Yeah...I just wish we could have given it a nicer death, considering what it endured."

"We aren't the responsible ones, here." Eric reassured. "Kepyet is the one to blame, leaving us with no other choice."

"We have what we came for." Justice sighed. "Let's get out of here – and resurrect Jasper!"

Eric nodded as Justice already began walking toward the entrance of the laboratory. The moment the duo had stepped back into the labyrinth Justice stepped over Jasper's corpse and twisted the skull icon. A splattering sound was heard as the door slammed shut – tearing a few of the vines and pressing their tips into the opposite wall. White smoke oozed from the vines toward Jasper's body. Justice lurched backward to Eric as Jasper's body absorbed the smoke. Jasper's eyes flew open as he inhaled his first breath.

"Jasper!" Justice effused as she ran to her companion and helped him climb onto his feet. Jasper held his hand over his heart – checking its beat.

"I'm alive?" Jasper perplexed. "I'm alive! So it worked?"

Justice rapidly bobbled her head forward and back. "Yes, yes! It worked!"

Jasper peered at the vines. "It did work! Did

you guys get the heart?"

"Yeah." Eric answered. "It was an...interesting fight."

"So, you did have to fight the elemental?" Jasper asked. "What was it like?"

Eric spoke as Justice attempted to. "Disturbing." He said. "The fight was disturbing."

"Tell me the story!" Jasper requested.

"Uhh...no." Justice and Eric chorused.

Eric continued speaking. "It consisted of things that I will never un-see."

"I would rather not refresh the memory." Justice agreed as Jasper pouted.

Justice was impressed by Jasper's recovery. He sacrificed his life in a ritual and literally died, yet the moment he was resurrected he returned to his usual self. Justice removed the torch from her back and ignited it. Although between the three of them it wouldn't be difficult to find their way back to the beginning of the maze Justice thought it best to not risk being affected by the sensory illusions again.

***

Ellis was sitting at one of the escritoires frantically flipping through the pages of multiple books. Teigao came into the library and approached.

"Magic books?" Teigao asked.

"Eh." Ellis answered. "Since you don't want to help I figure if I can learn some spell work I can do it myself. It can't be that hard – can it? One of these has to have a "for dummies" course."

"Ellis I'll be honest with you, there's more to my reasoning behind not approving of taking on the Sons of War again." Teigao said.

Ellis slowly rotated in his seat and leaned on

his left arm upon the table. His eyes narrowed as he addressed Teigao. "I'm listening."

"The forces there – they are indeed the last of The Sons of War." Teigao mumbled. "And the most fierce."

"Just men!" Ellis interjected. "With the right weapons and your Blessed hocus-pocus we can be rid of those bastards!"

"Their founder." Teigao uttered. "He's a god. A son of Ares."

"Like a literal son or just his namesake like the other freaks?" Ellis quaeritated.

"I did just say he was a god." Teigao mocked. "The name is Deimos."

"Thought the gods were on your side." Ellis leaned back against the desk.

"Not all." Teigao slowly paced around the room. "Some wanted no part in the chaos here, though that cowardly few left the planet. Except one – Deimos. He's a god of -"

"Battle terror or some shit like that." Ellis interrupted. "Pretty obscure but I read about him once...when we were real young Kaleyla read me some mythology books when babysitting me. As adults after the war we re-read some of those when work was slow. Thought he was just a made-up figure though, coming from misinterpretations of other myths and whatnot."

"Well he's unfortunately very real – and the war was just what he needed to become exceptionally powerful." Teigao elaborated. "Hid in the shadows, started The Sons of War, then wasn't heard from until now. He's too great a challenge for us, with a mere thought he can force us into a state of psychological torture. Even with my blessings I'm not immune."

"I knew there was more to that anxiety spell the other day than pollution." Ellis growled. "There has to be some way to defeat him though, roided up on fear or not he's still a pretty insignificant deity."

"Kepyet." Teigao breathed. "Our misfortune has quite a reach, the answer to both the greatest, unrelated threats is Kepyet. Continue studying the devourers, I know enough about Deimos to know that he doesn't want extinction. He needs people – a lot of them. Deimos will do what he can to harvest as much terror as possible until his agenda comes into fruition. We have time, we must be wise...we must not allow impulse to betray our rationality."

"Right." Ellis muttered. "Be sure to convey that to the people Deimos and Anat are going to kill."

Ellis waved his hand as if to swat Teigao away as he returned to studying the tomes on the desk. Teigao shook his head as he vacated the library.

***

Ronny and Unity approached the Phlegethon. Their phantom eyes burned as they trekked downhill toward the infernal river. The Phlegethon was a river of ardent lava, each bubble that popped on its surface released tormented screams of the souls trapped within the inferno. Unlike the calm Styx, the Phlegethon had an active flow with violently cascading waves and ripples. Above the river was a tempest of reddish-gray clouds.

As Ronny and Unity neared the lava a silhouetted figure appeared from the smoke downriver. The being was wearing a charred, black robe and riding a small, stone boat. Each of the being's hands held fireballs the size of apples

– which controlled the flow of the river. The fireballs obnubilated as the spirit slowed to a stop at the bank. Its hood cast a shadow over its face – and all Ronny and Unity could distinguish was the severely burned bottom jaw.

The spirit scrutinized the duo. "That oar..." It spoke in a broken, haunting voice. "Where is Charon?"

"Gone." Ronny answered. "I captain his ferry now. Phlegethon, I presume?"

Phlegethon cackled. "Charon commanded the Styx for countless millennia, now a human man wields the oar? How times have changed... What brings you here – spirit of the Styx?"

"I've heard the souls of elementals fall upon your banks." Ronny mentioned. "I'm searching for one in particular."

"A most unusual quest. What desire would the Styx have with an elemental?" Phlegethon catechized.

"It is my business." Ronny said sternly. "I seek a fire elemental that goes by the name "Sal". He died several Earth months ago. Have you encountered him?"

"Sal...?" Phlegethon chuckled. "Most unusual for a fire elemental to choose a nickname to accommodate mankind's inability to pronounce anything in their language. I do not have the elemental you seek, a fire elemental has not appeared on my banks since the gods and the Interdicted One had their war."

"Impossible." Ronny contended. "Sal sacrificed himself to save a couple of my allies. I saw the charcoal outline of his salamander form myself."

"That elemental never stood on my banks." Phlegethon asserted. "I did see a relatively powerful creature wandering near the Styx some time ago, however. There was another spirit with him – possibly a human."

"Where?" Ronny demanded. "And how long ago?"

"I have kept minimal track of time since the war." Phlegethon confessed. "Follow your river to where it meets the Acheron. There is a field near there which once held the great baetylus mines, there is also a disabled portal to Muspelheim in the region."

"Muspelheim?" Unity blurted. "The land of fire in the Norse religion! Perhaps your elemental friend seeks power from there?"

Phlegethon sniggered. "That would require rebuilding the portal. When the Interdicted One first rose to power it was in that field. He used the baetylus to outlast his first opponents. Before climbing back to Earth he made sure that portal was destroyed beyond repair. Surtr would have been irritating competition. Not to say a fire elemental wouldn't attempt to reconstruct the portal out of desperation though."

"So, that's where we go." Ronny announced. "Thank-you for your assistance."

"Anything for the ferryman of my sister Styx." Phlegethon bowed.

Ronny and Unity began their returning trek to the River Styx. Phlegethon conjured his fireballs and disappeared into the smoke emanating from his respective river. Once the pair were back onboard the Stygian ferry Ronny tapped the oar and the boat was propelled downstream.

"A second being..." Ronny mumbled.

"You believe it is "our" son?" Unity queried.

"It would make sense for Sal and Callum to

meet up and travel together." Ronny said.

"And the exhausted baetylus mines and the Muspelheim portal?" Unity snarled.

"Crazy ass stunts isn't a foreign behavior to those boys." Ronny smiled. "Let's reach them before they do anything stupid."

CHAPTER 13

Anat and Deimos stood at the edge of the cliff overlooking New Ur. A row of comet rocket cannons were set up behind them, with snipers between each artillery vehicle. The burned logs from when Sal protected the city were spread haphazardly behind the Sons of War, and their airplane was parked in a nearby clearing. As the sun set Anat gazed over the city - almost in a dwaal.

"What are you pondering?" Deimos asked.

"Nothing relevant." Anat replied. "Just when Seth stood here he set in motion the events that lead to this moment now. Our hunt for the fire elemental, our conflict with the Blessed and loss of two bases...two armies...my reunion with Ellis, possession, mutilations, seat of leadership, then our adventure leading back here."

"The way fate ties together...it's always interesting." Deimos muttered. "Let us write the conclusion in our favor."

"And you're certain the conclusion will go as written?" Anat glared at Deimos from the corners of her eyes. His visage reflected from the blue metal which had replaced her scleras.

"I'm the last living god that isn't in hiding." Deimos said. "There is no other way it can go."

***

Ellis vacated the library. Teigao sat in the ballroom reviewing material on the planning table.

Ellis yawned. "Well, couldn't find anything."

"Our luck as of late." Teigao said.

The clash of a door opening followed by muffled chatting was heard from the next room. Eric, Jasper, and Justice entered the ballroom from the staircase.

"How'd it go, kids?" Ellis inquired.

"We obtained the heart!" Justice effused. "It's already on the pedestal and absorbed into the ritual."

"Was it hard?" Ellis asked.

The trio just exchanged glances as they laughed nervously.

Ellis glared away for a second then looked back to his friends and chuckled awkwardly. "Okay? You bested a labyrinth...killed a life elemental...no epic tale of heroism to share?"

Jasper shrugged. "They won't tell me about the elemental either. The maze was pretty trippy though!"

"Wait – you didn't help fight the creature?" Ellis interjected.

"Well I was dead..." Jasper spoke. "Like...literally -"

"What?!" Ellis interrupted again.

"He was the lucky one." Eric remarked.

Teigao sniggered – as he knew enough about life elementals to guess what happened during the fight.

Meanwhile Anat and Deimos retreated behind their cannons. Deimos leaned against a charred tree and offered "Do you want to do the honors?"

"With pleasure." Anat purred as she looked over their soldiers and over the city. "Remember – only flatten half the city. Take your aim...lock the barrels in place..." The Warson troops adjusted the comet rockets to target their desired sections of the city. Steam whistled from the interior crevices of each cannon as the pure fire vaporized the moisture in the air. "Fire."

***

Ellis was about to pester his friends to tell the story of how they defeated the life elemental – but the citadel shook violently.

Teigao stood and clenched his fists as Ellis asked "What the hell is that?!"

Everyone equipped their weapons as they charged to the exit. They opened the citadel's doors and laid their eyes upon the attacker – one of Kepyet's sky sentries!

Teigao and Eric pushed the others aside to stand in the front as the sentry's guns took aim at the group.

"What?!" Justice screamed. "How is that thing operational?!"

"Revenants..." Teigao uttered. "Although they typically didn't pilot the sentries we believe they were trained on them in case of emergencies."

The deer revenant leaped from a lower platform on the sentry. He approached the Blessed coterie. Eric and Ellis immediately aimed their guns at the creature.

"Don't shoot." The revenant pleaded as he raised his hands. "For your sake more than mine...one bullet hits me and the five of you will unite into a single pound of ash."

"What is this?!" Teigao growled.

"The sword the girl carries." The revenant answered. "We need it. It is all we desire...The Monk does not view you as adversaries."

Justice shoved Eric and Teigao aside as she approached the revenant – aiming Kepyet's sword toward the monster. "Funny, we can't say the same!" Justice hissed. "We need the relics you plundered more than you know! I am NOT relinquishing this sword."

"I sensed weight in the word "need" there." The revenant observed. "You mean it...though we need the sword for something significant. The Monk...he recently endured what you humans would refer to as a "near death experience". He had an epiphany regarding the devourers. That the only chance Earth has against them is Kepyet, but to resurrect him we must complete a ritual – that sword is a part of it. The final part."

Justice lowered the weapon. "You're attempting to summon him, too?"

"Lies!" Teigao thundered. "He's manipulating you!"

"We served Kepyet!" The revenant laughed. "Why wouldn't we desire to summon him?"

"I demand to meet The Monk!" Justice called. "Then we can decide who summons Kepyet."

"Kid...we're short on time!" Ellis begged. "The Sons of War are attacking New Ur...some fancy new weapons and they have a god with them now!"

"What?!" Eric panicked.

"We have time!" Teigao assured. "I will not leave Skyrook undefended. Justice, Ellis, and Jasper...you three go and meet the monk."

"Hey, now..." Eric barked. "Shouldn't they bring along some extra firepower?"

"Not necessary." The revenant and Teigao chorused.

Teigao pushed one of Eric's arms down. "The sword isn't easily destroyed...it could easily survive a barrage from the sentry's guns. A single shot would...as that creature stated...reduce us to ash. That...monk person...wants us all alive."

"Unfortunately." The revenant answered. "But for Kepyet we would gladly disobey our new master if you don't conform. Come with us, with the sword, and I promise we won't harm you. Any of you."

"One condition!" Ellis yelled. "Spider-lady wears a mask."

"Flattering." A feminine voice from speakers on the sentry growled. "We can hear all of you. I'll...reluctantly...conceal my arachnid eyes. Just get your asses onboard. I'm impatient, trigger-happy, and currently have my fingers pressed against a very, VERY big trigger."

Four ropes dropped from one of the edges of the sentry below an opening. The revenant grabbed one of the ropes and offered the remaining ropes to the other three. Justice and her companions each grasped one then the ropes were lifted into the airship.

The room they entered within the sentry was small and empty with only one other door. As the deer entered the central chamber of the sentry the turtle revenant entered from the same door carrying a grenade launcher. Both doors slammed and locked as the turtle aimed his weapon at Justice and the two men.

Ellis aimed his handgun at the turtle. "I knew this was a trap!"

"No trap! No no, just making sure trip is smooth!" The turtle cackled as the sentry began to move. "Your weapons, put them away!"

"What if I shoot first?" Ellis threatened.

"Ellis..." Justice grumbled.

"The grenades can be remote detonated, too!" The turtle bragged. "I die, they still go boom!"

"He's right." Jasper confirmed as he examined the turtle's weapon. "This room appears indestructible too – just put the gun away, Ellis."

"Listen to your pet!" The turtle advised.

Ellis reluctantly holstered his gun.

***

New Ur had been reduced to half its size. The half nearest the plateau remained intact, but nothing remained of the other half. A giant, smoldering scorch mark defaced the ground where much of the city once stood. Nothing remained beneath the layer of black ash. The citizens of New Ur gathered as close to the rear cliffs as possible - cowering in fear.

Anat leaned against one of the cannons. "Beautiful...but wasteful using such power here."

"The Blessed will deliver themselves to us in good time." Deimos reassured. "I ordered the snipers to allow a few plebeians to escape, word will spread."

"Word of exactly what they will face once here." Anat worried.

"Descriptions, perhaps. But no certainties, nor access to anything that could compare." Deimos said. "We play the waiting game now. Once the city is starved we will demand the sulfur. At that point we will be met with the least resistance, and nobody will chase us and escalate the situation."

"There's room for error, especially when pissing off the Blessed." Anat opined. "But...you're a god, I'm just a human girl. What do I know?"

"Perhaps our success will rectify that attitude." Deimos hissed.

***

The sentry shook as it landed, and the turtle lowered his gun. "We're here!" He cackled.

Both doors opened. The sunlight from outside was discombobulating, usually polluted clouds dimmed the sun's radiance but it seemed as if the sky here was clear. As the turtle raised his weapon the deer and spider revenants entered the airlock.

"Gun down." The deer ordered. "They'll follow us."

The turtle lowered his weapon with hesitation as the deer and spider vacated the sentry. Ellis, Jasper, and Justice followed the revenants outside. They gasped at their surroundings. The sky was clear and blue, lush green flora surrounded and blanketed the mountain. They stood on a stone bridge leading into an ancient temple. The temple was cube-shaped and constructed from stones. Rows of windows opened into each floor of the structure. The three humans marveled at gorgeous landscape which enveloped them – awestruck.

"How..." Ellis gibbered.

"This place was untouched by the war." The deer explained. "The beauty only exists as far as your eyes can see. Just beyond that fog at the bottom of the mountain exists the desolation you're accustomed to. This sanctuary's days are numbered...the health of the outermost trees is deteriorating. The Monk awaits our arrival within the temple.

"Kepyet left a sigil here?" Justice inquired.

"Within the temple." The deer answered. "It was never recorded or spoken of."

"This is a volcano..." Ellis realized as they approached the temple entrance.

"Observant." The spider complimented. "It's mostly dead. The lava pool within the temple is fueled...but only for so long."

"So, I have a question!" Jasper spoke, dismissive of Ellis' concerns. "You guys are creatures that were tortured, right? But you're a spider...like, was anyone who ever just squished one susceptible to whatever Kepyet did to create you things?"

"Sigh..."You things."" The spider voiced. "I'm not giving your species a pass on those of us you executed out of irrational paranoia, but no. The previous owner of this body plucked my legs off one at a time before killing me. When it is time for my second death I will beg my assailant to rip this body apart before delivering the killing blow."

"Brutal..." Jasper quavered as they ventured upon the temple's entrance. The revenants stopped walking.

"The monk waits." The deer noted. "Enter the temple, there are two paths. One straight ahead and a descending stairway. Take the stairs."

"You aren't coming with us?" Justice asked.

"We have other chores." The deer answered. "The monk trusts the three of you will approach him willingly."

"Right." Ellis, Jasper, and Justice chorused.

Justice was the first to turn around and enter the temple. Ellis and Jasper reluctantly followed – concerned about who...or what...they will meet.

The only light within the temple was generated by the lava below. Following the light and the heat down the stairs the trio made their way to the bottom floor of the sanctum. They were able to maintain a tolerable distance from the lava's heat in the basement. The pool of lava filled the depression in the center of the room with an additional set of stairs between the lava pool and the brick floor that Justice and her companions stood upon. An ominous figure climbed out from the boiling, thick, orange liquid and onto the stairs.

He wore the body of a golem, one more advanced than the usual models. This golem's body was perfectly sculpted into the shape of a human man. His skin was the brown hue of the ceramic from which his body was crafted. The Monk wore a kilt crafted from adamant weaves and donned a long, thick beard of adamant wool. His orange eyes shined as bright as the lava. A smile crossed The Monk's face as he approached the trio.

"At last!" The Monk cheered. "You guys are here! I hope my henchmen weren't too rough with you...I told them to go soft..."

"Who are you?" Ellis growled as he equipped his pistol. "And I want a clear answer! I'm done with secrets!"

The Monk exploded with laughter as Justice pushed Ellis' arm down.

"Haha!" The Monk expressed excitement. "Chill, guys. Not literally – because you know, lava."

"Wait!" Justice stuttered. "Awful joke...informa – Sal?! Is that you?!"

"Indeed it is!" Sal giggled. "I'm so relieved to see you three are still alive!"

"Sal?!" Jasper perplexed.

"Say what?!" Ellis whined. "You died though! Saving us...so thanks for that – but we saw the -"

"Scorch mark of my body...I know..." Sal interjected. "I was weakened but I didn't die. I dropped my mortal form altogether, merged with what remained of the geothermal heat...and swam around in the mantle for a while. What is left of it anyway. Sensed some biological warmth – followed it to this temple. I was able to regenerate much of my energy here, can't return to my mortal form but I found this abandoned golem. The revenants taking refuge on his mountain found me – and we became friends."

Justice embraced Sal. "You're alive! Thank-you for saving us!"

"Yeah don't get all sappy just yet." Ellis advised. "So, you came back – why didn't you and the peanut gallery return to Skyrook? We could have used you – well...on that subject – why did you hide behind that ridiculous name? "The Monk?" Really? Sounds like a pop culture villain of some sort. Plus you sent your goons to steal the artifacts we were after!"

"I mean no harm, let me explain!" Sal begged.

"So, get explaining." Ellis ordered. "You aren't going to pull a Basil on us!"

"I couldn't just return to Skyrook right away." Sal admitted. "My spirit was dependent on intense heat for the longest time – and this golem can only retain so much. I was trapped in this temple, but while outside of a corporeal vessel my intuition intensified...intuition intensified...ha, that's kind of fun to say. Intuit-"

"Yeah, yeah..." Ellis badgered.

"Hmm." Jasper mumbled. "Intuition Intens-"

Justice finally let go of Sal as Ellis struck Jasper's forehead with two of his knuckles.

Sal continued speaking as Justice stepped back – suppressing a blush. "So, with my great intuition...I saw just how severe the threat of the devourers was. Bakasura approaches our world – and we were wrong about Tiamat. She can actually return to Earth on her own accord, unlike the others. All it takes to release her is a single leviathan. If she desired she could have spawned months ago. No divine weapons remain and that sword has an obvious limit on uses."

"We know all this." Ellis groaned.

"So, the Blessed must as well." Sal figured. "There is only one way to save the planet from the devourers...and that is to -"

Justice interrupted. "Summon Kepyet. We know..."

"You do?" Sal stuttered. "I thought you guys were just trying to gather his relics for cleanup or something! Know where the other sigil is?"

"That's kind of a stupid assumption..." Jasper teased.

"Considering we work with Teigao I can see where Sal came from, there." Ellis confessed.

"How do you know there's another sigil?" Justice wondered. "And it's in Skyrook's basement, by the way."

"Two of the pedestals activated." Sal replied. "Your doing?"

"So, they are universal?" Justice confirmed with herself. "The life elemental heart was. Eric and I had to kill the poor, tortured creature – and no I won't describe the fight."

"It gave live birth to bloody clones of you during the battle, didn't it?" Sal guessed.

"Well...yes." Justice chuckled nervously, before remembering that Sal is also a type of elemental.

"WHAT?!" Ellis and Jasper reacted to Sal's correct assumption.

"And who is Eric?" Sal inquired.

"He's at Skyrook." Justice answered.

"He's cool." Jasper added as Ellis said "Another Blessed prick, but better than the others."

Justice leered at Ellis. "The egregore was Kepyet's own doing. It possessed that lady that leads The Sons of War. Forced her to deliver it to our sigil."

"I see." Sal nodded. "Well – we have the other two relics all ready to be added to the ritual. Only thing left is the sword!"

"Are you still bound here?" Justice asked.

"Not anymore – my soul is strong enough to travel now. Why?" Sal quaeritated.

"Teigao wants to be present when Kepyet is summoned." Justice replied.

"Probably to kill him!" Sal feared.

"No, he knows we need him." Justice assured. "Out of courtesy I would prefer if we complete the ritual at Skyrook."

"I'm not sure..." Sal sighed. "But if you trust him, I suppose we can do the deed there! I get to bring my new friends though!"

"Joy." Ellis sarcastically effused.

"It will be fun!" Sal claimed unconvincingly. "Besides some extra muscle never hurts."

"How many revenants do you even have?" Jasper catechized.

"Five." Sal replied. "The three you've met, a raccoon, and a bull. Go on and board the sentry – I'll round my buddies up and join you shortly!"

Ellis and Jasper vacated the room. Sal grabbed Justice's shoulder before she could step away.

"Yes?" Justice asked.

"You're certain of Teigao's intentions?" Sal queried. "From what I've heard and sensed about him – he might be able to slay Kepyet in his freshly emerged, weakened state."

"I believe so..." Justice contended her own doubts. "I know he intends to have the ritual site as secure as possible in the event Kepyet isn't appreciative...but Teigao wants the world saved and although he isn't too thrilled about it he knows Kepyet is literally the only option."

"He's used Styx water before...Teigao that is." Sal worried. "If the bad blood between the two men escalates, would you be willing to turn your sword on Teigao? And the other Blessed?"

"Honestly I don't know." Justice said. "If it came down to it...the planet comes first. I am very fearful of what Kepyet may do after the devourers are dead though." She teared up. "Really though – why did you keep it a secret that you survived? You could have sent a messenger to at least inform me and Ronny!"

"You said it yourself. The world comes first – I couldn't take any risks, not to offend. And Ronny died before I found this body – but I heard he ferries the Styx now?" Sal answered.

"Yeah." Justice pouted. "I still struggle to understand your logic, but I trust you."

"You kids coming?" Ellis shouted from the top of the stairs.

CHAPTER 14

Both the Blessed and Sal's forces were all gathered within the sigil room of Skyrook. The mask and ring had already been included with the ritual. Justice stood by the final pedestal holding the accursed sword. Teigao and the blessed held large rifles – ready to fire them if needed. The revenants struggled to resist their urge to fight the Blessed, especially because they knew that each Blessed weapon contained bullets dipped in water from the Styx. Under Sal's orders they wouldn't instigate a battle, but each revenant positioned one hand to grab their gun and the other a blade. Jasper and Ellis leaned against the door frame – watching the event with their curious eyes. Sal's glowing eyes assisted with combating the dimness of the chamber as he leaned against the desk that once held the flash drive.

"Justice – are you ready?" Teigao asked. "We know not how the fiend will react or behave."

The deer yelled at Teigao "Might go smoother if you didn't have a bunch of guns with spirit destroying bullets aimed at him!"

"We'll only use them as a last resort." Teigao reassured. "Not to mention how small of a window we have, Lyth shot him with a Styx water bullet when he was in his prime and it barely hurt him."

"Let's just hurry." Ellis requested. "Sooner we get him back the sooner we can save New Ur."

"Could just send me in again." Sal commented.

"Deimos is too powerful." Teigao said. "Justice – place the sword, finish the ritual."

Justice's body shook from nervousness as she gently rested the sword onto the pedestal. She almost felt sick from the anxiety of what she was doing. Kepyet was among the most dangerous and unpredictable demons to have ever surfaced – and now she was summoning him back. The choice wasn't entirely hers and a dozen other people were involved with the sin being committed, but Justice was the one finishing the ritual so she felt the most responsible. She slowly peddled back as the pedestal claimed the relic. Black fire began to swirl around the center of the sigil – but nothing else seemed to be happening. Teigao and the Blessed nervously aimed their rifles at the center.

"Did I do it right?" Justice asked. "Are we missing a step?"

"His name must be spoken." The spider explained. "I'll allow you the honor."

"Of course..." Justice quavered as she took a deep, nervous breath. "Alright...here we go..." Justice exhaled a good ten seconds before taking another breath. She struggled to speak, but eventually forced the words off her tongue. "Kepyet!"

The black fire bounced between the pedestals and formed a pentagram as the candle lights flickered violently – contorting the shadows on the ceiling. All the black fire condensed into the center of the sigil then hardened into a black, reflective, amorphous substance which slowly twisted into the shape of a person. In a flash of black light the substance detailed itself into Kepyet. Demonic wings sprouted from between his armor and cloak as he collapsed onto his hands and knees. A gentle stream of smoke poured from the sides of his mask and his eyes flickered with a black static. Teigao approached the demon with his rifle in hand.

Kepyet chuckled in his weak voice. "Still under the same blind leadership I see." He snickered again – with his head still lowered. "Shall I reveal your true name? No...no...I will permit your illusions. Teigao...always so cautious. Is all of this necessary, or a proper way to welcome a man back into the world?"

"I'm surprised you still refer to yourself as a man." Teigao remarked.

"Heh..." Kepyet wheezed. "That's all I was...all I remain through the eyes of the gods, and fools such as yourself who remain in their service"

"Hypocritical, as usual!" Teigao barked. "It's almost sad – is this a mind game, or have you sincerely convinced yourself that the fates of your loyalists were any different than those that followed the pantheons? So much for their redemption."

"Intentions!" Kepyet snapped – still struggling to fully recover his energy. "The redemption I promised was liberty, the redemption you accepted is slavery."

The bull revenant threw one of the Blessed soldiers aside and grabbed their gun. As he did so the raccoon and turtle attempted to disarm a couple other Blessed. The spider equipped her pistol and knife. She shot the bull between the eyes as she threw her knife into the neck of the raccoon. The deer aimed his pistol at the spider as she shot the turtle between the eyes. Sal conjured a fireball which he hurled at the deer – blasting the flesh clean off his skeleton. The spider dropped her gun and raised her hands as the Blessed aimed their rifles at her (except Teigao who remained fixated on Kepyet).

"What just happened?!" Justice perplexed.

"LOWER YOUR WEAPONS!" Kepyet ordered as he raised his face to peek at the spider. "That is loyalty."

"You idiots shouldn't wield Styx water." The spider snarled. "The others have been conspiring to kill Kepyet for months. They didn't have a legitimate plan until you shitwads decided to bring Stygian water here. Figured they would slay Kepyet and plunder what power of his remained."

Eric aimed one of his pistols at the Spider. "And we are supposed to trust you don't have a similar agenda?"

"Kepyet's power is a heavy burden." The spider said. "One I'm not willing to bear."

Kepyet twisted his face toward Teigao. "If your aim is to slay me – pull the trigger now. There are only a few more moments where it remains possible by your hand."

"Yeah, dude!" Sal approached Teigao. "Enough of the charades, we get it, you really don't like the idea of working with your mortal enemy. Honestly the only person in this room comfortable with Kepyet being here is the pet spider we shared!" The spider revenant growled at Sal as he continued. "Let's put these guns away, let the man-demon recover, and go save New Ur, then the world?"

Kepyet struggled onto his feet as he chuckled at Teigao. "This elemental is wise, I advise you to take his words to heart and dampen your hostility toward me. I am vengeful, but I am also done with you, Teigao. My revenge manifested as your failure to realize the gods' agenda nineteen years ago."

"Kepyet!" Justice roared. "You don't account for the rest of us! The hell you put us through, the evil acts you forced me and my friends to commit! The false promises you made to my mother, setting up Basil to kill Ronny, torturing the life elemental!"

"There it is..." Kepyet interjected. "I've sensed your tension, that aching desire to call me out. My plans, meticulous as they were, still had flaws and unintended consequences. The plans enacted were along the only route of assurance I would be brought back. My promises to your mother weren't broken, the conditions simply weren't met in time. Basil was as foolish as he was zealous – but you personally saw to him facing your namesake. Your mother's fire certainly burns within you."

Kepyet drew his sword and leaned on it as if it was a cane. Teigao and the Blessed kept their weapons aimed at him.

"I'm with the fire elemental." Ellis shouted. "You Blessed are acting like little dogs. Either bite or stop barking. We have a city to save and that will be much more difficult if the mask is full of your magic bullets."

Justice stared at Kepyet – not knowing how to feel. She wanted to hate him for all that he put her through, but she was also fascinated by the dark being. Kepyet was a legend who's very mention would cause the hairs to stand on the back on one's neck. He also knew her parents personally and could put what she read about them into the context of who they were outside of the records they left behind. She was as intimidated by him as she was curious – after all Kepyet was the slayer of pantheons. The Blessed slowly lowered their weapons.

"Alright..." Teigao prepared to give everyone orders. "To take down Deimos we -"

"He's been feeble and slumbering for years." Kepyet interrupted. "You could not even find him, days ago you possessed the strength to slay him and didn't act. Was it your emotions? Your memories and experiences of trauma? It is my turn. Teigao – you and your golden monkeys are to remain here. My spider shall keep you company AND ensure you don't do anything stupid. I can and certainly will survey you through her five eyes. Jasper..." Jasper's eyes widened and his heart skipped a beat upon hearing Kepyet speak his name. "You will drive me and Justice to New Ur in your Exile." Kepyet turned to Justice. "You have many questions for me, I will answer some on the flight." Kepyet faced Ellis. "Ellis – you and the fire elemental will accompany us to New Ur in the Cannon." Teigao was furious that Kepyet undermined him, but realized there was little he could do.

"Deimos is an enemy of yours, right?" Ellis asked.

"During the war he hid." Kepyet replied. "I didn't care enough about the lesser gods to track him down, but Deimos definitely is a rival, as is his faction."

"So, I have a demand." Ellis continued. "The leader that refers to herself as "Anat", she's mine."

"You are granted your duel." Kepyet assured. "I'm aware of your...special...plan for it."

"What is he talking about?" Justice glared at Ellis.

"Wait!" Jasper drawled. "Why don't we all just take the Cannon?"

Kepyet limped to Jasper before answering. "Because I have a fondness for cool vehicles, especially those that mimic the aesthetics of the classic automobiles."

Jasper subtly grinned and whispered to Justice – who had already began her eye roll. "He thinks my car is cool."

"How leisurely..." Teigao disapproved. "Why not simply teleport to New Ur?"

"My powers are still collecting themselves and repairing the tether." Kepyet spoke. "We have time to take the practical route to where I will play the impractical role of superhero."

Kepyet ascended the stairs – still limping. Ellis, Jasper, Justice, and Sal followed the dark being through Skyrook and outside. Jasper ran ahead to start the Exile and drove it to the entrance of the citadel. Justice sat in the passenger seat and Kepyet reclined in the back seats. Ellis and Sal entered the Cannon. As Sal took his seat Ellis climbed into the back.

"What are you doing?" Sal asked.

"Getting something." Ellis mumbled.

The sound of the twisting gears within a lock was heard, followed by the creaking of aged hinges. Sal peered into the back but could only distinguish Ellis's back as he knelt on the ground. Ellis returned to the front of the cannon with a sword sheathed in leather. A layer of rust covered most of the hilt – minus an emblem on the pommel which was a red horse encased in a glass circle.

"A sword?" Sal perplexed. "I think we will need more than that to fight The Sons of War."

"It's not for the army, I have guns for that." Ellis lectured as he rested the sword next to himself as he sat. "This is for Anat."

"I assume it has value...to both of you?" Sal guessed. Ellis nodded as he started the Cannon. Sal returned the incline. "Never took you as the sentimental type."

The Exile began its flight – the Cannon trailed only a few hundred feet behind.

"I almost purchased one of these once." Kepyet commented. "I'm delighted that some Exiles endured this long."

"Want to know what modifications I made?" Jasper offered.

"Can you two talk about cars later?" Justice growled. "Kepyet killed hundreds..."

"Thousands, my dear. That's even putting it softly." Kepyet interrupted.

"...of gods." Justice finished, irritated. "He's back and the first thing you talk about is cars?!"

"The girl has a point." Kepyet admitted. "Quaeritate away, Justice."

"Can you still resurrect the dead?" Justice

immediately returned. "And I demand an honest answer!"

"Not yet." Kepyet said softly. "I hope you can take solace in knowing that even if I could the power would be of no use to you."

"Explain!" Justice ordered. "My parents, my brother, Ronny!"

"Ronny ferries the Styx now, I cannot steal him." Kepyet explained. "I am unable to sense your father, and the souls of your mother and brother are currently entitled to other beings. I can only resurrect loose souls."

"What other beings?!" Justice cried.

"That's a great question." Kepyet snickered. "My senses don't reach far enough for the answer, and as devastating as it is to admit that is the truth."

Justice chose to believe the demon. She panted for a moment while trying to piece together her next question. "What were my parents like?"

"Peculiar to say the least." Kepyet chuckled. "They would use that exact same phrase to describe myself. Your father was an intellectual, adored his reading. When his nose wasn't buried within the pages of a book his hands and eyes were fixated on an experiment. Every problem he encountered became an obsession until he discovered a solution. If he couldn't give a university level lecture on a question someone asked him he would devote countless hours studying whatever the subject was. As you may have read in his journal his temperaments did occasionally conflict with my bias in favor of spirituality. Our combined minds though – we were on the verge of the greatest, most long-awaited discovery of mankind!"

"The stone." Justice confirmed. "Do you know how to create it?"

"Nay." Kepyet pouted. "Though prior to my first death I did develop a theory. The stone isn't relevant to the present. When the time is appropriate I will act on my theory, and if you get over your hatred of me you are free to partake in my experiments."

"I don't hate you..." Justice said with doubt behind her words. "I don't know how I feel or should feel toward you. You're a monster and played a major part in desolating the planet and put me and my friends through a living hell...your intentions though, I don't know what to make of them."

"I take no offense." Kepyet reassured.

"My mother?" Justice sighed. "Can you tell me about her?"

"Ahh...Unity." Kepyet reminisced. "She had fire like no other. I say this as a close friend of Lucien's, it took an exceptionally special kind of woman to love and remain so devoted to your father. They argued as much as your companion Ellis smokes."

"Holy crap, man!" Jasper interrupted. "How much do you know about all of us?"

"I can see in your thoughts that you literally don't wish for me to answer that." Kepyet bragged. "Anyway – as much as they quarreled there was no resentment. Their love was genuine and rare for the time. Unity was a curious one, her capacity to learn was almost equal to that of your father's but her greatest desire was a normal life. Subconsciously, anyway. She did take an interest in our research, but due to the nature of our experiments Lucien and I both did what we could to keep her uninvolved. Unity was kind, but her kindness wasn't blinding. Anyone who attempted to take advantage of her sweet nature found themselves disappointed. Unity...her devotion and will were so strong. After I became the creature you see before you she stood up to me. Unlike the others that exhibited such behavior she possessed no powers or allies. If the two of you ever meet your pride in each other will be mutual."

"Hey...uh...Kepyet..." Jasper muttered. "We're almost there, will Deimos...like...sense you and shoot us down?"

"No." Kepyet answered. "I'm cloaking my presence from him. He will be unaware I'm there until it's too late."

"What exactly is the plan for after we land?" Justice inquired.

"An epic comeback for me, a gift for Sal, a lesson for you, and a duel for Ellis." Kepyet said.

"And me?" Jasper asked. "What about me?"

"Aren't you familiar with the "Dark Lord" archetype?" Kepyet inquired.

"Yeah...?" Jasper croaked, having no idea where Kepyet could possibly be going with his comment.

"We all need a driver." Kepyet insisted.

Jasper simpered as Justice giggled. She suppressed her laughter as well as she could because she didn't want to admit to herself that Kepyet had made her chuckle, however the task suddenly became less strenuous upon the realization that Kepyet was being serious.

CHAPTER 15

Anat and Deimos watched as the Exile and Cannon soared in from the mountain overlooking the remaining portion of the city.

"That's them!" Anat announced. "Fire!"

"Stop." Deimos ordered. "You're no coward. Isn't this a personal matter for you?"

"Give me the controller for the cannons!" Anat begged. "That will make this personal!"

"And less fun." Deimos replied. "I want to feed on their anxiety as you shoot and cut them down."

Anat hissed through her teeth as she drew her pistols. The Exile and Cannon landed in front of the city.

"What the hell?!" Ellis quavered. "How! There's nothing, not even ruins!"

"Pure fire..." Sal whispered. "They discovered how to make it. No mortal was meant to – but they somehow found a way..."

"Can you control it?" Ellis asked.

"Yes, thankfully." Sal answered. "But if it fuels all their weapons then it will be too volatile for me to even handle."

"Aren't you a fire elemental though?" Ellis catechized.

"Yes." Sal spoke. "But I also lost my mortal form, this golem keeps me alive and it can't handle nearly as much flame as my body could."

"Well shit." Ellis whined as he turned the Cannon off.

Jasper, Justice, and Kepyet had a similar conversation about the devastation and Sal's ability to harness the pure fire. In their conversation Kepyet admitted partial responsibility for recording the pure fire recipe in his notes during a state of madness. Jasper turned the Exile off then he and Justice vacated the vehicle as Ellis and Sal dropped out of the Cannon. They lined up and faced the hills beyond the ashes where the Warson siege squad stood.

"She's up there..." Ellis stated. "With that fear god."

Deimos and Anat approached the edge of the cliff.

"Only the four of you?" Deimos shrieked across the mile of ruin. "I suppose I was wrong in my assumption that the entirety of the Blessed would try to stop us. Has Teigao really become such a coward? Or is that him cloaking his aura in the back of your little car?"

"Deimos..." Anat uttered. "Something is wrong, something really doesn't feel right!"

The planet shook violently as the moon briskly swam across the sky and in front of the sun. Deimos nervously exhaled into growl.

"No..." Deimos panicked. "No, not possible!"

Kepyet exited the Exile and pushed his way in front of Justice and her companions.

"Kepyet!" Deimos's voice boomed across the field. "What is your goal here? What false promises have you made to those poor mortals and the fire elemental? You do know elementals are also susceptible to my powers, especially ones as weak as your friend there."

"I am not ignorant of your power, Deimos." Kepyet shouted back.

"As if it matters. Pure fire can tear through you!" Deimos warned as he raised his right hand. "Everyone, fire upon Kepyet!" Deimos lowered his hand – gesturing his soldiers to attack. Kepyet tapped his foot. The Warson soldiers did nothing.

"Are you all deaf?!" Deimos roared.

"A letter off." Anat hissed at Deimos as every Warson soldier collapsed – including the artillery crew.

"Jesus Christ..." Ellis's voice quaked as Justice and Sal watched in shock.

"What happened?" Jasper gibbered.

"He killed them all..." Justice mumbled.

"I underestimated you!" Deimos confessed. "No matter – a mistake easily rectified!"

Deimos leaped from the cliff and glided in the direction of Kepyet. Kepyet held his hand toward Deimos and a vortex of black fire swirled at his fingertips. The orbs within Deimos' torso extinguished as a sickly greenish-gold aura was torn from his body and into Kepyet's fire. Deimos' body decelerated to the ground – landing only a meter from Kepyet's feet. Kepyet released the vortex and it vanished in a puff of smoke. Anat activated her wings but when Kepyet tapped his foot again they broke from their sockets before

Anat's feet were even lifted from the earth. She growled as she sprinted toward the Warson vehicles.

Kepyet looked at Sal. "The pure fire is yours to extract, I've blessed you so that you may conjure both your elemental body AND the humanoid husk you met these people in." Kepyet turned to Ellis and said in his crisp voice "End this."

Kepyet waved his hand as Ellis unsheathed the special sword – teleporting him near Anat. Kepyet then gestured Sal to step toward him. The fiend placed his hand on the golem's chest and released a burst of dark magic from his palm. Sal's golem body crumbled away as his last human body regenerated in its place. As Kepyet lowered his arm Sal stepped back in shock, but grinned. The fire elemental spread his arms and as he did so the Warson weapons were ignited. In an instantaneous flash every spark of pure fire was absorbed into Sal's body. Justice placed her hands over her mouth – unsure what to make of what had occurred.

"You've been back not even an hour..." Justice gasped.

"I channel energies from both my realm and the gravitational movements of this one." Kepyet replied. "Deimos was arrogant, and in his hauteur inadvertently offered himself to me, granting more than enough of the proper energies and essences required to restore our elemental friend."

"You did more than restore!" Sal cheered. "I feel better than I ever have! I feel as if...there's a full star within me! No other elemental had this sort of power – why me?"

"You supported me when it mattered most." Kepyet answered. "The devourers are powerful, their vampiric abilities challenge my own."

"And you can draw energy from gravity!" Jasper added. "Wait – is that what the eclipse is for? Gravity's reaction when interfered with?"

Kepyet's mask cracked into a subtle smile. "Justice, you and Ellis have been wise to keep this kid around. He interprets the world around him in a special light. Now if you three will pardon me – there's an ubiquity of curious eyes I'm obligated to address."

Kepyet's wings sprouted from his back and he leaped into the sky above New Ur. Everyone in the city watched the dark being in incredulity.

"Survivors!" Kepyet began. "Your eyes do not deceive you despite your hearts wishing it so. I, Kepyet, have returned to your realm. The remaining Blessed have no option other than to follow me, and The Sons of War have been reduced to their final member, unable to ever be reestablished. You all see me as a demon, but I am why you are all still alive! Fate has granted me a second chance to be a hero – as I speak the great devourers return to Earth. My allies and I are going to stop them. Be warned, however, of the consequences of animosity. Human lives are worthless, simple things to take."

Kepyet returned to the ground.

"Some speech..." Justice snarled as the eclipse ended.

"Your approval isn't a concern." Kepyet riposted. "I'll be at Skyrook. You three can drive back. Four if your friend Ellis survives, if not...Sal can finish the job."

Kepyet vanished. Justice panicked and attempted to run up the hill – but Sal and Jasper grabbed her.

"We have to help him!" Justice cried.

"I sense his body heat." Sal answered. "I also sense his foe's, they're engaged in a one-on-one duel."

Justice clenched her fist as Jasper added "Yeah that, but also it's a personal thing. If we help Ellis and she dies...it would eat at him."

"And if he dies?!" Justice snapped.

"Well we believed him dead before...and it would be an honorable death. Really think Ellis wants to go out an old man, or be swallowed into a void by some gross monster?" Jasper commented.

Justice lowered her face. "That was devastating...but I do see your point. Let's load the Exile into the Cannon while we wait."

Meanwhile Ellis raised the sword and ran after Anat as she fled toward the vehicles. She sensed Ellis approaching and twisted her body around with her hands aimed at Ellis. The magnets in her robotic hands drew her guns to her palms then she pulled the triggers. Ellis smirked as the bullets were attracted to the blade of the sword.

"Remember this?" Ellis asked.

Anat shook with rage. "You said you lost that!"

"No..." Ellis corrected. "I actually said I haven't seen it. That bit is true – I kept it in a safe all these years."

"Snake." Anat hissed. "The magnetic and reactive gravitational energy of the blade won't keep you safe from explosives!"

"Come on!" Ellis begged. "Doesn't Anat still have some honor?"

"It's a duomachy you want?" Anat chortled, still enraged. "I'm willing to abide, if you're going to be reasonable. Terms?"

"Sword and dagger." Ellis stated as he excavated a dirk from his belt. "To the death."

"No other way to have it." Anat exhaled a lengthy breath. "I accept. We leave no loose end! The defeated dies. True to your terms...don't hold back...I won't, not again." Anat removed her cape and dropped it onto the ashen dirt.

"I don't intend to." Ellis growled with certainty as Anat removed the two swords she carried on her back and dropped them onto the ground. Next she unclipped several handguns and even a couple dismantled rifles. After those were tossed into the dust she excavated nunchucks, a whip, a truncheon, another pistol, a miniature pistol, two electronic weapons, a dismantled crossbow, and yet another pistol.

"Shit, Anat..." Ellis shook his head as she drew a sword similar to Ellis' from her back. Unlike the weapon Ellis carried the hilt of Anat's had no detail, and the blade was only half the length. She pressed a button near the blade and it extended to the length of Ellis'.

"Sword and dagger!" Anat purred as she equipped a red dagger from her lower back. "The demon sent you up here, the fight is yours to begin."

Thunder echoed across the landscape as the swollen clouds released their stress. A heavy rain collapsed upon Ellis and Anat.

Ellis assailed Anat. He prepared to lunge at her, but she jumped and kicked Ellis in the chest. Ellis spread his arms apart as he landed then lifted his legs into a backwards roll to evade Anat's stab at the ground where he lay. He rolled to his side as she continued her attack by stabbing her dagger toward him. As he regained his footing he used his own dagger to beat Anat's sword away – then his sword to parry her incoming dagger. Anat stepped back to avoid the stab as she swung her sword to Ellis' face – slicing his right cheek. The cut drew blood but wasn't much deeper than a cat scratch.

Anat used her robotic arms to twirl her weapons like the fins of an electric fan. Ellis dived forward and below her sword. He kicked himself between her legs as she attempted to slice his. As Ellis retracted his feet he attempted to cut the backs of her knees, but she jumped into a back flip behind him. Anat once again stabbed her sword into the ground hoping it would land in Ellis, but he rolled out of the way just in time and beat her dagger away as he regained his footing.

For the next few moments their weapons parried. The pinging sound of raindrops bouncing off Anat's armor caused auditory distractions and difficulty following the sounds of their weapons clashing. Anat kicked Ellis in the shin – throwing off his footing. Albeit Ellis caught himself in time to avoid a lethal strike Anat still managed to land two quick incisions on his left cheek the same depth as the wound on his other one. Anat jabbed her dirk toward Ellis' side, but it was beaten away by his own dagger as they parried each others' swords.

Anat leaped and twirled her body into a kick – lifting her leg so that her foot struck the top of Ellis' head. Ellis collapsed and crawled on his back away from her as she threw her dagger into the ground. After the dagger landed an inch from his groin Ellis kicked himself backwards and Anat crouched forward to retrieve the dagger and lunge her sword at Ellis. He flipped himself onto his stomach – kicking her sword away with his foot as he did so. Ellis pushed himself onto his feet and knocked both of Anat's weapons away with his sword as he turned to face her. Anat dropped to the ground and spun on the toes of her left foot – using her right leg to attempt to kick Ellis back down. Ellis jumped to avoid the strike and jammed his sword into the ground inches behind Anat's back mid-twirl. She felt the breeze from the incoming strike and stood as his weapon landed. Anat stepped aside and rotated her body into a stab with her dagger – which Ellis beat away. Once again the two clashed their weapons with identical strategies.

Ellis managed to slide his dagger-hand past Anat's sword. Even though he failed to strike her with the blade his fist bumped her jaw. Anat's hand twirled as she pulled it toward Ellis – stabbing her sword across the back of his shirt. She stretched her arm with the flat of her sword against Ellis' back – pulling him around to her side. Anat retracted her saber as her body contorted in attempt to drive the dagger into Ellis' chest. Ellis ducked and retreated past her dagger as she swung her blade toward him. He deflected her sword with his as he attempted to stab her eyes with the dagger. The tip of his dagger pierced Anat's mask but she stepped away before it could cause noticeable damage. As she evaded the strike she gracefully twirled her sword between herself and Ellis – lacerating his shins.

Anat remained persistent with her attacks as Ellis struggled to parry and evade them. His blood had gently colored his pants red – but the cuts weren't unbearable. Anat's attacks grew more brisk and erratic. Ellis entangled his weapons with hers then as they tugged their blades apart she kicked him in the stomach. Ellis ran backwards in a failed attempt to avoid falling. Anat remained still to catch her breath.

"I thought you didn't intend to hold back?" Anat breathed.

"I'm not!" Ellis roared as he struggled to his feet.

Anat's soaked bangs slugged over her face. The reflective blue machinery in her eyes flickered from between the hairs. A gentle film of water collected and dripped from the metal studs below her eyes. Thin steam rasped out from the joints of her robotic hands as the batteries boiled the rainwater.

"You're going to die!" Anat panted. "You challenged me with the belief that sword would distract me! Fool. Idiot. It had meaning to Kaleyla, not me. She's dead...but when I drive my sword through your throat don't expect to see her."

"Oh, I don't!" Ellis returned. His beard grew heavy from the rain and his own bangs struggled into his face. "I've accepted she's gone. You're blinded to that realization – must be that blue crap filling your eyes!"

"Shut up." Anat ordered. "Don't disappoint me...come now. Fight me." She quavered as Ellis reentered his combat stance, resisting the weight of the water his garb absorbed. "Let me put you out of your misery...I can see it...beyond the cuts."

"Less obvious than yours." Ellis remarked.

The blue crowns of Anat's teeth sparked as she clenched them together. "FIGHT ME!" She screeched.

Ellis charged at Anat then the two clashed

their weapons in an identical pattern again, but this time significantly faster. Anat was caught off-guard by Ellis' sudden match of her speed, yet he struggled against the strength and unnatural movements of her robotic hands. He realized that half of his defensive stunts were improvised. Ellis was forced to back peddle upon realizing her mechanical hands had him at a disadvantage. Anat noticed Ellis' passive footwork and became more aggressive with hers. Ellis noticed her attack pattern had an opening, unfortunately a brief one. He timed when she would be open next and made his move.

As both Anat's weapons drifted away from each other Ellis slipped his dagger from Anat's sword – risking his thigh. Her weapon barely missed his hip as he lunged the dirk at her chest. Anat caught what he was doing and realized the dagger could penetrate her armor and carve the top of her pectoral. She leaned back an exiguous distance and puffed out her chest – causing the dense metal plate between her cleavage to modify the degree of Ellis' incoming blade. His dagger jammed itself into her collar, but didn't cut through her uniform. Ellis continued to push his dagger forward which lifted Anat off the ground. When his attack concluded she slipped from the blade and fell onto her back.

Ellis prepared to stab his sword into her. Anat ignored the aches from collapsing and rolled onto her side – stabbing her dagger into the ground. Ellis realized his strike would miss so he retracted his sword as Anat extended hers and balanced her body on her dagger – using it as an axis to spin around. He jumped to avoid her sword but the instant his feet returned to the ground her legs had reached his position and tripped him. Ellis collapsed face-first and clashed his dagger with Anat's as he landed. They beat each other's swords together in a stunt which propelled both of them back onto their feet. The tips of their daggers clicked together as both combatants flicked the weapons upwards. Anat and Ellis waved their swords around each other for a moment before the long weapons touched and twirled. As they released each other's swords the two beat their daggers together before transitioning back into the usual attack patterns.

The largest issue facing Anat and Ellis was that their combat styles were the same. Anat's had grown more aggressive over the years while Ellis' more evasive, but the differences were as negligible as their moves predictable. Anat had the advantage of flexibility, reflexes, robotics, and improved instincts while Ellis' advantage was emotional stability. They simultaneously mustered the same idea and raised their weapons in an attempt to strike each other's shoulders with their forearms. This led to them clashing forearms as if they were the blades of swords. Realizing the method wouldn't go anywhere Anat and Ellis entangled each other's weapons into a double-twirl before stepping back from one another in order to reset the fight pattern.

Anat jammed her sword into the ground and used it as a pillar to cartwheel over. Ellis dodged the attempted strike of her dagger followed by both attempted kicks. As she completed her attack Ellis knocked her sword away with his dagger then twisted his body to evade her dagger. Anat and Ellis proceeded to engage in a double entangle once again, but this time Anat successfully disarmed Ellis of both weapons.

Ellis reacted by falling forward and grabbing Anat's hands – preventing her from striking him with her blades. She attempted to drill her hands away from his but Ellis had pressured her wrists in such a way that she was unable to rotate them. Anat flipped one arm over the other – spinning Ellis onto his back. He reacted by slamming his feet onto the ground before collapsing then focusing his strength into his upper-body to swing himself forward. While maintaining his grip Ellis returned to a standing position and flipped Anat over his head. She landed on her back but tore her hands free from Ellis upon landing. As she regained her footing Ellis retrieved his sword and dagger.

Anat focused her strength into her sword-arm and swung her weapon – targeting the point she knew Ellis would raise his weapons to deflect. The clash caused Ellis to be pushed sideways so that his back faced Anat. She threw her arms below his shoulders then curled them back toward herself – locking Ellis against her. Anat tightened her muscles – dislocating both of Ellis' shoulders. Ellis squirmed free of Anat's grip and cussed to himself while his arms flopped and struggled to maintain a grip on his weapons. He spun his body to use the momentum and lift his sword-arm to block Anat's incoming attacks. His hope was that she would try to kick him as a follow-up.

Ellis' desires came to fruition as Anat leaped into a rotating, double-kick. He angled his body so that her first kick would strike his left shoulder. The impact spun him around. As Ellis twirled he leaned back to place his right shoulder in the direction of Anat's second foot. The kick landed and Ellis was once again facing his foe with both shoulders knocked back in place. He prepared to strike her while her back was turned but she executed a flip and her heels kicked Ellis' hands away. Before he could recover Anat twirled around and punched Ellis in the chest with her dagger-hand. The tip of the blade sliced along the bottom of Ellis' chin. Anat attempted to slash his neck with her sword but he used his dagger to parry the slash.

As Ellis attempted to reestablish his stance Anat flipped her sword around in her hand and slid her palm along the blade. Once her weapon was fully extended she tightened her grip and swung the saber like a mace – striking Ellis on his pectoral with the hilt. Ellis attempted to stagger backwards but Anat whipped her sword around for a similar strike, this time the hilt's blow landed on Ellis's side and knocked him to the ground. He tried to stand, but Anat positioned her hilt between his feet so that each side of the cross-guard was below an ankle. She flicked her sword upwards – sending Ellis into the air feet-first. He landed face-first into the ashen ground. Ellis coughed as he accidentally inhaled the fine powders. When Anat approached he pushed himself back up – but Anat used his discombobulated state to slash him back and forth across the abdomen eight times with her dagger. His costume prevented her knife from digging into his organs but the lacerations were still deep and drew a significant amount of blood. Ellis knocked her dagger away with his sword then twisted it so that it would parry her dagger as he lunged his dagger forward.
Anat rotated her sword to deflect Ellis' dagger as

he recovered his own saber and attempted to slash her face. She turned her head and caused Ellis' blade to slice two of the three metal dots below her right eye. Electricity burst from the tech on her face and shocked Ellis – forcing his reflexes to release the sword. She used her dagger to force Ellis' sword to jam into the ground while using her saber to parry Ellis' incoming dagger. Anat stepped on the pommel of Ellis' sword to elevate herself enough to land a damaging kick to his gut. Ellis staggered back as blood from the cuts on his stomach sprayed over Anat's boot. She slashed her sword across the top of his chest. The incision wasn't deep enough to reach his skin but the force twisted Ellis so that his back was turned to his foe. Anat lowered the blade of her sword to align with Ellis' neck then channeled all her strength and will into her sword-arm to deliver the decapitating, killing blow.

CHAPTER 16

On a calm evening mid-2030 fourteen-year-old Kaleyla was babysitting nine-year-old Ellis. Ellis' family home was a larger, newer building a block away from the town hall. The city they lived in was small, and more of a town than a city. It shared a lake with a neighboring town. The building creaked in tune with the gentle winds outside as the blood red light from the sun setting behind smoke-contaminated clouds dimmed. Computerized lamps inside the house brightened to compensate for the obnubilating natural light. The two were playing with a few of Ellis' action figures, Ellis was controlling the villainous character.

Kaleyla pressed the buttons on the backs of the two figures in her hands which caused them to swing punches. When the fists struck Ellis' toy a computer within the doll activated a sound system. "Argh!" The toy screamed as its rubber skin changed colors as if the character had been bruised.

"And now you die!" Kaleyla growled – impersonating one of the figures in her hands as she brushed her golden blonde hair from her face.

"No!" Ellis whined. "They wouldn't kill him! The team always tries to capture villains!"

"But if they killed them things would be better in the long run." Kaleyla replied. "Villains ALWAYS escape."

"Some get redeemed." Ellis argued. "And whenever a hero does kill they turn bad or make things worse."

"Not always." Kaleyla opined. "But okay, when you're older you'll understand that the good guys don't always do good things. They can't."

"They can always try!" Ellis stated.

Kaleyla smiled at her young friend. "Sure." She peeked at the blank television screen inside the wall as she set the action figures down. "Time display?"

The television detected her voice and "8:34" appeared on the screen.

Ellis picked up the other two toys and began carrying them toward the cabinet containing the rest of his action figure collection. "Still a few hours before my parents get home."

"You're supposed to be in bed by ten." Kaleyla lectured. "I'll let you stay up until they get home again but you better do a better job at fake sleeping!"

"They didn't blame you!" Ellis recalled. "Well…"

"I got a lecture from them about letting you have too much caffeine." Kaleyla interrupted.

"Not like you got in any more trouble though." Ellis commented as he walked toward an opulent mahogany cabinet.

"And I would rather never." Kaleyla said. "Speaking of which – what are you doing?"

"My dad keeps his liquor in here!" Ellis blurted as he fumbled with the lock on the exquisite piece of furniture. "I don't suppose you have a paperclip?"

"Why on Earth would I have a paperclip on me?" Kaleyla grumbled. "Leave it alone, you're nine! Way too young to drink."

"I have before...I like rum! Whiskey and tequila are pretty good, too!" Ellis spoke as he attempted to pick the lock with his fingernails. "Are you sure you don't have a paperclip?"

"A paperclip could damage the lock." Kaleyla groaned. "The key has to be somewhere."

"My dad has it." Ellis explained.

"I doubt he takes it everywhere with him." Kaleyla said. "Maybe it's in his study?"

"Maybe!" Ellis effused. "Wait – are you seriously helping me get into it?"

"Up to you, I let you have ONE drink...and you go to bed at ten-thirty." Kaleyla bargained. "The drink should make you tired by then. Fair?"

"What about a cigar?" Ellis grinned.

"Hell no!" Kaleyla shouted. "The smell would linger too much, stick in your clothes, and I'm pretty sure your dad would notice a cigar gone more easily than one of his drinks depleted."

"Fine, fine..." Ellis pouted as they walked into his father's study.

The study was small - half the size of a bedroom. An office chair rested in front of a desk with a filing cabinet next to a computer monitor. The wall next to the desk was a solid face of books. A loveseat sat against the wall adjacent to the books. The wall across from the book shelf and the desk was cluttered with maps and motivational posters. Ellis searched around the desk as Kaleyla scrutinized the books.

Ellis grabbed something from a container near the monitor as Kaleyla felt around between a couple tomes.

"I found a paperclip!" Ellis cheered as Kaleyla rolled her sparkling blue eyes.

"And I found a key." Kaleyla waved the key she retrieved from between the books.

"Is it the right key?" Ellis quaeritated.

"Well, it was between a cocktail encyclopedia and a bartending guide." Kaleyla snickered. "Only one way to know for sure, though. Put the paperclip back, please."

They returned to the living room then Kaleyla fit the key into the lock. After a series of clicking noises the lock released the doors of the cabinet. Ellis marveled at the alcohol as if he was an eighteen-fifties pioneer who had just struck gold. The reflection of his black hair adorned the glasses and bottles with dark, translucent stripes.

"ONE." Kaleyla said sternly.

"I know, I know." Ellis whined as he grabbed a small glass which he filled to the brim with rum. "Drinking like a pirate tonight!"

"They technically drank grog." Kaleyla corrected. "Don't drink enough to be hungover tomorrow, either. Remember we have our tournament in Kung fu class tomorrow afternoon."

"I can handle a glass!" Ellis claimed. He took a sip then coughed.

"Certainly." Kaleyla teased.

"Aren't you going to have any?" Ellis offered.

"Yeah, no thanks." Kaleyla said as Ellis struggled

with another sip. "I don't want any alcohol in me when I kick your ass tomorrow."

CHAPTER 17

Ellis saw the tip of Anat's sword as it emerged from the edge of his peripheral. His instincts were familiar with her speed and realized that an attempted block or parry would be as useless as trying to duck. In a single exhale Ellis blasted all the wind from within his lungs as he fell backward. His sore shoulders curved inward when he did so. Once Ellis was even with Anat he opened his shoulders and jabbed his dagger to the side. Anat completed her attack with her forearm barely an inch from Ellis' face. Ellis had stabbed his dagger across Anat's throat – killing her. Anat's arms fell to her sides as Ellis removed his blade from her neck. A moist tearing sound galloped from her neck as Ellis' dagger slid from the track-like cut. The sword and dagger fell from Anat's robotic hands as she collapsed. Ashen dust from the ground powdered her face upon impact, and the fine soot of the ground thickened from the blood which erupted from her neck. As the rain came to a sudden end there was an instant of complete silence.

He panted for a moment, struggling to ignore the stinging sensation zipping along his cuts while collecting his sword. Ellis knelt above Anat and inspected the armor covering her abdomen. He rolled her onto her back. The machines in her eyes whizzed in attempt to configure themselves for the change in lighting, but sans a living brain to communicate with the blue metal completely sealed itself – crossing over her black-dyed irises and closing above her pupils. Once he discovered the armor's lock he removed the metal plate which covered her side – revealing the thin leathers and dense fabrics beneath. He detached the section of plates which covered her abdomen. Ellis returned to his feet and held the sword over his head. He closed his eyes then thrust the sentimental object through her corpse and into the ground. The light from the sun discolored the horse figurine within the pommel to a blood red.

The sound of a roaring engine skied across the landscape as the Cannon hovered in from behind Ellis. Jasper was in the driver's seat with Justice and Sal in the back.

"Ellis!" Justice shouted. She paled upon noticing that Ellis was covered in his own blood and staggering. "Are you alright?!"

"Yeah..." Ellis squelched. "Nothing that won't...ugh...heal...eventually." Ellis limped toward the Cannon. Sal reached down to help Ellis climb into the passenger seat. "Burn her."

Sal snapped his fingers and Anat's body combusted into an ardent, flickering, aquamarine flame.

"What about your sword?" Justice asked.

"It's hers." Ellis panted. "I kept it all these years to return it...this situation, close enough."

Sal rested his hand upon Ellis' shoulder – channeling his magic. All of Ellis' cuts cauterized.

"That will stop the blood." Sal assured. "Your injures are pretty extensive though, you need Blessed medical technology...or Kepyet's healing...right away. You're a paper cut away from dying of blood loss."

"Heh." Ellis coughed. "I was a cut away from losing my head back there."

"You beat her, though!" Jasper exulted.

"It's finally over." Justice said softly. "No more Sons of War, no more Anat."

"Only the devourers." Sal ruined the mood. "The threat most worthy of concern."

"Isn't that what..." Ellis interrupted himself as a wave of pain sparked through his abdomen. "Shit..." He inhaled slowly.

"Easy..." Justice advised.

"Isn't that what Kepyet is for?" Ellis asked. "Fighting those things?"

"Yes." Sal answered. "But he might not even be strong enough."

"He killed a small army with a thought!" Ellis chuckled. "Not to mention devouring that god...and restoring you."

"Restore? Dude he improved me! I'm more powerful than any elemental ever was!" Sal gasconaded. "But the devourers are unique in their power, even us elementals struggle to comprehend exactly how they work and what they can do. Kepyet may not be enough."

"He better be!" Justice growled. "After everything we did to bring that bastard back."

"Resentment!" Sal laughed. "But not

unwarranted. Kepyet has plans though, and we all have a part to play. He needs our trust. If you can't trust him...at least trust me."

The cannon arrived at Skyrook. Sal aided Ellis with walking into the citadel. Nobody was inside the lobby.

"Anyone here?!" Sal shouted.

Eric entered from one of the halls. "Yeah...Woah! What happened?"

"It was Anat." Justice replied. "She's gone...but Ellis needs help – NOW!"

"Kepyet and Teigao are bickering in the next room." Eric said.

Ellis vanished from the room and reappeared in the ballroom. Kepyet and Teigao were sitting on opposite ends of the table. Ellis spawned next to Kepyet as the fiend raised his hand to touch Ellis' chest. With a flash of black light all of Ellis' injuries were healed. The moment Kepyet released his hand Ellis was teleported back into the lobby.

"Where did he..." Jasper started as he noticed Ellis. "...oh, you're better?!"

Ellis spread his arms as he inspected his body. He then examined his scarred hand with the robotic fingers.

"Really?!" Ellis groaned as he faced the ballroom door. "You couldn't replace my fingers?!" He shook his desecrated fist at the door. "I know you could have fixed this, too!"

Justice clenched her fists and ran toward the door, but was teleported back to her original place.

"Yeah..." Eric sighed. "Kepyet has a teleport field around the room."

"What could he and Teigao be talking about that is so classified?" Justice asked.

"Who knows." Eric shrugged. "I'm sure one of them will share whatever plan they've conjured...eventually"

"At least he healed Ellis." Jasper commented.

Eric changed the subject. "So...are the Warsons finally gone? For good?"

"Yeah." Ellis answered. "Kepyet killed them all, except Anat who he left to me."

"How come you never told me that sword is what you kept in the safe?" Justice asked Ellis.

"Well..." Ellis sighed sadly. "I had my hopes that the sword would only be relevant under more positive circumstances, but I didn't want to jinx my hopes by speaking about them and the sword remain in the case forever. I suppose hanging onto the thing did serve a purpose, to what extent it effected the fight I can't say."

"Why didn't you keep it?" Jasper inquired.

"What would the point have been?" Ellis returned. "Technically it was HER sword. I don't need sentimental objects to remember people by, never saw the purpose in that."

"Like my father's journal?" Justice teased.

"That's different, kid!" Ellis blushed. "That's a document you can use and refer to!"

"You could have used her sword." Sal butted into the discussion. "It was a pretty well-crafted blade. Just saying!"

"I've grown more fond of guns and other things that go "boom!"" Ellis chuckled. "Especially now that age is starting to hit me, eventually there will be a time when my body won't keep pace with my mental reflexes."

"You're still relatively young." Eric commented. "Just have to stay in shape, maybe work on keeping your lungs intact. We also have Kepyet now."

"Immortality isn't my thing." Ellis admitted. "I'll survive as long as I practically can, would rather keep magical stuff to a minimum, though."

The doors to the ballroom swung open. Kepyet and Teigao stepped out of the room. Teigao approached Eric as Kepyet walked toward one of the front corners of the chamber. Several bolts of black lightning burst from Kepyet's body and scuffed the floor.

"What was that?" Justice catechized.

"Nothing worth worrying about..." Kepyet mumbled as he teleported onto the walkway and exited the lobby.

"...Yet." Teigao added.

"What do you know?" Justice's eyes narrowed.

"Enough." Teigao uttered. "Even the wraith himself has weaknesses." Teigao returned his attention to Eric. "A word?"

"No!" Ellis growled. "I'm getting pretty fucking sick of demanding this – but no more secrets!"

"It's not a mortal matter." Teigao assured.

"Neither is anything that's happened the last several mon...last two damn decades!" Ellis snapped.

"Eric lost his power when we faced Vulcan!" Jasper pointed out. "He's a mortal now, unless you've been lying even more to us!"

"I was chosen to use Kepyet's sword." Justice said. "And to be the leading role in resurrecting him. I may be a mortal girl, but that god killer upstairs wanted me to be pretty involved in non-mortal matters!"

"I'm not even mortal!" Sal whined. "What's the excuse for my exclusion?"

"I'm only speaking with Eric." Teigao barked.

"I'm demanding a say in this, too." Eric stepped back. "We promised no more secrets. We're all in this together, now. Whatever you need to tell me you can tell them."

"Very well..." Teigao seethed. "Kepyet intends to accelerate the arrival of the devourers. Having control over when they emerge may grant us an upper hand. That being said, some of them will require great amounts of power to summon and sustain long enough to slay. Kepyet possesses the power to summon and keep them here but he isn't even sure of his ability to slay them all. I am. I remember his patterns back from the war, and his ability to quickly adapt against greater foes. I know not what game he is going to play and involve us in, but I can't shake the concern of him once again becoming a rival. If he turns on us I have a way to defeat him, a vial of Janus' blood. If consumed it will temporarily give the drinker the god's power over doorways. It can be used to detour the flow of the Styx onto Kepyet."

"Oh, yes!" The spider's voice echoed from the next room.

Everyone was startled by her intrusion. The spider marched toward the group with a small vial of golden blood in her hand.

"Hand it over!" Teigao bellowed.

"You don't trust us." The spider whimpered. "There is so much distrust here. But it seems that you, Teigao, are the least trusted here. Before you and Kepyet had your little tête-à-têt he instructed me to retrieve this."

"You lie!" Teigao quavered. "If he wanted it...if he even knew it existed he would have teleported it into his hand and crushed it!"

"When he killed Janus he knew something was

missing." The spider giggled. "He wanted ME to retrieve it for this exact moment. To make a point."

She smashed the vial onto the ground. The golden blood flickered as its energy was exhausted. Teigao balled his fists.

"You do have a choice if you trust my master or not." The spider said. "But we won't have any plans of betrayal."

"I should kill you where you stand!" Teigao yelled.

"I think everyone needs to take a moment..." Justice tried to intervene.

"Do it!" The spider laughed. "See how well that works out for you. Kepyet has dozens of plans and has foreseen a multitude of futures, in many of them you aren't vital to our success. Neither am I so really all killing me, and in doing so getting yourself killed, would accomplish is making the resources more manageable."

"Enough of this crap!" Sal interjected. "The devourers are the enemy, not each other."

The spider smiled as Teigao growled through his teeth. They vacated the room in opposite directions.

"Well...I need some rest." Ellis announced. "It's been a long day."

"Literally!" Jasper added as he followed Ellis to the living quarters. "Kepyet froze time like five or six times...we've been in today for..."

"Too tired for this shit." Ellis cut Jasper off.

"I'm going to see if I can ease tensions with the arachnid." Eric said.

"I'll help, I know her pretty well." Sal joined Eric.

Justice shook her head. The constant

bickering between everyone had grown irksome. It was also concerning as they had argued over the same few subjects almost daily for over a year now. The hostility was distracting and all the distrust could lead to failure against the real enemies. She acknowledged her own animosity toward Kepyet and how that could get in the way – but how was she to overcome these feelings? His sins and what he put her through? Would it be proper for her to cut him some slack by assuming that in relinquishing his humanity that his moral compass had also been lost? Justice decided to find Kepyet and speak with him, hoping to comfortably arrive at better terms.

Justice ventured through the corridors leading onto the ramparts. She hoped that Kepyet wished to be found, because if he desired solitude he would conceal himself. This also meant that if she found him that it would be by his intention. Justice struggled with the unnerving sensation of knowing that seemingly nothing happens outside of Kepyet's designs and predictions. Sure enough – upon her first step onto the rampart she saw Kepyet leaning on the rail – looking out into the field.

"There is beauty in this desolation." Kepyet mumbled. "Pondering the ghost of what there once was. An answer to the many theories and assumptions made by man in regards to an apocalypse. Two hundred millenniums of humanity...nearly four eons of life since the first prokaryote swam within the primordial waters...all ends here." He paused for a moment. "How willing are you to defend what we have left? To secure a leap of faith that, once this is over, there may be a chance to rebuild?"

"Most life is gone, all is infertile." Justice commented as she approached the crystal railing and leaned upon it beside Kepyet. "I can't give you an honest answer for what I would do to buy us time. I don't even know myself."

"You're too welcoming of the grim." Kepyet sniggered as he raised his left fist. Justice peeked at his hand – noticing that there was something within his palm. Kepyet opened his hand to reveal the flash drive containing his alchemy notes.

"Is that what I think it is?" Justice marveled. "What use is it to you, now, though?"

"Records." Kepyet replied as the drive vanished. "And study material for yourself. With the power of a philosopher's stone we may be able to revive life."

"You could also resurrect many of the dead, can't you also grant fertility?" Justice inquired.

"I can do many things...having taken the powers of every god I've slain. Unfortunately there are safeguards which were put in place long ago. Not necessarily preventative measures against your suggestion...but cause for complications not even I could manage. There are also the elder ones...primordial beings which predate existence as we understand it. They care not for what occurred here, I could have cut down every god and titan without appearing on their radar. But if I were to reset the natural order of things..." Kepyet sighed. "There is a loophole and that is the power of a philosopher's stone."

"And you know the last ingredient?" Justice asked.

"I might. The concept of the stone may have been misinterpreted by our ancestors." Kepyet spoke as if he was concealing information, but

Justice wasn't comfortable enough to call him out. She did feel unease upon hearing "our ancestors" coming from behind his mask and had to remind herself that Kepyet was once no less human than herself. Although the being currently standing beside her was a demonic wraith of sorts, twenty years ago he was a human man named Cooper Thomas. Justice wondered what visage hid behind the mask – if any. The face of a monster, a skull, or just a middle-aged man?

"My father trusted Cooper." Justice uttered. "Would he have trusted Kepyet?"

"You accept the distinction." Kepyet praised. "That is where your mother struggled. I'm not entirely certain, but your father was both an intellectual and a man of practicality. He would have understood my intentions had I chosen to include him in my crusade, though I doubt he would have supported my methods."

"That isn't what I asked..." Justice growled.

"Trust comes in many forms, child." Kepyet said. "Lucien would have trusted my intentions, my goals...even if he didn't support my endgame. He would have trusted how far I would go to succeed. He would have trusted my word...factoring in those breeds of trust...the answer is no. The paradox that he would have trusted me enough to not trust me."

"So, how can you expect me to?" Justice hissed.

"I expect you to trust yourself." Kepyet replied. "You have superior intuition, admirable instincts. It is time to utilize those traits."

"I suppose you trusted me with your resurrection." Justice sighed.

Kepyet took a step back from the rail. Several

bolts of black lightning sparked from his body and scorched the ground between Justice and himself. His sword appeared below his right hand. Justice glared at the shadowed weapon.

"You miss this." Kepyet said. "The feel of my accursed blade."

"I don't know what you're talking about." Justice lied, though unaware of her own answer.

"Yes you do..." Kepyet teased. "It's a fine weapon. Although wielding it possesses a burden of unease it syncs well with the spirit."

"It's...it is your sword." Justice stuttered as the castle reddened from the sunset.

"I can be generous." Kepyet mumbled as he waved his free hand. The Pyroguard's Blade manifested in Justice's palm. "Duel me for it."

"You truly are mad." Justice refused. "I'm just a human girl...a mortal human girl. You're...you."

"At this point are you seriously so fearful of a greater foe?" Kepyet laughed.

"You killed a highly trained army with a thought then consumed the soul of their god." Justice argued. "I was butchered by Anat – another human with no magical powers."

"You also felled both a Centimane and my top general." Kepyet taunted.

"Luck on both counts." Justice attested.

Kepyet gestured his left arm – possessing Justice's right arm to raise her weapon and point it at the fiend.

"I'll be fair." Kepyet assured as Justice willfully kept her sword pointed at him. "I'll fight like a mortal. Like a human. None of my powers, no enhanced abilities and no additional senses will be used to give me a combat advantage. Here is my offer to you, Justice. If you can land a single hit on me...even if it's just a scratch...just a tap...I'll give you my sword."

"You're certain I desire it." Justice breathed.

"You may decline." Kepyet offered.

Justice didn't wish to decline. She couldn't comprehend why – but she did want Kepyet's sword. Whatever magic remained within the weapon had seduced her spirit. The weapon was more than sword...although Justice didn't know what other uses the object had she subtly realized its importance.

"One hit?" Justice whispered.

"Less than that even. One particle of your weapon contacts one particle of my body." Kepyet confirmed.

"And if you hit me?" Justice queried.

"I won't." Kepyet assured. "Because you aren't going to let me. Hit me."

Confused by Kepyet's statement Justice thought it best not to confuse herself further by asking more questions. She raised her weapon then attempted to strike Kepyet.

CHAPTER 18

Anat rested face-down in the black gravel of the underworld. She awoke then slowly rose to her feet. Immediately feeling something wasn't quite right she examined her hands – albeit red in color, they were flesh! She contemplated her hands, then slowly scrutinized her surroundings. The area was foggy, and the sky a pestilent tan with swirling red and black clouds. Her clothing was a pale gray imitation of the black shirt and pants she wore beneath her armor. Anat lifted her right leg and bent it back and forth as she swayed it side to side. She listened carefully for the sounds of metal and wires, but heard nothing. Before she could figure out what was happening a voice in the distance startled her.

"Why are we slowing?" A woman's voice barked.

Anat sprinted toward a boulder in the opposite direction from where the voice came from.

"A soul." A man's voice answered.

Anat hid behind the boulder – feeling vulnerable without any weapons or knowledge of what was happening. She peeked through a small hole between a curve on the rock and the ground. The fog cleared to reveal a river as the ferry of the underworld approached the bank. Ronny and Unity stood at the bow.

"I don't see anyone." Unity stated.

"I sense them." Ronny returned. "They're confused...hiding."

"So, leave them?" Unity suggested. "They obviously don't wish for us to find them."

"I know you're out there!" Ronny shouted, ignoring Unity. "Don't be afraid, I don't charge for passage. You will be in good company while we figure out a resting place."

Anat remained still as she realized that she had died. How, though? She had honed her fighting skills more than Ellis had. Her health surpassed his, as did her ambition. Where was her mistake? Anat had no intention to rest. She had devoted her life to fighting and that is what she decided to continue to do. Perhaps the afterlife could present new, more interesting opportunities.

"Ronny..." Unity nagged. "They aren't interested."

"Beyond those hills is the Phlegethon." Ronny said. "Do not go there...the fires destroy a soul beyond death. Don't touch the water from this river...the Styx, either. One touch rips your soul apart and only leaves a phantom madness of who you once were behind...forever as part of the river. Approach the water and call for the ferry, when you decide to come onboard."

Anat heard Ronny's words, but refused to

board the boat. The Phlegethon sounded interesting to her. Fires? Fire has use in the mortal world...perhaps there are similarities she could exploit.

"Still nothing." Unity groaned.

Ronny sighed and tapped his oar. The ferry drifted away from the gravel then accelerated downstream. Anat ventured over the dunes as the fog gradually re-infested the landscape. She used the sky as a reference to ensure she continued in the same direction. About a mile from the first hill she saw a river of ardent flames. The ground rumbled in response to the violent bursts of energy from the Phlegethon.

Anat approached the flaming river. The lack of heat made her feel uneasy, but then she considered that it must not mean much because she barely felt anything at all. Is death really this boring? Vexation momentarily replaced her bewilderment as she realized THIS was the fate of everyone she had slain. They should have endured worse treatment, and their pain should have followed them beyond the grave!

She poked the liquid fire with her left pointer finger. The entire finger vaporized and channeled a surge of pain through her body. Anat fell backwards and onto a strange white rock concealed by the gravel. Upon landing the finger was replaced with a powdery stone copy of itself. Anat rolled onto her side then stood – examining the prosthetic. She felt the stone with the fingers on her right hand. It was hard, and dense. The texture was like limestone, but the hardness was greater than diamond. What was this material, and why did she suddenly feel as if she had command over it?

Anat focused on the stone finger and imagined a knife. The material vibrated and smoothly, albeit slowly, transformed into a knife. She then imagined a claw, and the material took shape. When she relaxed her mind the stone returned to being a finger. She noticed the empty white stone on the ground then caressed it with her prosthetic finger. Unfortunately she couldn't modify the material that wasn't a part of her body. Out of curiosity she reapproached the river and motioned her stone finger toward the fire. The river's seemingly non-existent heat softened the stone. It became gelatinous as it neared the otherworldly flames. She retracted her hand with a smile. The stone rehardened.

She crouched down to dig into the gravel with her hands. Below the gravel was a fine powder-like substance. The grains were small and light like ash, but easy to pack together – like clay. What luck! Anat dug the hole as close to the flaming river as she could without touching the fire. Once the barrier between the river and her hole was only a centimeter in width she transformed her finger into a mattock and struck the top of the barrier. Fire from the Phlegethon slithered through the impression and into the hole. Anat dug another hole – this time she brushed the gravel away from the material beneath it before digging. This new hole she dug into the shape of a bardiche.

Anat gripped the larger stone in the ground. She struggled to lift the rock. The stone was roughly the size of a beach ball but felt as if it was much larger. Anat held the ore above the fire in the hole she had dug until it became amorphous. Once the rock started to drip she tossed it into her other hole. It took the shape of the container before hardening. Pleased with the result, Anat lifted the half-weapon from the mold then placed it on the ground – flipping it onto its side. She carefully dug a hole beneath the almost-bardiche as identical in shape and depth as possible. Anat moved the item aside then prospected the ground around her. Surely, there must be more of this mysterious material?

Unbeknownst to Anat, the ore she discovered was baetylus, and she was near old mining grounds. Although the once rich seams had been exhausted billions of years ago there were still a few traces of the material. Anat found another small boulder no more than a hundred feet from the first rock. This one was slightly larger, but she was still able to carry it. To regulate the size she allowed the rock to drip into the fire for a moment before tossing it into her second hole. As the second half of her bardiche cooled she held the flat side of the first half near the fire until it softened. Once Anat noticed the first sign of melting she slammed the two halves together – completing her weapon.

Anat's new bardiche had a short handle, but a viciously long blade with an elegant, slender curve. The weapon was far from light, but the craftsmanship allowed the weight to be used to gain momentum and strike with as much precision as power. Satisfied with her wicked new toy, she strolled along the Styx – carrying her bardiche across her torso like a scythe.

***

Ronny and Unity parked the ferry on the shore of a field. To their right was a narrow stream which connected the Styx to the Acheron, and to their left was an extended channel of the Styx. Crumbled baetylus gravel, drained of its life-altering magic decorated the landscape. A stream of red smoke arose from a depression in the distance.

"Curious." Unity remarked. "Could it be the portal to Muspelheim?"

"Energy from it." Ronny answered. "I believe there would be more of a show if the portal was open. That does prove activity though. Let's go."

Ronny and Unity traveled across the field toward the crimson gas. The tainted pink ground mimicked the fog and the sky, forcing dependency on their other senses. Within the crater was a circle of broken pillars with Nordic runes carved into them. The gems within the runes once glowed, but had long lost their radiance. A puddle of water from the Styx menaced the far left curve of the crater – dripping from the bend of the river along that edge. Two ominous figures stood in the center of the crater attempting to direct the smoke. They instantly halted their actions to address Ronny and Unity.

The taller creature stood over eight feet. Two skeletal, bat-like wings extended from his spine. He wore a blindfold over his eyes. A series of small, walnut-colored horns formed a crown along the top of his bald head. His skin was ivory, and the flesh had rotted from his cheeks and most of his jaws. The top half of his face maintained its skin – forming a mask over the skull. A strip of flesh rested below his nose and supported the small patch of lip above his two front teeth. The heads of several dead serpents dangled from beneath his jaw bone. Armor crafted from a black synthetic fiber covered the fiend's body. Bundles of long, red feathers protruded from behind each shoulder, and ticking, silver watches dangled over each kneecap.

The second creature was significantly shorter – not even as tall as Ronny. A worn, beige towel covered his face and a gold hood concealed the top of his head. His body was covered by a plain, red vest. Gray sleeves enveloped his arms and red gauntlets protected his hands. The shorter creature wore the same type of armored trousers as his companion.

"Impossible!" Unity screeched.

"You know them?" Ronny growled.

"What have we here..." The taller monster cackled. He had the voice of a heavy, lifelong smoker.

"You're both dead!" Unity screamed. The darkness of her eye sockets seeped through her flesh as she shouted, and her teeth momentarily withered.

"Who are they?" Ronny catechized.

The black around Unity's eyes faded, but her flesh began to chap.

"The tall one...that is Pleonex!" Unity quavered. "The shorter one is Gehenna. He looks different, he changed his armor. The blind one though – he was a master hypnotist. They're both supposed to be dead!"

"Technically the two of you aren't all that lively!" Pleonex laughed. "What brings you here, to us? Don't you have a boat to sail?"

"Just following a lead." Ronny answered. "But now that we're here – I can't bring myself to allow you to repair that portal!"

"How did you survive?!" Unity hollered. "Gehenna – you were run through with water from the Styx! One drop is enough to shred a soul!"

Gehenna twisted his head back and forth between Unity and Pleonex, almost as if he was confused. Pleonex tapped his knees together - causing the arms on his clocks to turn. Ronny and Unity were out of range, but Gehenna appeared to lose all independence upon hearing the tap. A scimitar appeared in Gehenna's right hand. Ronny's oar encased itself in metal in response. Gehenna charged uphill toward Ronny – who remained still in a defensive stance. Meanwhile Anat noticed the cloud of red smoke. With her interest piqued, she jogged toward the crater. Eventually she reached a point where the only way ahead was across the Styx. Anat charged as quickly as she could and skipped across the river in two leaps. Upon the first footfall her left eye disintegrated, and upon the second her incisors. Both her teeth and eye were replaced by baetylus which shifted colors to mimic the appearance of her original organs.

CHAPTER 19

Justice and Kepyet sparred on top the ramparts of Skyrook. Kepyet barely moved, but his subtle contortions and minor actions in footwork allowed him to evade the majority of Justice's attacks. Those he couldn't dodge were deflected and parried. Occasionally Kepyet would attempt to strike Justice with potentially lethal maneuvers – disrupting her focus. Justice decided to apply her creativity to the battle.

Knowing that in most duels the objective is to kill she switched her focus toward crippling strikes. Justice jammed her sword downward toward Kepyet's foot. As he twirled his weapon to block the attack Justice flicked her sword upward to Kepyet's armpit. He spun his blade to knock her sword away. Justice used the power of his strike to accelerate her twirling slash at his knees. Kepyet casually folded his left leg back to allow Justice's sword to pass millimeters below his knee. As her weapon passed between Kepyet's legs he replaced his left foot on the ground and bent his right leg back. Realizing her attack failed Justice motioned her sword toward Kepyet's right elbow. He twisted his body to the side as he whipped his blade up to knock hers away.

"You can do so much better." Kepyet taunted.

Justice ignored the fiend's remark as she persisted. The challenge was to land a single hit. Perhaps a scratch would be easier? She stepped back while lashing her sword across Kepyet's torso – still missing him. Justice performed a check step in hopes of startling Kepyet during her lunge. He remained still and calmly beat her sword away. Before she could react he beat her sword a second time – forcing her arm beyond the back of her head. As Justice recovered her weapon Kepyet jammed the point of his sword against her neck. The poke was deep enough to be felt but didn't penetrate her skin.

"Keep trying." Kepyet ordered as he pulled his sword away in preparation for another strike. "In a real duel you'd be dead, never allow a foe to force your weapon out of your line of sight. If it does happen then act defensively, retrieve your weapon after you're a safe distance from your opponent."

"How is this even fair?" Justice whined. "You're how old?"

"Eighteen years younger than my Earth age, countless decades older factoring in how I managed time on my island. I mimic the experience of souls I consume, but none of that is relevant. In this moment I am a man with a sword, and it is in such moments your concerns would be wise to lie." Kepyet replied as he twirled his weapon toward Justice.

Justice leaned back as she spun her blade away from Kepyet's. She had hoped that the parallel positioning of their weapons would have allowed her a strike to his wrist – but he retracted his arm barely in time. As Justice's sword extended to the previous position of Kepyet's wrist he took advantage of her opening and beat his blade against hers before sliding it down to her weapon's guard. Once Kepyet's blade tapped the guard of hers he swung his sword out – pushing Justice's away. She ducked to evade a strike to her neck then launched herself upwards to headbutt. Kepyet's mask cracked into a smile as he stepped back to dodge. Kepyet hopped backwards to avoid the following swing from Justice's sword. She was finally taking the fight more seriously - meaning the proper time had come.

Justice and Kepyet clashed swords at a more rapid and ferocious pace. An atypical sensation overcame Justice while they dueled. She couldn't comprehend exactly what was happening to her, but she felt somewhat invaded. Normally this would have offended and angered her, but in this case her subconscious urged her to accept it. Was that her natural reaction? She wondered if Kepyet was possessing her or executing a subtle form of mind control. The purpose of this fight was still lost to her – yet she persisted with the duel and the set objective. Had she become an unwilling participant in an experiment of his?

The racing thoughts delayed a realization – that Justice was now holding up her end of the fight! Her moves were mostly instinctual, and with every clash of their swords she felt her muscles gain the ability to pull off more complicated maneuvers with the sword. Kepyet was teaching her how to fight and uploading each move into her mind. Justice retreated and lowered her blade.

"Tired already?" Kepyet teased.

"You said you wouldn't use magic!" Justice blurted. "You're doing something to my mind!"

"Language, my dear. My claim was that I wouldn't use my powers to give me an advantage in combat." Kepyet corrected.

"Toying with my mind is -" Justice began before Kepyet interjected.

"Giving YOU a combat advantage. My fighting knowledge is being uploaded into your mind." Kepyet explained. "Unless you would prefer to further rely on luck to carry you against superior foes."

Kepyet staggered upon finishing his sentence with a cough. Black lightning sparked from his body into the ground for a moment – this time the surge lasted noticeably longer than the previous incidents.

"And that?" Justice snarled. "What is that about?"

"Nothing...nothing to do with you." Kepyet assured as he recovered.

"It's still something. I would like to know what's going on, the Blessed don't really follow it but we're trying to have a no secrets code around here...and you're technically a team mate now." Justice said.

"More like team leader!" Kepyet laughed. "I'll tell you this much. The corporeal human vessel is limiting...even when it's three-quarters baetylus."

"Will that be a problem?" Justice worried.

"Million dollar question." Kepyet answered. "I

recommend that you get some sleep. Tomorrow is a big day."

"You're summoning them so soon?" Justice quavered.

"Only Bakasura..." Kepyet reassured. "He should be feeble...and easily slain."

"And then what?" Justice asked.

"There's Lotan. Once he falls the only significant devourers remaining are Tiamat and Apophis. Those last two may or may not be hiding behind an army of leviathans." Kepyet explained.

"And you can take them all?" Justice said doubtfully.

"Perhaps." Kepyet mumbled. "I still own this sword, but it's merely a tool. Consider the relevance of my planning, you stand beside me this moment for a reason. Soon you will realize your part."

Kepyet snapped his fingers. Justice was teleported into her bed as her uniform was swapped with her sleeping clothes. Before she could fully comprehend what had transpired this evening she fell asleep. Kepyet gazed across the night sky from the rampart.

"A curious, determined mind...fit for survival." Kepyet muttered. "You would be proud of her, Lucien."

"You do know he's Styx waste." A playful, yet mysterious voice said in a heavy Haitian accent from behind Kepyet. The being concealed himself in a shadowed corner.

"Of course." Kepyet answered. "And I see you survived all these years...as planned."

"It was my plan to survive, friend." The phantom chuckled. An orange spark flickered in front of the being's face. A cloud of tobacco smoke blew past Kepyet's mask.

"I haven't been able to taste or smell a cigar since..." Kepyet sighed.

"Oh, mortal pleasures!" The creature giggled. "I'm no mortal but still get the effect. You've fallen completely apart!" The creature burst into laughter.

"I'm killing Bakasura tomorrow." Kepyet said. "Tiamat will eventually rise again. Before my...previous departure...I entrusted you with something."

The phantom released another puff of smoke. "Yes...yes, yes, Kepyet. I still have it. But know I have the upper hand of our deal now. The favor I acknowledged was storing the treasure, I have not forgotten your sins!"

Kepyet raised his right hand; the cigar was teleported into his fingers. The baetylus around Kepyet's lips faded as he took a drag from the cigar. He crushed the wrapped tobacco in his hand as the flaky black material wrapped back over his decaying lips.

"I don't need my taste to know yours is still poor." Kepyet barked. "Play your games...but Tiamat will be after what I've given to you. Be my foe and I'll ensure it's recovered before you fall into her belly."

"Shit." The phantom snickered. "Your overconfidence competes with only my dick in size!"

"Your crudeness confirms your health." Kepyet groaned.

"I want more from our deal." The spirit growled. "You know where to find me when the time comes that you're willing to negotiate."

The spirit vanished, Kepyet shook his head

before returning his gaze to the night sky.

CHAPTER 20

Cooper Thomas was resting on the floor in the center of his meditation room. The chamber was mostly circular with an exquisitely carved mahogany door as the only exit. A series of windows wrapped around the entirety of the room looking out into the lush green forest surrounding his home. Brightly colored roses of different hues bloomed all throughout the narrow garden between the building and the trees. Sparkling granite stones haphazardly marked the small ponds. Two incense sticks burned between each window within the room. One stick of each pair was smokeless while the other produced a thick fog. Cooper sat on his knees.

An ardent light penetrated his windows. The flare burned his eyes, but he opened them nonetheless in an effort to discover what had just happened. Cooper found himself standing on a stone platform near the edge of a cliff. Massive, golden statues of judicial scales surrounded the platform. In a state of confusion he examined his surroundings. Between two of the scales there was a golden door. As Cooper approached the door it swung open. Rather than walking into the room Cooper was transitioned into the area. The visual sensation was like pointing a camera through the door then zooming in.

The chamber was dimly lit by the reflected sunlight radiating off the orichalcum and golden walls. Waterfalls dropped from the ceiling along the wall into small ponds and fountains. Potted flora with fat leaves decorated the wall space between the falls. A couple Greek klines sat by a table in the center of the room, each one holding royal blue pillows and cushions. A kylix filled with wine appeared on the table. A soft, but stern feminine voice echoed into the room from the next corridor. "Sit." She ordered.

Cooper approached one of the klines and reluctantly reclined onto the ancient couch. The goddess Nemesis entered the room. She smirked upon identifying her guest. "Cooper Thomas...do you recognize me?"

"Scale statues, these recliners...Greek...you're also blind. You are...Nemesis?" Cooper guessed.

Nemesis curtsied. "Indeed."

"This is a dream...I must have fallen asleep." Cooper muttered under his breath.

"You are in a deep meditative state." Nemesis smiled. "Are you doubtful?"

She marched to the center of the room then rested upon the kline across from Cooper.

"I'm in my house...was..." Cooper mumbled. "Is this real? Or is it a dream?"

"How real are your other dreams?" Nemesis purred as she sat up in her seat. She reached her arm across the table to caress Cooper's cheek with her hand. The awkwardness of the gesture made him feel uncomfortable, however the unnatural softness of her skin was calming. Even the minor scrape from her fingernails felt oddly therapeutic. She retracted her arm. "Real enough?"

"I can feel in my dreams...but this is...curiously different." Cooper confessed. "Surely, there is a purpose?"

"A wise assumption." Nemesis answered. "There have been suspicious activities happening as of late. From what I have perceived Zeus has been in regular contact with Amun-Ra and and Odin. The different pantheons never interact, not for thousands of your years. If anything he would have sent Hermes...not the case."

"And why is this business of mine if it's even classified to yourself?" Cooper inquired.

"I'm a goddess of justice, my duty is to ensure all is fair and kept in check...as directed by the natural balance of the universe and the edicts set by the elder ones. I feel...disturbed." Nemesis paused. "There is great potential in you. I read your heart, Cooper. The age of your soul, your will, your psychic awareness, what you intend to gain in contrast to the great loss I feel in your heart. I am forbidden from acting on my feelings, it's not pleasant being interdicted from doing my assigned divine task."

"Understandable, but why am I here? I'm a mortal man." Cooper stated.

"I can offer you more." Nemesis said. She raised her right hand and the gold in her aura condensed into a glittery ball of light. "I feel there are dark times ahead for man. You may be able to accomplish what I am unable to try." She released the orb into Cooper's body. His eyes flickered with gold light for a couple moments, when the light works came to an end his eyes faded to a beige color. "You resist?" Nemesis snarled.

"I do." Cooper answered. "There must be someone more worthy than I."

"I offer it to you." Nemesis argued.

"And I am honored, sincerely." Cooper assured. "But I refuse the gift. It interrupts my own balance."

"You aren't new to sacrifice." Nemesis hissed.

"My familiarity with its toll works against your plea." Cooper said. "I apologize for offending you, I don't mean to come off as ungrateful...but I will not use your essence."

"I leave it with you..." Nemesis pouted. "Along with the choice to embrace it or not... I recommend you accept it, though. In the coming years it WILL be needed if my intuition is correct. It always is."

The room collapsed and Cooper's eyes flew open. Finding himself back in his home, he fell onto his back. He felt a rumble against his hip as his phone went off. Cooper reached into his pocket and excavated his smartphone. He pressed the notification button and a hologram projected from the top of his device. It was a simple box with laser-projected text in the center. The top corner of the text read "Lucien" and the main body read "Cooper, I just learned that I'm going to be a father! I know you might be worried it might get in the way of our research. Don't, though. Now I have more reason than ever to complete the project! I need us to succeed, I want a better world for my child to grow up in. Correction - *perfect world."

Cooper deactivated the holographic screen as he dropped his phone. He examined his hands. Gold static flickered between his fingers.

"Dammit." He uttered. "Is this your way of putting pressure on me?"

CHAPTER 21

Ellis stood outside Skyrook smoking a cigarette while watching the sunrise. He marveled at the way the clouds warped the sun's hue to a blood red and how much of it reflected off Skyrook and onto the stale grass. The spider stepped outside beside him then lit a cigarette herself. Ellis resisted eye contact.

"I don't get it." She proclaimed. "These little things are so awful, all the chemicals. Not to mention what smoke inhalation does to lungs."

"It's simple." Ellis said. "I'm entitled to a minor pleasure in this hell. I don't give a damn about the side effects, doubt they'll hit me before I get killed anyway." They both took a puff from their cigarettes. "What about you?" Ellis spoke quickly. "You're smoking too. Doesn't that burn your...however many eyes?"

"The body isn't mine." The spider giggled. "I don't care about this bitch, Kepyet even granted me immunity from medical death. This body could have cancer that lasts far beyond the point in which it would be fatal...I would personally be fine while the girl suffers. I hope for that. Though I don't agree with it I understand why the fearful race that is man squished my kind. The torture though, not necessary."

"How could a girl like that be so diabolical?" Ellis queried.

"Your old friend was worse." The spider remarked. "I don't have answer for you."

"Aren't you a bit of a psycho yourself?" Ellis asked.

"I was a predator." The spider answered. "Hatched to hunt and survive. That was the purpose of my life, just a gear in the ecosystem."

"And now?" Ellis blew out a gust of smoke.

"I'm still figuring that one out." She replied.

"Aren't we all." Ellis chuckled. "Kepyet and Teigao seem to have it together."

"Kepyet." The spider confirmed. "The Blessed are pawns without a king...or a board."

"Have a name?" Ellis asked.

"Never had a use for one." She smirked. "Your language is constructed well enough to allow it."

"Awkwardly." Ellis groaned.

"Would you be more comfortable with me if I had a name?" She smiled.

"Probably." Ellis shrugged.

"I was a cousin of the tarantula." She explained. "How about "Tara"?"

"I like it." Ellis confessed. "I can almost think of you as a person, when I don't see your spider eyes anyway."

"Flattering." Tara groused.

Ellis and Tara continued to watch the sunrise while smoking their cigarettes in unison. They stood less than a foot away from each other.

Justice stepped outside. "Hey Elli..." With widened eyes she paused. "You two are getting along?"

"We bonded over the activity you hate." Ellis chortled.

"Also my name is Tara now." Tara added.

"What was it you wanted?" Ellis asked Justice.

"Right..." Justice blinked in an addled state. "This is a thing now, alright. Okay, well...sorry, you two are seriously getting along?"

"I wasn't the one with the problem to begin with." Tara opined. "He was just salty over me beating you guys to Atlantis...and he doesn't like arachnids."

"She's alright I suppose." Ellis said.

"Well I'm glad you guys are on good terms?" Justice shook her head. "As I was saying, get ready soon. Once Kepyet and Teigao are done with their umpteenth argument we're heading out to where Kepyet wants to raise Bakasura."

"Alright, I'm going to need one more smoke before this nonsense." Ellis answered.

"I'm prepared to leave whenever." Tara said.

"Well...make haste." Justice ordered as she strolled back into the castle.

"How do you like being human?" Ellis asked Tara. "I mean...close to."

"It's different." Tara admitted. "Arachnid brains are very, very different from your human brains. I can't exactly describe it because of how different they are. I had great instincts, some memory...even basic emotion. Ability to reason is where it got tricky, that was mainly tied in with hunting instincts. Though much of that was sensations and reactions programmed into my

DNA. I also recall having a much different perception of time."

"Which mind do you prefer?" Ellis pestered.

"They both have their advantages and disadvantages. It matters not how I feel about it personally. I wasn't meant to have a human-like mind. So much in this time is out of place." Tara perceived.

"Make the most of what you have now." Ellis implored.

Hours later everyone in Skyrook convened in the ballroom. Kepyet stood with a minor hunch and thin streams of sickly dark smoke steamed from the cracks in his mask. The zipping sounds of static electricity echoed throughout the building as Kepyet's armor conducted the ominous charge from within his soul. Albeit everyone noticed the odd condition Justice felt as if she was the only person phased by it. Kepyet's attempt to reassure her wasn't successful. Teigao pouted in the corner of the room – expressing his disapproval of Kepyet's plan.

Kepyet ambled to the center of the room. "Is everyone prepared for this?"

"Do we have a choice?" Eric remarked.

"Sure!" Tara replied. "My master won't punish you should you choose to be a coward."

"Not that I fully support this..." Ellis started. "But I'm not seeing a better option. As suicidal as this is the best way to take down a greater enemy is to catch them off-guard."

Tara stood next to Ellis as she acknowledged his comment with a soft smile. Sal opened his mouth to state his opinion.

"Our combined might should be enough for Bakasura." Sal assured. "It might even be fun!

Pulling that thing out before he's ready, we can taunt him! It's like catching someone with their pants down!"

"Where did you learn that expression?" Justice quipped.

"Remember I lived with Ronny and Callum for many years." Sal answered.

"Are you done chattering?" Kepyet snarled. "Time counts."

"I have a question!" Jasper yelped. "Why are we doing this in New Jericho?"

"The walls are difficult to devour." Kepyet replied. "It's also remote. The odds of interference are minuscule. Can we go now?"

"Please." Ellis and Tara chorused, then awkwardly glanced at each other.

"I'll stay here." Teigao declared. "Someone needs to survive when this foolish stunt fails."

"Survival doesn't always constitute victory." Kepyet disparaged. "Let's go."

Kepyet clanked his gauntlets together. As the vibration of the sound wave faded the party appeared within the walled, barren field of New Jericho. Ellis, Eric, Jasper, Justice, Kepyet, Sal, Tara, and the remaining Blessed soldiers examined their surroundings while their brains readjusted from the teleport.

"Spare no time." Kepyet ordered as he utilized his telekinetic abilities to throw a pile of colorless debris from a stone foundation. The land shook from the gravitational shifts when Kepyet forced the sky into his trademark eclipse. He opened his wings in addition to releasing torrents of cloudy lightning from his body. Gesturing his hands like conductor's batons he directed the foul energies into a point. Kepyet maintained the charge until he was too weak to stand. The fiend collapsed as an unnatural, almost mechanical screaming noise bellowed from within the small hole Kepyet had burned into the ground.

Everyone stood back from the scorch mark. Ellis and Tara awkwardly bumped shoulders when instinctively stepping toward the same spot behind themselves. In a puff of the noxious devourer gas a leviathan appeared.

"Aww hell..." Ellis groaned. "Not those things again!"

Five more leviathans sprouted from Kepyet's mark. All six of them fixated their eyes upon the kneeling demon. Kepyet kicked himself onto his feet and with a snap of both fingers disintegrated all the creatures. Sal conjured a spark in each hand but allowed them to extinguish upon witnessing Kepyet slaying the beasts.

"Damn..." Jasper marveled.

Kepyet channeled more energy into the hole.

"Bakasura!" Kepyet roared. "You cannot hide behind Apep's drones forever!"

Kepyet collapsed from exhaustion. The screaming noise was again heard, this time louder. Devourer fog sprayed from the hole then condensed into a different creature. Bakasura emerged. He stood roughly four meters in height. A gold trench coat flopped around his back and sides. His fat belly protruded outward. Bakasura's skin shifted between phantom white and bruise blue. Tiny fangs were visible within the centers of his dark eyes. Incisors dangled from the nostrils of the monster's pudgy nose. Large, unkempt hair crowned Bakasura's head. A few chunky, slobbery tongues squirmed from his scalp - each one barbed with haphazardly grown teeth. The bottom half of Bakasura's circular face was occupied by his grotesque mouth which lingered between an uncomplimentary frame of thick, tire-like, chapped lips. Two fuzzy yellow tusks desecrated by brown cavities bent outward from the corners of Bakasura's palate. His bushy, grimy black beard merged into his tick-infested chest chair. Countless mouths of various sizes appeared and reappeared on the giant's stomach. A tattered brown loin cloth immodestly covered his groin. The legs of black insects were indistinguishable from the lengthy pubic hairs bursting from the edges of the rancid breechclout. His hands and feet were smaller than what was natural for a humanoid of such stature. Pillars of drool squirted from each mouth as it faded in and out of reality.

Bakasura shook the earth with his screeching roar. The force of his ravaging skreak struck fissures throughout the ground. Kepyet prepared to throw a bolt of black lightning at Bakasura but the devourer skid toward the fiend posthaste with his fist balled. Kepyet was punched with enough force to torpedo him through the first pane of the great wall.

Sal ignited both hands as Ellis and Tara drew their pistols. Jasper frantically dug through his satchel in search of grenades. Justice equipped the Pyroguard's blade as Eric clipped his hand cannon together. The Blessed soldiers aimed their weapons at the devourer – unable to determine where to focus their fire.

Bakasura roared as he shifted his attention to Sal – who threw a massive, but quick plane-sized fireball at the devourer. Bakasura's stomach opened into a mouth to swallow the flame. Sal channeled more flames into his hands as Bakasura opened his jaws to spit the initial fire back at Sal. Sal embraced the attack as it raised the temperature within his body. This time Sal channeled the flame around Bakasura – who inhaled the fires into his many mouths. Once Sal was drained of energy he ended his attack ready to accept Bakasura's return. In a steady beam of heat Bakasura fired the attack back into Sal. As he accepted the sun-like inferno Sal felt like a god. Bakasura ended the attack by launching a sizable mouth at Sal – scooping him into it.

The mouth closed for a moment but reddened then combusted before it could swallow. Sal fell from the mouth's debris – having used nearly all his strength to liberate himself. Bakasura's filthy facial mouth curved into a smile as he threw two more mouths at Sal. The first engulfed a boulder which the second regurgitated from above – crushing Sal. The fire elemental crawled out from beneath the rock as Bakasura leaped to the location to crush Sal's body beneath his shin. Sal's draconic tail burst from his lower back and squirmed as Bakasura mangled his bones.

Bullets peppered Bakasura as Ellis, Tara and the soldiers began their attack. Bakasura approached them but was cut off by a black lightning strike from Kepyet – who climbed from out of the wall. Bakasura opened his stomach's largest mouth to exhale winds with the strength of a hurricane – blowing everyone except Kepyet onto their backs. Sal struggled to heal beside the boulder. All the Blessed soldiers forced themselves to sit up well enough to shoot at the devourer. The tongues on Bakasura's head flicked outward, and several others manifested alongside them. In an instant of crude terror the giant tongues invaded the mouth of each Blessed soldier and adhered to the backs of their throats. The tongues reeled the soldiers into the mouths on Bakasura's head – devouring them.

Bakasura chuckled a laugh which could only be described as the sound of a backed up hose struggling to clean an outhouse. "Kepyet..." Bakasura growled.

"Demon." Kepyet returned.

"May as well just call me "brother"." Bakasura teased. "I was not yet ready to be summoned again. But I am glad you have called me, nice of you to bring me snacks."

"All I've brought is your execution!" Kepyet barked as he charged at the devourer with his sword.

Bakasura grabbed the blade of Kepyet's sword then lifted his arm – taking Kepyet with it. Noxious ooze dripped from Bakasura's palm onto Kepyet's mask. Kepyet charged a black fireball in his left hand then pelted it into a mouth on Bakasura's chest. A flash of light burst from Bakasura's mouths as he whined and dropped Kepyet. Upon landing Kepyet telekinetically lifted Bakasura to slam him into the ground. Ominous ooze splattered from the devourer. Kepyet raised his sword but one of the tongues in Bakasura's hair lashed out at Kepyet and wrapped around his body like a lasso. Bakasura stood while the tongue retracted into a mouth concealed within his hair. Kepyet teleported from the tongue to behind Bakasura in hopes of landing a strike to the beast's back, but Bakasura launched a miniature mouth from the back of his ankle that ate through the center of Kepyet's chest then flipped back to pass through his head along its return to Bakasura's leg. Kepyet had only fallen halfway to his knees before Bakasura twisted his body into a kick – shattering the side of Kepyet's mask. The dust from the landing concealed Kepyet's face.

The devourer reached toward Kepyet but an explosion knocked out a chunk of his shoulder. Bakasura leaned backwards as Jasper approached with several grenades. He threw another but this time Bakasura caught it in his mouth. The explosive was swallowed before it could detonate.

Bakasura lumbered toward Jasper. Justice sprinted beneath Bakasura with her sword – severing his legs at the knees. The devourer tumbled to the ground but caught Justice with one of his tongues. Before he could retract the slobbering appendage the tongue was severed by a miniature cannonball. Justice landed beside Bakasura's head then leaped forward to evade his attempt to trip her with his tusk. Several more cannonballs pelted Bakasura's back as Eric approached.

Eric dropped the hand cannon because he depleted his ammo, but instantaneously equipped his pistols. Ellis, Eric, and Tara bombarded Bakasura with bullets. The barrage kept him down but didn't seem to do much more than scratch him. Justice continued to run away from the devourer when she realized Sal had recovered. A tidal wave of fire swept over Bakasura – incinerating him.

Everyone lowered their weapons to catch their breath but Kepyet's voice thundered "Not yet!"

A stray drop of devourer ooze grew into a fully

recovered Bakasura with three mouths floating around his visage. The mouths darted by Ellis, Eric, and Tara – ripping their guns from their hands. Jasper prepared to excavate one of his guns but one of the mouths stole his bag – throwing it a fair distance from him. Black lightning struck the mouths before they could fixate on anyone's body.

Ellis, the one closest to Bakasura, equipped his sword. Bakasura jerked his body sideways – smacking Ellis with his plump stomach. Ellis collapsed onto the ground. Bakasura opened his mouth to allow a frog-like tongue to whip around Ellis. Tara jumped in front of Bakasura last second to cut the tongue with her knife. She succeeded but Bakasura elbowed her into the air. He bent his head upward – catching Tara in his mouth. A beam of fire blazed through Bakasura's throat – forcing him to cough Tara out before he could swallow. Sal readied another attack but Bakasura exhaled another hurricane – blasting everyone away.

"You saved me." Ellis said to Tara as they tried to ignore their bruises. She replied with a simple smile.

Kepyet flew into the air – his mask had reformed. The shadow of a massive phoenix trailed behind him. Kepyet's demonic wings opened as a wave of black fire was released upon Bakasura. The creature inhaled Kepyet's flames then conjured a black fireball from a mouth on his wrist which he used to strike Kepyet. Kepyet plummeted for a moment but opened his wings in order to glide toward Bakasura with his blade. Bakasura ducked as Kepyet passed overhead but a mouth protruded from the top of his head and bit Kepyet in half. Kepyet's legs regenerated as he landed.

Sal growled with his hands ignited. Bakasura's stomach opened into a mouth while it stretched to the ground. A stream of dirt squirted from a mouth on the back of Bakasura's ankle and struck Sal – burying the fire elemental in a mound of dust. Justice and Tara assailed Bakasura but lost their footing and tripped in their attempts to evade the mouths Bakasura started to launch from his body. Kepyet teleported in front of Bakasura then slashed the monster's stomach open. Bakasura whimpered as Kepyet butchered him.

Droplets of Bakasura's blood morphed into more mouths – some of them even had tiny arms and legs! Kepyet raised his sword – summoning a furious downpour of black lightning strikes upon the Bakasura spawns. One floating droplet transformed into an arm that punched Kepyet's cheek. A second arm generated a couple feet parallel to the first; the second arm grabbed Kepyet's throat to whip him onto his back as Bakasura's body reformed. Bakasura opened his mouth to inhale Kepyet. Kepyet used telekinesis to seal himself to the ground but the lower half of his body degraded into a swarm of pebbles and dust particles as Bakasura inhaled him. The dark warrior's body briskly regenerated at the diaphragm – but while Bakasura was rejuvenating Kepyet's life force was being siphoned. As Kepyet struggled to maintain his place in existence the point of deconstruction crawled up Kepyet's torso.

Justice prowled behind Bakasura and sliced off the back of his head. The devourer lost his grip on Kepyet while Ellis, Eric, and Tara joined Justice in cutting Bakasura apart. Sal ignited the growing pile of Bakasura's slimy flesh. Kepyet's body regained its form.

Kepyet charged an invisible cloud of black lightning along the tip of his fist as he punched Bakasura – disintegrating him once more. This time Bakasura's goo was launched farther than the eye could see as it faded into nothing.

The ground shook – tripping everyone. A microscopic droplet of Bakasura grew into the full creature. Bakasura embraced Kepyet – forcing the warrior's face into his stomach's mouth. Black fire enveloped Bakasura as he consumed Kepyet. The distorted energies sparking from the duo prodded the others away. If they stood too close the black lightning would shock them. Nobody's guns or explosives would activate.

Tara hissed and leaped toward Bakasura in a last ditch effort to rescue her master. Dark electricity wrapped around her like a cocoon – slamming her into the dirt near the others. Ellis rushed to check on her. Sal's eyes gleamed when the moon began its crawl from the face of the sun – clarifying that Kepyet was nearing defeat.

"Eyes closed and to the ground!" Sal bleated. "NOW!"

Everyone obeyed. The sun's light intensified. Everyone's skin burned as the ground smoldered. The top layers of the great wall vaporized and the next couple layers melted into lava. With the top half of his body gone Bakasura screamed. Smoke sprayed from the gurgling skin of the devourer. What remained of Bakasura melted into a pool with a couple lethargic jaws bobbing along the top. All that remained of Kepyet were his arms.

Ellis held Tara as she gagged – strenuously trying to open her many eyes. Justice and Eric prepared to lunge at the puddle with their swords while Jasper tinkered with a grenade.

"Did I get him?" Sal wheezed – holding his forehead.

The mouths sank into the puddle.

"I believe so." Justice gasped – hoping her body would recover from the heat wave. Confusion filled the girl when she realized her current concern for Kepyet. Was she fearful that defeating the other devourers wouldn't be possible without him – or had she become attached to the devil which was once her parents' best friend? A knot tightened within Justice's stomach. If Bakasura could end Kepyet then attempting to battle the remaining devourers would be nothing short of suicide.

Sparks hissed beneath the dust near Kepyet's arms. A vacuum formed on the location – coloring the wind black during the suction. Kepyet reformed – but kneeling and gasping.

"Sal…" Kepyet whispered.

"Hey…" Sal answered. "Good to see ya alive, my dude!"

"Everyone except Sal…back…" Kepyet commanded.

Justice and Eric exchanged confused glances but obeyed. They lurched away from the pool – but still faced it. Jasper had entered a dwaal over his tech – cussing at himself while fumbling with the device. Ellis remained oblivious to everything happening as he tended to Tara.

"Sal, your fires are reigniting." Kepyet perceived. "With me – let's finish this bastard!"

"NO!" A stentorian feminine voice bellowed. The

land surrounding Bakasura rippled. Kepyet and Sal where thrown back. A thundering rift appeared beside Bakasura – mustering itself from the bubbling goo.

The rift lasted long enough for Tiamat to step through in her humanoid form, but collapsed behind her. She raised her left hand – regrowing Bakasura. Bakasura bowed before the fallen goddess. Devourer ooze steamed from between the scales on her face; blood slowly dripped from her yellowed eyes. Her tail had been regrown but this new tail was covered with festering sores and burns.

"My lady." Bakasura praised.

"After millions of your years...the luxury of return." Tiamat purred.

"How?!" Kepyet perplexed. "You're supposedly too feeble to hold power the mortal world!"

"Yet...I stand before you." Tiamat replied. "You only know of feeble intimately."

"Tiamat!" Justice screeched as she approached the reptilian queen. "You were a creation goddess! What happened to you?"

Bakasura growled in preparation to assail Justice, but Tiamat gestured him to hold back.

"Being a deity..." Tiamat smiled ironically. "A status of a fool. Though that isn't understood among the race of man, is it?" She glanced at Kepyet. "There was the exception, but he stands not as one of you."

"I stand with this planet." Kepyet claimed.

"One of a great many." Tiamat said softly.

"Your master aspires to consume them all." Kepyet lectured.

"There is consistency in emptiness..." Tiamat answered.

"You'd be left starved and bored." Kepyet remarked sternly.

"But accomplished." Tiamat returned. "As is the goal of all sentient life."

"Accomplish what?!" Justice yelped. "Leaving nothing behind to last?"

"Your logic is shaped by generations of lies." Tiamat argued. "I was a creator, in a distance of time that would overwhelm you. Creation...life... At a point it will escape you, reject the benevolence of a guiding hand. It broke my heart and betrayed me."

"You can't judge everything based on the actions of one god!" Justice pleaded.

"There was a chain of events." Tiamat explained. "You have brought upon the subject of negotiation though."

"Negotiation?!" Bakasura growled. "Let's just feast upon them and be done here!"

Sal's hands reignited. "This dish has proven himself too hot for you to handle!"

Tiamat blinked her decaying, reptilian eyes at Sal. "Was that a joke about spices?"

Justice groaned.

Eric aimed his pistols at Tiamat's forehead. "We don't negotiate with monsters."

"I'll entertain it." Kepyet interrupted. "Tiamat...do state your proposal."

"Kepyet..." Tiamat mumbled softly. "I seek Marduk. Deliver his spirit to me, and I will allow you to be spared." She looked over the others. "Along with your pets here."

"Until the time comes for Apep to eat us!" Sal blurted.

"It's still a good deal for you." Bakasura's voice rumbled. "Unlike me, the great serpent doesn't play with his food."

"No deal." Kepyet declared. "You fall by my hand!"

Kepyet waved his right hand to conjure a magical barrier around himself and his companions. Using telekinesis Kepyet stole one of Jasper's grenades – overcharging it with ominous power while it drifted through the air. Kepyet slammed the grenade between Tiamat and Bakasura. The initial explosion was tantamount to a nuclear bomb, but the blast retracted into a point on Tiamat's hand. Kepyet knelt from fatigue as the shields around his companions faded.

"Was that it?" Tiamat taunted as Sal hurled a fireball at her. The flame did nothing. To retaliate she lashed her tail around Sal – lifting and crushing him.

Justice repetitively slashed Tiamat's tail but her sword could barely etch the scales. Eric fired his pistols at the same point Justice attempted to cut. A sinister smile crossed Bakasura's face as he grabbed Eric. Jasper desperately aimed his pistol at Bakasura but before he could squeeze the trigger Eric was flung into the mouth on Bakasura's stomach.

"Eric!" Justice cried as Kepyet severed Tiamat's tail – releasing Sal.

Bakasura launched a mouth at Justice but she disappeared. Ellis, Jasper, Sal, and Tara were also gone. Kepyet's mask cracked into a smirk.

"You've created cowards." Bakasura bellowed.

Kepyet ignored the devourer's comment as he filled himself with tenebrous energies. The dark warrior prepared to strike but instead collapsed face-first into the ground. Baetylus melted from parts of Kepyet's currently exposed skeleton. His bones cracked into a powder. Bakasura reached toward the fallen fiend but Tiamat pulled the beast away. Kepyet's bones healed then he forced himself upright as the baetylus slowly reconstructed itself.

"Well isn't that just beautiful." Tiamat taunted, her tail regenerated itself. "You can conjure what it would take to murder us, but your body is unable to harness such might."

Kepyet's palms sparkled with thundering black magic. He stepped in to shock Tiamat but her tail snagged his waist then threw him between her and Bakasura. When Tiamat released her tail she grabbed the back of Kepyet's collar to fling him over her head and scalp-first onto the ground. Once Kepyet landed upon his back Tiamat placed her reptilian foot on his chest.

"Bring me Marduk." Tiamat ordered. "I have him, and I spare you...maybe your minions. That is my offer. You are a stone road of failures...do think on where you wish to lead."

Tiamat removed her foot from Kepyet while her tail whipped the air behind her – creating a rift. "Come, Bakasura." Tiamat said. "Let us grow our strength while our friend here contemplates his future."

Bakasura growled in acknowledgment as he accompanied his queen through the portal – which closed once they had passed through. Kepyet quaked the ground with an angry roar before teleporting away.

CHAPTER 22

Weeks into Kepyet's war on the gods Mount Olympus had been set ablaze. The bulk of the Blessed's forces were distracted defending other key locations across the planet – leaving only the Greek pantheon's guards to assist them against the Nutes and revenants raiding the kingdom. Thunder echoed across the sky as the countless sons and daughters of Zeus were slain by Kepyet and his forces.

Nemesis stood nervously within her chambers – ready to strike whatever is to pass through her door. The goddess feared whatever foe was capable of massacring such a radicated pantheon, although she had a feeling she knew who it was. Nemesis clenched her sword as her door, and the wall around it, popped into a cloud of dust. The red light from Kepyet's power-hungry eyes flooded the chamber.

"I've been here before." Kepyet announced.

"So, it is you..." Nemesis said somberly. "Why?"

"You know why." Kepyet replied. "Did you not predict this?"

"I don't know what I saw..." Nemesis quavered. "Are you here to kill me?"

"I can say I did." Kepyet spoke softly.

"I can't leave." Nemesis alleged. She blitzed Kepyet but before she could land her strike he jabbed his sword into her chest. The goddess dropped her weapon and tumbled to the floor as Kepyet retracted his. Her blindfold slipped from her face – revealing pale blue, crystal eyes. He sheathed his sword then knelt by her side – holding her up.

"I'm sorry...had you chosen flight..." Kepyet mourned.

"I couldn't." Nemesis coughed. "This though, it is not the power I granted you?"

"No." Kepyet confirmed.

"You no longer have it..." Nemesis observed.

"I found someone more worthy." Kepyet assured. "And I gave them half."

"And the rest?" Nemesis worried.

"Secured. I have respected your gift...and applied it to a goal of salvation. Just not yet." Kepyet said.

Nemesis simpered while allowing her sparkling eyes to close. "Good...I sense your heart...I may be the only one to understand all of this. Please, never lose track of your ambitions."

"I finish everything I start." Kepyet reassured. "Your sacrifice will not be squandered. I promise."

Calmed, Nemesis used the last of her strength to nod before dying in Kepyet's arms. He laid the goddess down then snapped his fingers – engulfing her body in fire.

In the present Kepyet appeared in the ballroom

of Skyrook – sitting on the floor. Justice sat in a chair against the wall with her head down. Jasper stood by his friend to comfort her. Sal leaned against the table across from Teigao. Teigao scowled at Kepyet and approached him. Kepyet fought to remain conscious as Teigao lifted the dark being by the neck then threw him across the room.

"Where is Lancast?!" Teigao barked as he marched to Kepyet again. One of Kepyet's wings sprouted from his back and pushed Teigao away. Kepyet used the wall to assist him back to his feet as his wing retracted.

"You were informed!" Kepyet growled.

"You saved these people!" Teigao seethed. "Not Eric?"

"Bakasura acted while I was weakened." Kepyet claimed. "Swallowed him before I could regain my strength."

"They should have been teleported here sooner!" Teigao roared. "You can see the future, you couldn't see this?"

"It's not always clear!" Kepyet alleged. "Tiamat's strength was underestimated, has been since before my time! The outcomes I have foreseen were calculated with the assumption that Bakasura would be the only foe we faced today!"

"And my other men?" Teigao hissed. "What about them?!"

"They instigated the devourer out of their own foolishness. Nobody should have assailed Bakasura without myself or Sal also on him." Kepyet opined.

"So, you knew they would be devoured." Teigao deprecated.

"The probability was significant but not yet determined." Kepyet clarified. "Their inability to be tactful wasn't a fault of mine."

"I should slay you where you stand!" Teigao raged.

"Try it..." Kepyet instigated. "See how you fare against the devourers without me..."

"They wouldn't be a problem if it wasn't for you." Teigao said. "And now you've proven to us that not even you can defeat them."

"I still have a couple more tricks up my sleeve." Kepyet assured.

"At what costs?" Justice drawled as she stood and walked to Kepyet. "You've already counted off my parents, my brother, your own top generals, and now Eric! Not to exclude the over-eight billion people!"

"And had I not acted the gods would have abolished us all!" Kepyet returned.

"And right now?" Justice quavered. "The gods left after the war, why did you have to have the devourers summoned and come back?"

"The Blessed would have made no attempt to restart the world...I have a few ideas, but they require both the Philosopher's stone and all threats vanquished!" Kepyet asserted.

Justice didn't like Kepyet's answer, but she believed him. She trusted that his intentions were in the right place, but his moral compass was misguided...if it even existed.

"Perhaps you could have laid the foundation for your resurrection without having Basil summon those things." Teigao said. "You're tricky enough."

"You can judge in retrospect all you want." Kepyet replied. "What matters is that I am here now as a result of the course of the actions I did take. Here are a few facts about the current situation. Bakasura and Tiamat are still weak, had the dragon not intervened Sal and I would have slain Bakasura. Lotan and Apophis remain too weak to cross into our world, and Apophis can only make the crossing if all the other devourers are dead. I can conjure the energy to slay Tiamat but my body is currently unable to harness it. Tiamat is too weak to remain in our world for long, it may be a while before any devourer crosses over again. When she does arrive her desire is to devour the soul of Marduk. I am inclined to believe that she will hold off until that happens."

"Didn't you kill him?" Teigao groaned. "Our one bargaining chip."

"Yes but he's not necessarily out of play." Kepyet grinned under his mask. "I saved his soul – knowing its value to Tiamat, in the event she would be trouble."

"So, where is it?" Justice sighed. "And you better tell us!"

"With a deity I didn't napoo." Kepyet answered. "Marduk's soul is safe with Baron Samedi."

"You've got to be kidding me!" Teigao whined. "You left our most valuable asset against those monsters with that hedonist?!"

"Baron Samedi?" Jasper butted in. "Isn't he that zombie guy with the cigar and whiskey?"

"I'm pretty sure it's rum." Sal blurted. "So, a Loa survives? Interesting..."

"I'm skeptical." Teigao confessed. "Eighteen years and he hasn't made himself known? The Baron was a showman. With so much death the entire planet is the perfect stage, enough to make him the most powerful deity."

"We had an agreement." Kepyet said. "I'm certain he's partying somewhere and sneaks himself the occasional newly-dead soul."

"Could he help us fight Tiamat?" Justice inquired.

"He could, but I doubt he will. He doesn't exactly view me fondly and if he were to fight the devourers it would be after I'm gone." Kepyet answered. "Off topic, but where are Ellis and my spider?"

"She goes by "Tara" now." Jasper and Sal chorused.

"Down the hall." Justice tilted her head toward their direction. "She's still pretty weak...Ellis is tending to her...oddly."

"I think he likes her." Jasper said.

Teigao shook his head. "As if there wasn't already enough madness on the premise..."

"Well, collect them." Kepyet ordered. "There's more to my plan and I need everyone here."

CHAPTER 23

Gehenna and Ronny clashed weapons. Unity creeped back and watched – reluctant to fight. Pleonex cackled loudly at the bottom of the hill. The ticks and tocks of his watches synchronized with Gehenna's attacks.

"Pleonex controls this warrior!" Ronny realized. "If we can silence the clocks we can discombobulate him!"

Ronny swung his oar downward to Gehenna's legs, but Gehenna skipped over the strike and would have cut Ronny's head with his scimitar if the other end of the oar didn't deflect the curved blade. Unity picked up a nearby stone and charged into the crater – preparing to throw the rock at Pleonex. Pleonex sighed while aiming one of his watches at her.

"Lady? Bean, I think!" Pleonex shouted while releasing a violent sound wave from the watch. Unity fell to the ground and entered the fetal position.

"Unity!" Ronny screamed while struggling to fight Gehenna. "What did you do to her?"

"She thinks she's a bean now!" Pleonex laughed maniacally.

Gehenna lashed Ronny across the stomach while he was distracted. The strike was excruciating, but not deadly. Ronny grew concerned though about what would happen if he was butchered here in the underworld. Is there a second level of death, or would he just suffer until he was diced into a million pieces and dumped into the Styx? Gehenna prepared another strike but Ronny fell back with his oar swinging outwards – smacking Gehenna across the face. Ronny felt resistance when retrieving his oar – Gehenna's mask had caught on the end and unraveled from beneath his hood. Ronny's deathly face grew even more pale upon seeing the visage of his rival – it was Callum! A gray fog glazed over the boy's eyes. Noticeable creases in flesh webbed across his skin – possibly scars from when Kottos crushed his head.

"Callum!" Ronny cried. "It's me, Ronny!"

Callum ignored his surrogate father and raised his scimitar. Ronny lurched backwards, now only engaging in defensive moves. Pleonex stung the airwaves with his laughter.

"He can't hear you!" Pleonex bragged. "His mind is mine! It is true that the real Gehenna belongs to the Styx, but I programmed his combat skill into this puppet! Now, Gehenna, kill the ferryman!"

Ronny struggled to protect himself as Callum's attacks grew more rapid and ferocious. While Callum persisted with his assault Ronny pleaded with him, but his words had no apparent affect. It was obvious that Callum had been under Pleonex's control for some time and that his mind was recessed deep within the psychological prison of which Pleonex was warden. Callum used his free hand to push Ronny's oar aside and knock him down, he then raised his scimitar for what he intended as a finishing strike. As Callum lowered his weapon it was blocked by a large, ax-like blade.

Anat stood over Ronny holding her bardiche. She flung her weapon upwards – throwing the scimitar from Callum's hand. Then she pulled her bardiche to her side in preparation for a lunge.

"What?!" Pleonex hissed.

"Wait!" Ronny begged. "Don't kill him!"

Callum reached for his weapon but Anat gripped his wrist with her free hand.

"What?" She asked with a puzzled expression.

"He's hypnotized!" Ronny explained. "That's my boy, don't hurt him!"

Anat flicked her hand around – flipping Callum's arm so that his body followed onto his back.

"You're asking a lot." Anat groaned. "But very well."

Anat tore off her baetylus finger then threw it onto Callum's chest. The stone morphed into a net which wrapped around the boy's body. Each thread's end formed a stake which plugged itself into the ground. Anat's finger regenerated as she helped Ronny to his feet.

"You have allies?" Pleonex grumbled.

"We actually just met." Anat giggled. "I saw fighting, wanted in."

"And by what criteria do you choose your allegiance?" Pleonex inquired.

"My previous superior looked like a zombie, too. Wasn't a fan." Anat replied. "I presume you're the hypnotist?"

Pleonex threw a sound wave at Anat while Callum unsuccessfully wrestled the nets.

"Bean!" Pleonex blurted as Anat approached. "Egg! Tuba! Chicken! Hippy?" Anat smirked while Pleonex thundered the sounds from his clocks across the ground in her direction. "Why won't you submit?!"

"Hypnotism is just another form of lying." Anat purred. "I've been past believing lies."

"A serious foe." Pleonex complimented. "I haven't encountered such since Kepyet ordered Basil to betray me. I wonder...is it also his hand which guides your actions?"

"I guide myself." Anat snapped, readying her weapon for an attack.

"The fact you're here means you've lost a fight before, I will not be intimidated!" Pleonex growled upon equipping a set of vicious, metal claws. Each set of claws extended two-and-one-half feet in length and consisted of a double-edged metal blade. Green fog coated his boned wings. He flew into the air.

Anat's baetylus finger grew into a whip; she cast it into the deathly sky and caught Pleonex. With a tug she pulled Pleonex to the ground — slamming his body into the dirt. He liberated himself by shattering her whip-finger. She slammed her bardiche toward him but he blocked the attack with one of his claws. Ronny bounced his attention between watching the fight and the slow healing process of his abdomen.

Pleonex managed to regain his footing and nearly stabbed Anat, but she seized the offending claw between the blade and handle of her bardiche and used the momentum to pull Pleonex back onto the ground. He swung his other claw at her neck, an attack she blocked with her regenerated baetylus finger. Anat's baetylus eye flared into a fiery orange hue as it heated to lava.

"My throat is a no-no." Anat hissed as she knocked the claw away then proceeded to lop off Pleonex's hand with her bardiche.

The monster rolled onto his back in reaction to Anat's strike, then continued to roll to evade her next swing. As he contorted onto his feet he attempted to trip Anat with his right wing, but she just severed it with her ax. Pleonex tried to stab Anat with his other wing but she leaned forward and raised her bardiche – cutting that one off too.

Pleonex intentionally ran his claw between the blade and handle of her bardiche to pull his foe closer to him as he stepped toward the nearby the puddle of Stygian water. He twirled around – forcing Anat to step into the accursed liquid. She screeched as she tugged her bardiche – ripping the claw from Pleonex's hand. The top-left corner of her face sizzled and a ghastly smoke sprayed from her mouth. Her elbows and hips ignited into multicolored flames but didn't disintegrate.

"How?!" Pleonex quavered. "The Styx water ravages all it contacts!"

Thick, basalt-colored smoke obstructed the left half of Anat's face – distorting the orange gleam of the respective eye while blood covered and dripped from her right eye. A trail of smoke grew from the end of each strand of her hair.

"I must be special." Anat theorized. She jerked her foot back onto solid ground but pulled

Pleonex to her previous position. His body had eroded before his second foot was even lifted from the ash. Anat's body returned to normal as she glared into the pool of Styx water – watching the tormented shards of spirits shred Pleonex's armor.

Unity awoke from her condition as Callum's eyes lost their dark shells.

"Ronny...?" Callum whispered as Ronny sprinted to his location.

"Callum!" Ronny cheered. "Are you there, now?"

"Yeah...what happened?" Callum squirmed. "And why am I in this strange net?"

The net crumbled as Anat and Unity approached, Unity moving at a more frantic pace.

"Callum!" Unity cried.

Callum sat up. "Who are you?"

"Unity!" Unity wept with joy. "I'm your mother!"

"Mom?" Callum stuttered. "You're still alive! Or...whatever this is?"

"We're all dead here." Ronny chuckled. "It is good to see you again, we have been searching for you!"

Unity embraced Callum. "What happened to you, son?"

"I don't remember much..." Callum confessed. "Shortly after I died I heard this strange noise...I think I was hypnotized by some skeleton guy."

"You were..." Ronny confirmed.

"I remember bits and pieces of it." Callum said. "He wanted to enter Muspelheim...I think the plan was to re-enter the mortal world from there and bargain with Surtr."

The portal to Muspelheim lost the bit of power it had by the time Anat reunited with the others.

"Fail." Anat sniggered. "That thing isn't opening anytime soon."

"He was desperate..." Callum answered. "And who are you?"

"Yeah..." Ronny's eyes narrowed. "I'm wondering that too...you're the only being I've ever heard of who could survive contact with the Styx."

"No "thank-you"?" Anat pouted.

"I am grateful that you freed my son." Unity spoke out. "What drew you to this place? Are you a fallen angel or a Valkyrie?"

"I just saw the smoke." Anat shrugged. "It interested me so I thought I would check it out. Then I saw you guys fighting, combat is sort of my favorite thing ever."

"So, you're a psychopath." Callum remarked.

"Callum!" Unity yelled.

Anat smiled. "Observant...I've been called worse."

"We owe you much." Ronny bowed his head. "Please, come with us onto the ferry. Under my command it's a sanctuary until we can find another, secure, resting place."

"Hmm. Yeah. No." Anat declined. "I'll continue to explore this place...see if there are any other creatures that need slaying or folks that...god I've deviated from my nature...need saving."

"There's nothing out there...not anymore." Unity stated. "The longer you roam the madder you become...my own sanity isn't certain after the time I was lost."

"I'll take my chances." Anat argued.

"Is there anything I can do to repay you?" Ronny asked. "I am the ferryman, after all."

"Perhaps." Anat paused. "If you ever encounter

a man named Pradhan, allow him free passage."

"All passengers board my boat for free. I'm not Charon." Ronny assured.

"Then our business is done." Anat replied as she turned from the trio and began strolling away.

"Wait!" Ronny blurted. "We never got our answer...who are you?"

Anat stretched her body sideways so that they could only see her right profile from over her shoulder. She thought for a second, as the question bore more depth than she was comfortable exploring.

Anat contorted her lips into a soft smirk and said "The red horse."

CHAPTER 24

Teigao approached the exit of Skyrook. Justice caught him while she made her way toward the ballroom.

"Where are you going?" She inquired.

"Somewhere else." Teigao answered dryly.

"Obviously." Justice rolled her eyes. "Kepyet wishes to speak with everyone in a few minutes...or did he already-"

"I don't care." Teigao snapped. "And neither should you if you know what is good for you."

"It might be useful information against the devourers." Justice guessed.

"A fool's errand." Teigao mumbled with a woebegone expression. "The fiend, and that's all Kepyet is...a fiend, miscalculated our odds of success. He was so sure of himself earlier, damn certain that Bakasura would be dead right now. Instead, that creature is gaining incomprehensible power. Tiamat herself has become quite strong...and even if they are taken out we can no longer estimate the might of the others."

"Is that not why we need everyone together?" Justice pleaded. "I know you have powers you don't share with us, I can't help but feel that you can summon other demons, like that dog, which could be used to fight."

"It's wise to know your own limitations. I know mine, and I would suggest you learn yours." Teigao advised. "That is Kepyet's folly. It was his downfall then and it will be the nature of his downfall now, only this time he insists on taking the rest of us down with him."

"I like to believe there's a method to beating any challenge." Justice said.

"It is just that – belief. Belief alone failed mankind, instigated many wars, divided the public, fueled every failed experiment and tragic error." Teigao ranted. "I was the leader of The Blessed. That was my team, my faction, my responsibility. Now...they're all gone. We weren't like the Warsons, we didn't have sleeper cell reserves hidden throughout the planet to fall back on."

"Eric." Justice lowered her head sadly. "I restrain my grief."

"He was like family to me." Teigao sighed. "His father and I were close, Ricky Lancast was a damn good warrior and commander. Sunk one of Kepyet's flagships, against impossible odds. Helped me manage the utopia that was New Jericho...he even managed to recover that stupid flash drive from the black market traders it has bounced between. He believed we had succeeded in securing ourselves, and look what happened...under our noses a traitor brought an end to our city. Eric was important to me, I was there to watch him grow up and become the incredible warrior you knew. Then...like nothing...he was erased from existence. Do you think Kepyet feels remorse? His guilt is over his own loss, soiling his image of himself before an audience. Eric may not have even been an asset, for all we know his fate was calculated into the equation even in the event of success. That was the case with your parents and brother."

"I'm not defending Kepyet!" Justice snapped. "We have a common goal, an important one, and a mutual enemy."

"You sound too sure." Teigao remarked. "How do you know Kepyet hasn't arranged your death? Or Ellis'? Jasper really seems to be at risk since he's useless on the battlefield. The boy is clever but with Kepyet's magic what need is there for a weapons expert or engineer?"

"Well it is my job to protect them, if that is the case." Justice alleged. "I have the blood of my parents, they were close to the man Kepyet was before he became a monster. Perhaps there's a secret in my bloodline?"

"He was the same man." Teigao insisted. "Cooper Thomas isn't new to the actions of the devourers, he wrote a loved one out of existence in exchange for dark powers long before becoming Kepyet. The shadow of her memory lingered within that man's heart...eventually creating Kepyet. A human life is a worthless sacrifice...but to erase an existence...that is something else. It is the nature of the devourers. A power Kepyet uses but is unable to understand, his essence is still human...for the most part. He can only handle so much energy before it breaks him down."

"He's also a master at finding loopholes." Justice opined. "I have no love for him, he may be a rival – especially after allowing Eric to be thrown away, but the devourers are an urgent matter. I will hold Kepyet to his sins if...when we defeat the devourers. Perhaps the philosopher's stone will be of use...I know harnessing its power is my destiny."

"You look too far ahead, over too many obstacles." Teigao chuckled. "The problem with envisioning so deep into the future is that you open yourself to being caught off guard. Knowing what you do now of Cooper Thomas, is it not concerning?"

"Well..." Justice drawled. "If anything you have given me a more intimate understanding of his character, I pity him, in a way."

"Say you do defeat Bakasura and even Tiamat." Teigao began. "And drop any other foes along the way to the snake. Apophis is a being of pure chaos, insatiable hunger...exists only to destroy. His very being exists on the veil between that which exists and not does exist. A maelstrom of eradication which became conscious. Knowing what you do now of Kepyet – are you not afraid of what Apophis may offer him?"

"Kepyet's ambitions have always been to save the planet..." Justice alleged with doubt under her words.

"In a lost time there was a mighty god. A righteous entity – during who's epoch there was prosperity. He and his divine brothers educated their mortal worshipers in mind and hand – contemplating the universe and the intricacies of civilization with their brains and working the gifts of the Earth into beautiful creations with their hands. He questioned the seemingly malevolent actions of other gods, to the point his own morality drove him into declaring a war on the other pantheons. His brothers followed him, but these gods were outmatched and suffered a loss so great all records of their time in power have been erased. The name of that fallen god is forgotten." Teigao rambled. "Kepyet is not the first. The universe is large, he won't be the last. He's failed once already...do you really want to follow him into his next failure?"

"I act for myself." Justice paused. "I believe the answer is in the Philosopher's stone, and that there are ways to victory yet uncovered. I don't blindly follow Kepyet, but I have my faith that in following him for the time being I will make my own discoveries."

"So be it." Teigao pouted. "I hope you are right. You do have great potential, Justice. From the day you idiots first broke into New Jericho we all saw it. However, you can't convince me to remain a part of this."

"Very well." Justice realized there was no longer a point in trying to get through to the old wizard. "Where will you go?"

"I don't know yet, I will see where fate takes me." Teigao answered. "I do hope our paths cross again."

Justice nodded, unable to think of a proper response as Teigao made his way out the door. He had given her much to consider, and convincing reason to rethink her support of Kepyet. The demon was apparently even more unstable than even she realized, but what was she to do? She needs Kepyet to help her discover the Philosopher's stone and he is their only chance against the great devourers. Justice wondered – why her? Why did she have to be a survivor of the great war? Of all people why is she the one related to Kepyet's scientific partner? She mourned her brother and friends, how could she not despise Kepyet for labeling those close to her as expendable? He is even the reason she met them to begin with! Justice wondered if she could control herself if Ellis or Jasper were excluded from Kepyet's endgame.

The footsteps of the others congregating in the ballroom echoed into the chamber. Justice tried to ignore the noise from the airship's engines outside as she ventured to meet with the others.

Kepyet stood near the back of the room with Sal at his side. Ellis leaned upon the table between Jasper and Tara. Justice couldn't help but notice how Ellis and Tara were almost holding hands.

"So, what's this about?" Jasper blurted. "Are you going to lead us to another loss?"

"You can't have victories with that attitude!" Tara lectured.

"Forgive me for becoming sick of watching friends die left and right!" Jasper argued.

"Where is Teigao?" Ellis interrupted.

"He left..." Justice muttered.

"As if he was even here." Kepyet remarked. "Save your grief, everyone. We have a war to win...and I have formulated a strategy. I have always been a proponent of security measures...I laid the foundation for strong plans in the event my others fail. I didn't believe I would see the day the seeds I planted long ago would have a purpose, but here we are. The power I can wield isn't enough to defeat the devourers. It wasn't enough to defeat the pantheons I challenged either, which is why I once divided my power. I harbored the bulk I could, the excess was divided across my three generals. Basil, Pleonex, and Gehenna. Again, I must divide my power...but only certain souls, either by nature or blessing, are capable of surviving enough of my essence to be useful." Kepyet's body sparked. "I struggle to regulate the energies my soul manipulates, as some of you may have noticed. Defeating a devourer requires the full potential of my magic."

"So, who are you giving your power to?" Jasper asked. "Basil was proof that you have poor judgment of character!"

"There is method to what you interpret as my madness, child." Kepyet assured. "The first since my revival to receive my gift is Sal. A fire elemental, a powerful nature spirit who understands the importance of being responsible with great power." Kepyet paused. "The second – I choose Justice!"

"Me?" Justice stuttered.

"The daughter of my best friend!" Kepyet announced. "Your intuition is an asset, and you have proven yourself able to adapt to drastic changes in any situation. You also earn the trust of everyone you encounter, whether you realize it or not. I also have a secret – long ago a goddess, one I wish I could call a friend, gave me a gift. I wasn't worthy so I rejected it. Part of the gift – I passed onto you...prior to your birth."

Justice's eyes widened. "What do you mean? How come I never knew?!"

"You weren't ready." Kepyet answered. "In the ideal situation...in my hopes, you never would be...but fate has called for the gift to become active, complemented by mine! Embrace it!"

Justice's eyes flared into alternating black and blue lights. A twisty beam of white light swam around her body while a subtle, black flame rushed across the full surface of her skin. Justice fell against the nearest wall, but briskly recuperated.

"I don't feel anything now?" Justice stuttered.

"Give it time...it's power not meant for mortals to even comprehend, your spirit needs time to study the gift, away from your conscious mind." Kepyet explained.

"So, what good is this, then?" Justice barked. "I'm not sure I even consent to this!"

"You desire to have input in my plans, and to maintain the safety of your companions." Kepyet commented. "What better way to achieve that than by possessing not only a portion of my essence but also power I don't even have myself or feel worthy of?"

Justice wanted to argue with the ominous being, but she couldn't bring herself to engage him any further. She knew that he was correct, albeit she didn't understand how useful the so-called "gifts" were without her knowing how they function.

"As for my third choice..." Kepyet paused, and smirked under his mask. The subtle smile wasn't visible but the crowd unanimously sensed it was there. "I'm already aware you humans won't approve...but there's someone I need to resurrect."

To be continued.

Glossary

Abzu	Sumerian water deity who was Tiamat's lover
Adam's ale	Water
Bardiche	A battle axe with a long, curved blade and typically a longer handle
Breechclout	A loincloth
Facinorous	Wicked
Galère	A group of troublesome people
Incline	To nod
Kline	A long chair where the head / backrest is on a short end
Kylix	A cup with a long stem and wide, shallow bowl
Malison	Bad luck / a curse
Napoo	Bring an end to
Occipital knob	A bulge of the bone in the back of the skull
Tardiloquent	Speaking slowly

ABOUT KEN RA

Ken Ra came into this world the night (and day in some parts of the world) he was born in April 1993. Late March in the inverted year of 1663 the guinea was declared legal tender and used as such until it was replaced by the pound in 1816. In December 2015 Ken Ra graduated from college with a degree in Broadcast & Cinematic arts, and several months later he got a few screenwriting gigs ranging from simple proofreads and story revisions to writing feature-length scripts. He started writing his first novel (Skyrook Gorge – Hunger) in 2017. Ken Ra has always been fascinated with history, mythology, and spirituality. Many locations in the Skyrook Gorge series are taken from his recurring dreams. The cat this book is dedicated to taught him how to climb trees.

Skyrook Gorge

Ken Ra

Made in the USA
Columbia, SC
17 September 2022